THE SCREAM OF THE BUTTERFLY

Also in the Lars Winkler series

The House that Jack Built

THE SCREAM OF THE BUTTERFLY

A Lars Winkler Novel

JAKOB MELANDER

Translated from the Danish by Charlotte Barslund

SPIDERLINE

First published in Denmark as *Serafine* in 2014 by Rosinate & Co.
This edition published in Canada in 2015 by House of Anansi Press Inc.

House of Anansi Press
110 Spadina Avenue, Suite 801
Toronto, ON, M5V 2K4
Tel. 416-363-4343
Fax 416-363-1017
www.houseofanansi.com

The lyrics on page 393 are from "When The Music's Over," words and music by The Doors. © 1967 (Renewed) Doors Music Co. All Rights Reserved. Used by permission of Alfred Music.

House of Anansi Press is committed to protecting our natural environment. As part of our efforts, the interior of this book is printed on paper that contains 100% post-consumer recycled fibres, is acid-free, and is processed chlorine-free.

19 18 17 16 15   1 2 3 4 5

Library and Archives Canada Cataloguing in Publication

Melander, Jakob, 1965–
[Serafine. English]
The scream of the butterfly / Jakob Melander ; translated by Charlotte Barslund.

(A Lars Winkler novel)
Translation of: Serafine.
Issued in print and electronic formats.
ISBN: 978-1-77089-441-9 (bound). ISBN: 978-1-77089-442-6 (html).

I. Barslund, Charlotte, translator II. Title. III. Title: Serafine. English.
IV. Series: Melander, Jakob, 1965– . Lars Winkler novel.

PT8177.23.E53S4713 2015   839.81'38   C2015-904793-5
                                                     C2015-904794-3

Library of Congress Control Number: 2015934550

Cover design: Alette Bertelsen
Type design and typesetting: Alysia Shewchuk

We acknowledge for their financial support of our publishing program the Canada Council for the Arts, the Ontario Arts Council, and the Government of Canada through the Canada Book Fund.

Printed and bound in Canada

THE SCREAM OF THE BUTTERFLY

OCTOBER 1999

FOG STRETCHES ACROSS Prøvestenen. Drops of water glisten in the late evening air. The smell of minced beef, onion, and tomato still lingers between the buildings of the Margretheholm Refugee Centre. The residents have gone to bed and all is quiet. A Red Cross worker has just finished his last round. Soon the night shift will take over.

A door slams in the education block behind the main building. Bright voices echo between the red-brick walls, before they're swallowed up by the fog. A child runs down the steps from the education block and then sprints toward the door at the end of the main building.

The corridor inside is dark and deserted. The lights have been turned off in every room. A single, narrow beam of light coming from under the door closest to the exit casts a faint glow across the filthy linoleum floor—the room he shares with his sister Afërdita. Her blue bath slippers are lined up next to a pair of large, lace-up shoes on the mat outside.

Arbën puts his dirty running shoes next to his sister's slippers, then looks up and down the corridor before opening the door without making a sound.

The room is sparse, containing a bookcase with their few belongings and a table below the window. The orange curtain flutters in the draft from the cracked window frame. The floor is sticky under his bare feet; its surface shines in the light from the naked light bulb hanging from the ceiling.

The sound of someone breathing quietly.

Two naked bodies are lying on the bed. A crumpled blanket has been kicked to the end. His sister's eyes are staring at the ceiling. One arm dangles over the edge of the bed, her hand half open. Red flowers bloom on her chest. Dark, sticky leaves run down her arm, across her palm. Her finger forms a bridge between the stab wound in her chest and the pool spreading across the floor. A pair of scissors is buried in the flesh of her neck.

A calm face rests on her chest. The cheeks quiver with every breath. The nose and forehead are smeared with blood. Arbën's hand falls from the door handle and he steps back out into the corridor.

Red bubbles appear at the corner of the man's mouth. Then he looks up and their eyes meet.

LARVA

[Larva (from Lat. *larva*, "ghost; mask," to describe an
animal, first used by Linné, who considered the larva
a masked insect), a stage in the development of many
animals after hatching, prior to adulthood. Larvae
differ from adults, often having a completely different
nutritional biology . . .]

The Great Danish Encyclopedia

MONDAY, SEPTEMBER 23

1

LARS ARRIVED AT Frederiksberg Allé by Sankt Thomas Plads. He parked on the pavement next to the fountain, right outside the police cordon. It was dark and drizzling lightly. Curious onlookers, reporters, and police officers jostled on the sidewalk and crowded around the semicircle of parked cars under the lime trees. The light from the street lamps and the photographers' flashes flickered, bouncing to and fro between the wet tarmac and the underside of the yellow lime leaves. The whole scene lay bathed in a nervous and unreal glow.

"They say his head is almost..."

As Lars got out of the car, a woman took a cigarette out of her mouth and started jogging toward him. She was around forty, her hair tied back with a scarf. "Hey, Lars. Have you got a minute—"

He waved his hand to make her go away, held up his badge to a uniformed colleague, and was allowed through the cordon. A press photographer was busy climbing a tree in front of a neigh-bouring apartment building.

Lars walked through the arched entrance and into the stair-well of number 28. A constant stream of police officers guided the way.

The broad oak door on the second floor opened onto a small hallway with checkered floor tiles. It was full of coats, hat shelves, and shoes. A narrow door to the right led to a guest bath-room with an old-fashioned toilet. Everything was tasteful, but slightly shabby. This was old money — Frederiksberg aristocracy. The house belonged to Kirsten Winther-Sørensen, managing director of her own clothing company, and Mogens Winther-Sørensen, mayor of Copenhagen, long-standing member of the Radical Party, and son of the party's chairman, Merethe Winther-Sørensen, who was currently Denmark's finance minister.

Lars had tried to recall what little he knew about the mayor in the car on the way to the crime scene. Mogens Winther-Sørensen had been the mayor for more than ten years and, as far as Lars could remember, his time in office had been charac-terized by a pallid pragmatism. The Radical Party, despite its name, was actually at the dead centre of Danish politics. The capital's relationship with the Danish parliament was business-like and rarely dramatic, irrespective of whether the govern-ment at the time was right or left wing. But Lars knew nothing about the man himself and could only just remember what the mayor looked like. While they were still married, Elena had occasionally mentioned Kirsten Winther-Sørensen's clothing line, which was the extent of his knowledge about the mayor's personal life.

Perhaps he should have taken more of an interest in politics? Or his marriage? In the latter case, he had neglected it too long. Elena had left him and moved in with Ulrik in the spring.

Lars went through the hall, and continued straight ahead

until he reached the kitchen, where the police photographer was at work on his subject.

A man in his early forties with hints of grey in his dark hair was lying on the floor, staring at the ceiling with a mixture of surprise and pain. His pants had been pulled down around his ankles. His lower body was twisted, his hips at a ninety-degree angle to the floor. His dark, wrinkled genitals flopped over his pale thigh. The head had been almost severed from his body. A pennant of coagulated blood spread across the floor toward the kitchen cupboards. A single, extended spray of red reached from the floor, across the lower cupboards, over an open pizza box with three or four slices remaining—pepperoni, Lars noted, he had yet to have dinner—and up to the ceiling. Allan Raben, Lars's colleague for eight years in the Violent Crime Unit, was kneeling near the kitchen table with a measuring tape, sweating. There were several footprints at the edge of the pool of blood, close to the body. One set of prints—stilettos would be his guess—had trampled in the puddle before disappearing to the left. A soft whimper came from the adjacent room.

"Hi Lars." Wallid Bint shook his hand. His dark face was half hidden behind his mask, but Lars thought he could still see the gleaming teeth of the assistant from the Institute of Forensic Medicine through the white fabric.

Lars nodded and took a step back to make room. Bint's boss, Frelsén, was bending over the body, his hairnet stuffed into the back pocket of his protective suit. Pale tufts of hair stuck out from his scalp. The chief forensic pathologist now had several bald spots. Why hadn't he noticed that before?

"Frelsén." Lars greeted the pathologist. "What have we got?"

The pathologist straightened up, tugging at the fingertips of his latex gloves.

"Our killer entered through the front door by picking the lock. The victim was in the middle of an amorous transaction."

Frelsén pointed to the victim's pants. "A single cut with a sharp, heavy object. It took great force. The head has almost been severed from the body, but you don't need me to tell you that." Frelsén winked. "The upstairs neighbour came home with some friends after a night out and noticed the open door. He knocked and popped his head around, managing to catch a glimpse of the killer, who was leaving through the back door."

Frelsén gestured over his shoulder toward the door. Low moaning could be heard on the other side. "The second party to the transaction is in there with Sanne and Lisa." Then he bent over the body once more.

Sanne. So she was here too. He hadn't spoken to her since Midsummer's Eve. He had tried calling her a few times, but she never answered her cell phone, and she had recently been away for a month on holiday—with Martin.

"Is there anything to suggest that the murder was politically motivated?" Lars rummaged around in his pocket for his cigarettes. "There's a general election in less than two weeks." Even he couldn't have failed to notice the timing.

Frelsén snorted with derision.

"Local politics? *Danish* local politics?" He shook his head and turned his attention back to the victim.

Allan placed his hands on his knees and stood up to join Lars.

"Was the neighbour able to give us a description of the perpetrator?" Lars continued to fidget with the cigarette packet in his pocket.

Allan rolled up the measuring tape and made a face.

"He didn't have time to see much and could only make out that the killer was wearing dark pants. His friends stayed on the landing. They were fairly drunk at the time and their statements won't be worth all that much."

Lars left Allan in the kitchen and went into the room next door. A petite, dark-skinned woman with big, backcombed hair and heavy makeup was perched on a low sofa opposite Sanne and Lisa. She was wearing a deep-purple, sequinned dress that rode high up her thighs, revealing long, smooth legs.

He took a seat next to her.

"Lars Winkler, Copenhagen Police." He nodded quickly to Sanne and Lisa. "What's she saying?"

"Not much." Lisa scratched her coarse, dark hair. "Her name is Serafine Haxhi, and she arrived from Hamburg today."

Sanne avoided his gaze, pushing a train ticket across the coffee table. For a moment he felt giddy: her vibrant grey eyes and the dusting of freckles across her nose and cheeks wouldn't let him focus.

He put his cigarettes on the table and picked up the train ticket: *Arriving CPH 16:08*. He turned to the slender woman. Her high cheekbones and almond eyes—they were almost too much, too perfect.

"You're not his wife, are you?" Lars said to Serafine in English as he stuck a King's in his mouth. He offered her one while he lit his own.

The woman took the cigarette without looking at him. A row of badly healed scars ran up the inside of her left forearm. She followed his gaze. Then she stuck the cigarette in her mouth and hid her arm beside her thigh. She leaned over the lighter he kept lit between them, and inhaled. She shook her head, blew out smoke, and looked away. Lars put the lighter on the table and nodded toward the kitchen.

"What happened?"

Serafine took another drag of the cigarette while her eyes flitted around the room. She started picking at the hem of her dress, staring out of the window into the night.

"We didn't manage to get anything out of her, either." Lisa tossed her notebook onto the coffee table, grimacing "We don't even know how they met. There can't be much doubt that she was busy giving him a blow job when the killer arrived."

Serafine heard the word *blow job* and reacted immediately.

"No sex." Her fragile body started shuddering. Lars waited until she had calmed down.

"But then why are his pants around his ankles?"

"He came out from the toilet and…" She trailed off, stubbing out the cigarette in the ashtray with abrupt, stabbing motions. She took another cigarette from Lars's packet and lit it.

"Your accent. You're not German. Where are you from?"

Allan popped his head around the door just at that moment.

"Bint and Frelsén are done. Do you need them in here?" he glanced behind him. "Otherwise they'll take him away now."

Lars looked at Sanne and Lisa. Neither of them protested.

"It's okay. We've seen plenty. Is the police photographer happy?"

Allan nodded.

"Frelsén says the post-mortem will be tomorrow morning at nine. By the way, there's someone out here who wants to talk to you."

Kim A's figure loomed in the doorway, even Frelsén looked tiny in comparison. Lars made his excuses and went out into the kitchen, while Frelsén instructed the paramedics on how to handle the body.

"Kim. What are you doing here?" Lars ignored the outstretched hand.

"I was on my way home when I heard what happened on the radio." Kim A walked around the paramedics to the back door and out onto the landing.

Lars followed. "So, why are you here?"

Kim A put his hand on Lars's shoulder.

"I'm with PET now—a close protection officer to the minister. I thought she might want me to take a look at things with the election coming up. After all, he is her son."

Lars positioned himself between the body and Kim A, and watched the paramedics lift up the mayor and put him on the stretcher. A flash went off. A tall, balding man wearing steel-rimmed glasses and army pants stood hunched in the doorway, his camera set to continuous mode.

"Who let you in?" Lars pushed the photographer out into the hallway and summoned a uniformed colleague. "Make sure you get his name and the name of his paper, then escort him downstairs and drive him out to the middle of nowhere."

"Hey, listen, you can't just—" The photographer rotated the camera in his hand, trying to shoot more pictures from his hip. Lars blocked him.

"You've just contaminated my crime scene. I can do whatever I want. Get out!"

"Off we go!" The other police officer raised his hand and herded the photographer out of the apartment, following him down the stairs. Kim A was leaning against the wall, observing the incident. He chuckled.

"Cheeky, aren't they?"

Lars shook his head. The sound of the photographer's protests echoed through the stairwell.

"Like you said, you're with the Security and Intelligence Service now." He stuck out his arm, trying to usher his former colleague into the hallway. "I'm going to have to ask you to leave."

Kim A nodded at the pool of blood on the floor and the white chalk outline marking the position where the body had lain.

"So you have no suspects? How about the prostitute in the next room? Surely she must have seen something?"

"Time to go, Kim." Lars bundled him out.

Kim A disappeared into the stairwell. Suddenly the large kitchen was empty. Lars went back to Serafine, who had lit yet another cigarette. Lisa was sitting opposite, going through her notes. He could hear Sanne elsewhere in the apartment.

"Serafine." Lars sat down. "You're coming with us. We need the German authorities to verify the information you've given us." He turned to Lisa. "Has Bint fingerprinted her?"

Lisa nodded. Serafine turned her head, and stared out the window into the darkness, pressing down over the roofs.

2

IT HAD STOPPED raining by the time Lars and Sanne found themselves back on Sankt Thomas Plads. It was already nine thirty in the evening. The reporters had all gone home or to their offices to write and polish tomorrow's articles and features. There was no doubt what angle they were going to take.

Lisa had driven Serafine to police headquarters, where she'd been remanded in custody. Once she recovered from the shock, they would have to see what information they could glean from her.

Lars closed the door to the stairwell and followed Sanne out under the archway.

They hadn't been able to reach the victim's wife, Kirsten Winther-Sørensen. Papers found in the apartment indicated that the family owned a holiday home in Hornbæk, but also that the dead man's mother, Merethe Winther-Sørensen, lived in a house on Amicisvej, not far from where they were now. Breaking the sad news to the family was their immediate priority, although Kim A had probably already done that. And the post-mortem awaited them first thing tomorrow morning.

Lars took a deep breath and arched his back. The air was moist and cold, but it felt refreshing after the nauseating smell of blood and perfume in the apartment above.

Sanne's wispy hair had grown since the summer. He wanted to reach out and run his fingers through it. At that moment, the light from a street lamp fell across her face and he took a step back.

"What's wrong?"

Sanne gestured. A figure had moved out from the shadows under the lime trees.

"Sanne? Lars?"

"Ulrik?" Lars started buttoning his coat. Sanne said nothing, taking out her car keys.

"Horrible business." Chief Inspector Ulrik Sommer nodded up toward the second-floor windows. "And for this to happen now. We can't afford to put a foot wrong."

Lars thrust his hands into his pockets. Since when had that ever been an option?

"I've briefed the justice minister, who will be calling the prime minister, but I insisted that we would inform the victim's mother in person."

"That's actually where we're going now."

"Right... I thought I might come with you."

A taxi raced past them in the street, going well above the fifty kilometre per hour speed limit.

Sanne concentrated on her driving. Lars sat in the back, gazing up at the roof of the small Fiat 500. The lights on the dashboard made Ulrik, in the front seat, appear even more gaunt than he really was; his skin looked grey, sunken, and drawn. The chief inspector ran his hand across his face.

"Merethe Winther-Sørensen has been the leader of the Radical Party for more than twenty years, and served as a minister in several governments. Mogens has been lined up to take over from her since the end of the last century. As far as the party is concerned, he has chosen a very unfortunate time to get himself killed."

"You're referring to the general election, aren't you?" Ulrik nodded.

"No one knows what this will mean for the election campaign. Whatever happens, Merethe Winther-Sørensen has more than one reason to mourn her son's death, so show some discretion. Both of you."

Sanne turned onto Amicisvej. The light was on behind the ground-floor windows of number 17.

"Our friends from the media have already been kind enough to call her." Ulrik got out. Lars and Sanne followed him.

"It could have been Kim A," Sanne said, locking the car. "He turned up at the crime scene and talked to Lars."

Ulrik looked at him, and Lars nodded. Some way down Amicisvej, a man was leaning against a car, watching them. Kim A, perhaps.

It was Merethe Winther-Sørensen herself who opened the door to let them in. There was no need for them to say anything. Her eyes were milky and she was blinking constantly. Her white curls were a veil of candy floss around her small head.

"Please, come in." The finance minister led the way through the hall and down a passage. Her lavender jacket and skirt were ill suited to her short, broad body.

A small, desiccated man was sitting at a circular table in an overfunished drawing room, the pieces of a huge jigsaw puzzle spread out before him. He didn't look up when they entered, but kept his eyes on the piece in his hand, turning it over and over, trying to make it fit.

"I'm sorry for the loss of your son." Ulrik stopped in front of Mogens Winther-Sørensen's father, who looked up, squinting against the light.

"I don't have a son." Then he turned his attention back to his puzzle piece.

Ulrik looked briefly at Lars and Sanne. Merethe Winther-Sørensen pulled out an armchair.

"My husband always does puzzles when he's upset." She took a seat, leaving them the gaudy, floral sofa.

They fell silent. A clock was ticking somewhere in the house.

"Did that prostitute kill my son?" the minister asked Ulrik.

"A witness saw the killer." Sanne went on to explain how the perpetrator had escaped down the back stairs.

"I was woken up by a journalist from—just a moment..." Merethe Winther-Sørensen found a small notepad in her pocket and held up her reading glasses in front of her eyes. "*Ekstra Bladet.* She said it was a sex killing."

Ulrik rubbed his forehead.

"We don't know much yet. I'm afraid tomorrow and the next few days may well be unpleasant. Might I suggest that you turn off all your phones and let the party issue a press release?"

"Absolutely out of the question. I can't just disappear in the middle of an election campaign!" Merethe Winther-Sørensen looked outraged. "Will you be holding a press conference? I want to take part."

"I don't believe that's—"

"It's not up for discussion. I presume you're doing everything in your power to catch my son's killer."

"It'll be detective sergeants Lars Winkler and Sanne Bissen

here in charge of the investigation." Ulrik placed a hand on Sanne's shoulder and nodded in Lars's direction. "Sanne?"

Sanne straightened up on the sofa.

"The whole area is currently being searched, and all of the neighbours are being interviewed. There will be a post-mortem tomorrow."

Lars looked out of the window while Sanne spoke. The PET close-protection officer who may or may not be Kim A was still leaning against the car further down Amicisvej. Merethe Winther-Sørensen bent forward.

"About the press conference—"

Lars interrupted the minister as he continued to stare out of the window. The PET officer hadn't moved.

"Would you happen to have a phone number for your daughter-in-law? Or your granddaughter, perhaps? We'll need to talk to them."

Merethe Winther-Sørensen frowned. Then she wrote down a number on her notepad, tore off the sheet, and handed it to Sanne across the coffee table.

"This is the number for Sarah, my granddaughter. They're at their holiday cottage in Hornbæk. Would you please be so kind to not call for a couple of hours? It's probably best that I'm the one to tell them..." Merethe Winther-Sørensen trailed off and clasped her hand over her mouth.

"I think we had better..." Ulrik rose.

Merethe Winther-Sørensen got up as well.

"Yes, of course." Her facial expression was completely composed once again. "I'll show you out."

Two sombre portraits of thin men with pained expressions were hanging in the hallway. A more recent painting of Merethe Winther-Sørensen in yellow and mauve shades was hanging next to them. All three were placed at eye level on the wall facing the front door.

"That's my father, Mogens Winther-Sørensen. My son is named after him." Merethe Winther-Sørensen pointed to the individual portraits as she spoke. "And that's my grandfather, Holger Winther-Sørensen. And that's me of course." Lars was sweating. Suddenly, the hall felt oppressive.

The minister continued.

"My father served as a minister in Hilmar Baunsgaard's government. My grandfather served under both Kampmann and Krag. I had hoped that Mogens's portrait would hang here one day, too." She straightened her jacket. "I expect to be informed about the press conference tomorrow morning."

Lars watched while Ulrik shook her hand. Sanne hesitated, trying to attract his attention. Out of the corner of his eye, he saw her shake the minister's hand. Lars left without saying goodbye.

"A woman of strong opinions." Sanne said, buttoning up her jacket. She stepped out into the street and unlocked her car.

"Merethe Winther-Sørensen has controlled and toppled prime ministers. You don't want to make an enemy out of her." Ulrik looked at Lars as he spoke. Then he got into the passenger seat.

3

AN S-TRAIN LEFT the platform. The carriages accelerated and the light from their windows flickered across the building behind him. Lars stuffed his hands in his pockets and crossed Lundtoftegade, heading for the construction site that had spread across Folmer Bendtsen Plads during the late summer. An old Opel raced past him, spraying water across the sidewalk and up the legs of his jeans. Lars swore under his breath as he jogged along the fence surrounding the site. Soon the drilling would be all day and night. In six years he might be the lucky owner of an apartment with a Metro station right on his doorstep. But would he still be living here in six years? He hoped not.

They hadn't exchanged many words on the way back from their visit with Merethe Winther-Sørensen and her idiosyncratic husband. Sanne had dropped Lars and Ulrik on Sankt Thomas Plads before driving home. To Martin.

Lars turned the corner and reached the small passage between the construction site and the front of his apartment block. A drunk staggered out from the Ring Café just as he passed it and bumped into him.

"Hey – hey, man. Look where you're going." Lars caught a glimpse of bloodshot eyes, week-old stubble, and nicotine-stained fingers. A stench of beer and cigarettes briefly engulfed him before the guy moved on, stumbling around the corner toward Nørrebrogade while muttering to himself.

Once inside his second-floor apartment, Lars hung his jacket on a hanger, went to the bathroom, and washed his hands; he also splashed cold water on his face, but to no avail. The skin around his eyes was still puffy. His bones ached from fatigue and he was starving, but he had no appetite. The pennant of blood against the checkered floor cast a dark shadow over his field of vision. Coffee? No—it was almost midnight; he would never be able to sleep.

He kicked off his Converses, went into the living room, and turned on the stereo, flicking through his vinyl records until he reached Bowie's *Heroes*. He put the needle on "Neuköln." Somehow that track felt appropriate right now. He sat down on the sofa and leaned back. Bowie's breath moaned through the saxophone while Lars lit up a Blue King's.

What had it been like to see Sanne again? She had never responded properly to his offer of going with him to New York, and then she had suddenly left on holiday. With Martin. And now—well, now what? He studied the smoke rising toward the nicotine-stained ceiling. Someone was shouting outside. He heard a window slam shut. Best just to forget about the whole thing.

Lars got up. The dystopian romance of "Neuköln" turned into a simple exchange between congas and rhythm guitar, a pulse, a beating heart: "The Secret Life of Arabia." He was alive!

He turned on the tap in the kitchen and flicked the ash off his cigarette in the sink while he waited for the water to turn cold. Then he filled a glass and walked back to the living room. Maria's room yawned emptily at him. He still hadn't grown used to her absence. How lonely could you possibly be in a two-bedroom apartment in outer Nørrebro?

Well, now he knew.

He lay down on her bed and rested the cigarette on her desk. He inhaled her scent, which still lingered on the bedspread, and stared up at the posters of young men. He had no idea who they were: singers, actors, sports stars? There was no doubt that the idea of a year of high school in New York had been a good one, both for Maria and for Caroline, her friend who had been raped last summer. They had been staying with Lars's father in Brooklyn these past two months. Maria sounded happy whenever he spoke to her, and she talked about their classmates and the teachers at St. Ann's School. His father had assured him that all was well and that the girls were having a whale of a time. Only it wasn't the same as having her living here at home.

The day's events began to seep into his thoughts. Merethe Winther-Sørensen had been scarily intent on securing a place for her son in the line of great politicians, on adding Mogens to the illustrious Winther-Sørensen family dynasty. And now his body was resting in a temperature-controlled steel drawer in the morgue on Frederiks V's Vej in Østerbro.

Lars sighed, swung his legs over the edge of Maria's bed, and got up. He might as well get some sleep. They weren't going to solve the case tonight.

SEPTEMBER 1999

"**YOU CAN'T DO** this to me, Mogens, or to your father."
Merethe Winther-Sørensen half-rises from her armchair.
Berlingske Tidende slides onto the floor, the newspaper's sections
scattering across the deep pile carpet. The front-page story about
the government reshuffle, which has made her finance minister,
faces upward. There is a big colour photograph of Prime Minister
Poul Nyrup Rasmussen with his arms extended, the new team
of ministers gathered in front of his office. His mother, sporting
a silly grin, is standing right next to the prime minister.

Outside, above Amicisvej, the last bits of daylight are burning
out, pulsing orange and red over the roofs of Gammel Kongevej.

Mogens rubs his palms on his pants and takes a deep breath.
It's going to be a tough evening.

"I've made up my mind, Mother." He struggles to keep his
voice steady.

"After all the work I've done for you? That your grandfather and great-grandfather have done? Does none of that matter?" Merethe Winther-Sørensen sits down again. The last newspaper section, entitled "Free," flops onto the floor.

Mogens starts to sweat. All throughout his childhood, the demonic images of his grandfather and great-grandfather grew in his mind, spreading their sombre wings until they engulfed his whole world in their silent, stern embrace. No one escapes from the shadow of these idols who demand total obedience—and yet he is attempting the impossible. A strong sense of responsibility for the family project has been impressed on him ever since he was a little boy. This endgame fans a permanently guilty conscience, the knowledge that everything you do can always be done just that little bit better. And his mother knows exactly which buttons to push. She is a master.

But this time—for once—he will decide for himself.

"This isn't about my grandfather or great-grandfather. Or you. This is about me. What I want to do and how I want to live my life. And politics, the city council..." He rests his palms on his lap and stares down. "Well, it doesn't interest me."

"Shh." His mother hushes him. He can almost hear the ancestral portraits in the hall rattling in sheer outrage. "Don't say such things."

"But it's the truth. I'm not suited for it."

Merethe Winther-Sørensen raises her chin. The sound of her voice fills the drawing room.

"I have devoted my life to politics." Her gaze fixes on him. "What does Kirsten say?"

Kirsten?

"It's her idea. She can see how little time I have for Sarah."

Bull's eye. It takes a few seconds before she has recovered enough to breathe again. Then she pulls herself up on the armrests and staggers out of the room. Her heels clip-clop up the stairs.

Total silence ensues. Mogens closes his eyes and leans back against the cushions. A car passes by slowly outside. Victory is only partly assured. He needs her acceptance. A total break would be too costly — for both of them.

When Mogens opens his eyes, his father is looking at him.

"You have to give her something, son."

"What do you mean?"

Arne turns in his chair, lowering his voice.

"Your mother can't bear losing face. If this was a budget negotiation —"

"But how? Either I'm on the city council or I'm not. There's no compromise, nothing to negotiate."

"You could give her time to get used to it. Take administrative leave, perhaps? After six months, who knows? Maybe she'll have accepted it by then?"

Mogens's hand flops down on the sofa cushion. He had hoped for a permanent solution — a result. But his father is right. His mother won't surrender, not now. And the bottom line is that he gets away. Now. That's what matters. He can start his new life.

The sound of steps on the stairs returns. His mother sweeps into the drawing room, filling it wall to wall.

"I'm prepared to agree to a leave of absence, three to six months." She stops behind the armchair; stiff fingers grip the back. Her parchment-white skin is stretched taut across her face.

Mogens and Arne exchange glances.

"Six months, minimum." His hands are shaking.

His mother grimaces. Then she laughs so wide he can see her molars.

"This, just as I return as minister? No flies on you, are there? I hope you know what you're doing. And what are you going to do?"

"You'll find out." Mogens dries his sweaty palms on his pants again. He can hardly believe that he has gotten this far.

26

"Secrets, eh? Well, I suppose you need to rebel at some point. Before you come to your senses." She walks up to him and pats his cheek.

Mogens closes his eyes, fighting the urge to flinch. He'll ring his stand-in first thing tomorrow morning.

TUESDAY, SEPTEMBER 24

4

"SHE'S BEEN CLIMBING up the walls in there for the last three hours." The duty officer walked with Lars down the corridor of cells, keys jingling in his fleshy hands.

It was eight o'clock in the morning. Lars had had a restless night, slipping in and out of a dream where Sanne kept scolding him. Why hadn't he called her since the summer? He had woken up at five o'clock, his rage a knot in his stomach. He *had* tried calling her. She was the one who hadn't... He found it impossible to go back to sleep again, and when the alarm went off at a quarter after seven it had been a blessing in disguise.

The duty officer stopped in the corridor and flicked through the bunch of keys for the right one.

"Nobody in the other cells got a wink of sleep last night. And now she's demanding asylum. Can you believe that?"

The shouting coming from the furthest cell, muffled by the

heavy steel door, really did sound like "asylum," although the voice was slightly distorted by an indeterminable accent.

"If you ask me, she's terrified of something." The shouting inside the cell stopped the moment the duty officer inserted the key into the lock. "But she refuses to say what."

Serafine was curled up in the corner of the worn bench, arms wrapped around her knees. Her head rested on the graffiti-scrawled wall with DICK spelled in a hundred different ways. Then she started banging her head against the wall. There was a large blue bruise on her forehead, right below her hairline.

"I want asylum."

He took Serafine up to his office, and ordered coffee and a bread roll. She ignored the cheese and the jam, and buttered the roll.

Lars waited until she had stopped chewing.

"If you want asylum, I can help you apply." He fell silent, waiting for a reaction. She swallowed the last mouthful and said nothing. "But first I need to know exactly what happened yesterday." He took out the train ticket and placed it on the desk between them. "You arrived at Copenhagen Central Station by train from Hamburg yesterday at..." He turned the ticket around and read out loud. "4:08 p.m. You got off the train. Then what happened?"

Serafine looked straight at him, then raised two fingers to her lips and moved them away again in a soft arc.

Lars shook his head.

"You can't smoke in here. Later, okay?"

Serafine turned her head and looked out the window. There were traces of last night's rain on the windowpane, but a few blue patches had started to appear in the grey clouds above.

Lars leaned back. In his experience, most people wanted to talk. They needed an outlet to offload violent events. Even hardened criminals might feel a huge sense of relief once they started opening up. But the psychopaths and the brainwashed were another story. Gang members, and political and religious fanatics were as cold as ice; you would get nothing from them. But there wasn't anything to suggest that Serafine was a psychopath or that the killing of the mayor was politically or religiously motivated.

He clicked his pen in readiness, trying to catch her eye.

"The area around the railway station is littered with surveillance cameras; we'll find out what you've been up to sooner or later. You might as well tell me now."

Serafine looked at him with a faint smile, then shook her head. She turned to stare out of the window once more.

Lars tried another approach.

"Where did you meet the mayor? The victim?"

Serafine scratched the scars on her forearm, keeping her gaze on the window. He put down his pen, got up, and perched on the corner of the desk.

"Now listen. If you want me to help, you'll have to—"

The door opened. The colour drained from Serafine's face and she shook her head violently.

"No!"

"Lars?" A breathless Allan came in, waving a printout of an email. "We've had a reply from Interpol."

Serafine turned back to look at the rain hitting the windowpane. Lars cursed under his breath.

"And?"

"It matches what she's told us already." Allan placed the printout on the desk in front of him. "Serafine Haxhi. The Germans have her fingerprints. She and her family applied for asylum in 1999 in Ilmenau. I've checked, it's a town in the former East Germany, down by the Czech border. She and her sister disappeared shortly afterward." Allan looked up. "Are you getting anywhere with her?"

"Not a squeak. She wants asylum."

Allan leaned against the filing cabinet.

"I was just talking to the duty officer. Some of the things he told me..." He sighed. "What a mess. We won't get anything from her."

Lars hesitated. Allan was right, but there were still procedures.

"Why waste more resources on her?" Allan drummed his palms on the filing cabinet as he spoke. "Drive her up to the Sandholm Refugee Centre. Let her apply for asylum, if that's what she wants. Perhaps the centre's psychologists can get through to her. It'll be days before she's sent back to Germany, anyway. And then... Well, at least we'll know where she is, if we need to talk to her again."

Lars rubbed the bridge of his nose with his thumb and forefinger. Should he give it one last go? At that moment there was a knock on his door, and Sanne and Lisa entered. His tiny office was starting to feel crowded.

Lisa tossed today's edition of *Ekstra Bladet* on his desk. A grainy colour photograph of Mogens Winther-Sørensen's body on the checkered kitchen floor filled the front page. The dark stream of coagulated blood disappeared in the top right-hand corner. There was a laconic caption below the picture:

COPENHAGEN MAYOR IN SEX KILLING

So it had kicked off. Lars folded the newspaper and pushed it aside.

"Why don't we interview Kirsten Winther-Sørensen?" Sanne still had her jacket on. "She and her daughter are back from Hornbæk. And Ulrik wants a quick result."

Lars closed his eyes and held his breath.

5

THE WOMAN WHO opened the door was dark, Mediterranean-looking. She was big boned, but her movements were feminine.

Kirsten Winther-Sørensen stepped aside, letting Lars and Sanne enter. The kitchen smelled strongly of bleach and detergent. All traces of blood and the chalk lines drawn by the crime scene technicians had been removed from the cupboards, the table, the tiles, and the walls, but Lars didn't have to close his eyes to see the victim in a contorted position on the floor, the lower body naked.

Kirsten Winther-Sørensen ushered them through the room where they had tried interviewing Serafine last night, into a living room with whitewashed floorboards, wooden skirting boards, and impressive stucco decor. They sat down on one of the sofas in front of the large window overlooking Sankt Thomas Plads.

"My condolences," Lars began. It was a quaint, archaic expression that created distance rather than intimacy. But it was the right thing to say: an expression of sympathy to someone facing the greatest possible loss, while remaining strictly formal and devoid of emotion.

It was windy. Outside, the yellow leaves whirled past.

"Thank you." Kirsten Winther-Sørensen pulled her legs under her on the sofa, resting her elbow on the armrest. She was wearing a white outfit, presumably from one of her own collections, and looked surprisingly composed.

"We have to ask you some questions. I'm afraid some of them might be unpleasant." Sanne was doing the talking.

Kirsten Winther-Sørensen turned to look outside.

"Nothing can be more unpleasant than the call I had from my mother-in-law this morning."

She was either in shock or utterly indifferent. Lars tried to catch her eye without success. No one said anything for a while. The sound of quiet weeping was coming from somewhere in the apartment. Lars and Sanne exchanged glances.

"My daughter, Sarah." Her voice was flat. "She's finishing high school."

Sanne cleared her throat.

"All three of you were meant to drive up to the cottage together yesterday, but Mogens suddenly had to stay behind at the Town Hall..."

"He said something about an extraordinary budget meeting. I don't really keep up with politics."

A telephone rang in the distance; the muted weeping turned into mumbling. Kirsten Winther-Sørensen half-turned in her seat.

"Sarah? Who is it?"

"It's only Granny." There was a shift in her daughter's voice. She sounded almost... happy? Lars took out his notepad and turned his attention back to the interview.

"So it wasn't a scheduled meeting? Is that normal?"

"It has happened before, yes. We had agreed that he would follow later, but—"

Now Sarah's voice was coming from the adjacent room; she was walking around with the phone.

"I . . . I would like that. Tomorrow, did you say?"

"Sarah?" Kirsten Winther-Sørensen raised her voice. "What are you planning to do tomorrow?"

Sarah carried on with her conversation and didn't reply.

Lars was making notes. "Do you know anyone who might have wanted your husband dead?"

"No." Kirsten Winther-Sørensen twirled her wedding ring around and around, frequently glancing at the door to the room next door. "He called around five thirty to say the meeting had just finished. He sounded happy—said he just had a few things to take care of in the city. I had roasted a chicken . . ." She trailed off. Her jaw made a sudden movement, skidding to the side.

Lars waited, letting her regain her composure, before he continued.

"You're aware of the . . . circumstances? How we found your husband?"

Kirsten Winther-Sørensen straightened herself and looked up slightly.

"I've seen the headlines, yes."

Lars closed his notepad. He too had seen them: countless variations on *Copenhagen Mayor murdered. Hooker only witness.*

"We will need to speak to your daughter as well." He stopped speaking and listened. There was a single sniff from further inside the apartment. "But it doesn't have to be today. You should expect that the media will try to keep this going, so it would be best if you and your daughter . . . could avoid talking to them."

Kirsten Winther-Sørensen smoothed back her hair.

"You need have no fears on that account."

6

L **ARS POURED HIMSELF** another cup of coffee from the French press that Mogens Winther-Sørensen's secretary had brought into the mayor's spacious office. The room was adorned with PH lamps, herringbone parquet flooring, tall wooden panelling, and green fabric wallpaper. The Town Hall certainly did what it could to promote Danish architecture, craft, and design.

So far they had spoken to two city councillors from the Radical Party, along with one Social Democrat and one Conservative. None of them had noticed anything unusual and didn't seem to think Mogens Winther-Sørensen had been upset or depressed. He had chaired the meeting as he always did and hadn't brought up any contentious issues. Everything on the home front appeared to be fine. If the four politicians were to be believed, the victim had been a textbook mayor. Maybe that was what was bugging him? Mogens Winther-Sørensen's colleagues had depicted him as squeaky clean, but surely no one was that boring?

He abruptly put down the cup. The fine bone china clattered.

"Did anyone from the Danish People's Party attend the meeting yesterday?"

"The Danish People's Party?" Sanne lowered her notebook. "But the Danish People's Party and the Radical Party loathe each other."

"Exactly." Lars got up and popped his head outside to talk to the secretary. "Excuse me?"

Kristian Havholm wore a remarkably well-fitting, dark blue suit that camouflaged the problematic areas on his tall but slightly plump figure.

"You wanted to talk to me?" His smile was friendly; his handshake firm. He had short, blond hair and wore an oxblood tie. Lars was no expert on politics, but even he couldn't fail to notice that Kristian Havholm was a man going places.

Lars asked him to take a seat.

"As you've probably guessed, this is about the murder of the mayor."

Kristian Havholm's expression became suitably sombre.

"A tragedy. How awful for the family. He had a daughter, I believe?"

"You attended the budget meeting yesterday?" Sanne had picked up her notepad again. She had her pen ready.

Kristian Havholm nodded.

"What did you discuss?"

"As far as I recall, there were three items on the agenda." Kristian Havholm adjusted his tie with a flat hand and leaned back. "Delays to the Metro expansion, a temporary increase in the grants to improve the Brønshøj-Husum neighbourhood and…" He closed his eyes. "Some roadwork, I can't quite…"

Sanne checked her notes.

"In northwest Copenhagen: Tagensvej, from Tuborgvej down to Lygten."

"Yes, that's right: three completely uncontroversial items. Some of us had a few questions, but the mayor was able to answer all of them. Everything was voted through unanimously."

"Did anything happen at the meeting that you think might explain why Mogens Winther-Sørensen was murdered?"

"Nothing in the slightest. It would have been remarkable if that had been the case. There's nothing in Danish local politics worth killing for."

"And no problems otherwise? Political grudges, something on the home front perhaps?" Lars was fishing and he knew it.

"It's well known that our two parties rarely see eye to eye on anything, but you could always trust Mogens if you made an agreement with him. As far as the home front is concerned, I wouldn't know." Kristian Havholm's gaze grew distant.

Lars and Sanne exchanged glances.

"According to those of your fellow council members we've already interviewed, no one could put a finger on Mogens Winther-Sørensen." Lars leaned forward. "Do you share that opinion?"

"Ha! They're all terrified of his mother." His gaze grew distant again, then suddenly he continued. "I don't suppose Mogens was worse than anybody else, but as for the finance minister — you don't want to get on her bad side."

7

GREY CLOUDS DRIFTED across the sky, filtering the harsh, sharp light. Lars got out of the car and waited until Sanne had slammed the door on the passenger side.

A figure waved as it crossed the parking lot on the way to Rigshospitalet. Lars narrowed his eyes.

Then he recognized the red glasses and the short bob.

"Christine." He waved back. Christine Fogh stuffed her hands into the pockets of her white coat, jogging the last stretch. Sanne had come to a halt a few steps behind him.

"Hey Lars." Christine stopped, slightly out of breath. She nodded to Sanne. "What are you doing here?"

"Post-mortem. We're . . . Sanne?" He looked over his shoulder. "You go on ahead. I'll be with you in a sec."

Sanne hesitated. Her arm twitched briefly. Then she headed for the back entrance, bowing her head against the wind.

Lars turned to Christine.

"How are you?"

She tucked her hair behind her ear, but the wind blew it out of place.

"You never called."

"No...I've been a bit busy, you know." Even he could hear how feeble it sounded.

Christine folded her arms across her chest.

"Is it about the mayor?"

Lars nodded.

She wavered for a moment, shifting her weight from one foot to the other. Then she reached out and trailed her finger down to his forearm.

"So when can I expect to hear from you?" She didn't wait for a reply, instead taking a pen from her chest pocket and scribbling down a number.

"But..." Lars took the note and checked the number before stuffing it into his pocket.

When he looked up again, she was already on her way back to the hospital. She stopped briefly and lowered her voice.

"I think your colleague is watching us from the window."

Lars turned around, just in time to see Sanne's back retreat from the first-floor window. When he turned around again, Christine Fogh was between two cars, slipping into the shadow of the monolithic Rigshospitalet. He followed her sturdy figure with his eyes.

Sanne was waiting for him by the door to the morgue, fiddling with the handle.

"What did she want?" Her tone was casual.

"Oh, she..." He pointed to the door. "Shall we?"

Sanne hesitated, her hand still on the handle. Then she pushed open the door and marched down the corridor toward Frelsén and Bint, who were at the furthest workstation.

Frelsén plunged the scalpel into the body the moment they stepped inside the narrow cubicle. He made an incision from the breastbone down the stomach toward the pubic bone. Yellow fat oozed out on both sides of the cut; blood collected in the grooves in the steel table. Lars took off his jacket and put it down on a chair. It was hard to believe that the victim still contained so much blood. There had been several litres on the kitchen floor last night.

"Sanne, Lars." Frelsén didn't look up. "Glad you could come."

Lars stepped closer. Mogens Winther-Sørensen's face looked peaceful as he lay on the table. His black stubble stood out against his skin, which had the bluish hue of skimmed milk.

"No traces of saliva on the victim's penis or scrotum, and there are no other indications of sexual activity such as vaginal fluid. You didn't find a condom in the apartment, did you?" Frelsén looked at them over the rim of his glasses. They both shook their heads. "Right," he continued. "So if this was a transaction, they hadn't reached the delivery stage yet." He suppressed a giggle. Sanne shook her head; Lars said nothing. This was classic Frelsén.

"What about the cut to his throat?" Sanne took out a transparent plastic bag from her purse and held it up. "Our colleagues found this in the courtyard, some distance from the crime scene. The blade is bloodstained."

Sanne removed the knife from the bag and placed it on the table alongside the body. It was a Japanese cook's knife made by Hocho, heavy and with a broad blade, and suitable for cutting vegetables. The serrated edge was caked with a mixture of congealed blood and an indeterminable, stringy white substance.

Frelsén gave it the once-over.

"Ah, that looks interesting. I wonder what that could be." He put his glasses back on, and then leaned over the knife. "We found tiny metal fragments in the wound, so we'll see if we can match them to the metal alloy of the knife. We should have an answer for you later today or tomorrow." He bent over the knife once more. "But I'd still like to know—"

"Mozzarella." Lars was leaning against the wall. "Mogens and Serafine used the knife to cut pizza. The killer went for the first weapon available."

Frelsén raised his eyebrows, then returned to the deceased. Suddenly the knife was no longer quite so interesting.

"Time of death?" Lars sat down on one of the chairs along the wall.

"The upstairs neighbour saw the perpetrator leave the apartment around 6:45 p.m., which would fit with the body temperature. So, thereabouts, I would say."

"You'll send us the test result from the knife, won't you? There's a press conference at three thirty this afternoon. It would be great if we could introduce the murder weapon then."

Frelsén adjusted his gold glasses.

"I'll see what I can do."

Lars walked toward the car. It wasn't until he stuck the key in the ignition that he realized Sanne wasn't behind him. She was nowhere to be seen. He didn't spot her until he turned onto Frederik V's Vej. Lars drove up alongside her and rolled down the window.

"Jump in."

Sanne shook her head, stared down at the sidewalk, and continued walking. Lars followed her in the car.

"Sanne—"

"I just need a bit of air. I'll see you back at HQ." She looked toward Blegdamsvej and carried on in a straight line.

8

THE WIND SHAKES the woodwork outside, but the air inside her room is stagnant. Her eyes are sticky with caked make-up; her throat is dry. Her head is heavy and confused. The clock on her cell phone insists it's late afternoon. Her third leg rises; the nausea between her thighs. Lust, which doesn't belong to her, rages, ripping her body apart.

She looks around for something she can use to cut the thing off, but there is nothing in the small single bedroom they have given her that will do the job. There is just a bed, table, chair, and a small cupboard for her personal effects. She has nothing to put in the cupboard. The small parcel she was given upon her arrival at the Sandholm Centre sits on the table, containing a toothbrush, toothpaste, and sanitary napkins.

Her vision blurs.

She closes her eyes, pressing her fingertips against her eyelids until the pain comes and coloured dots dance in front of her. The bed merges with the kitchen, the checkered floor, the dead body, and the night in the strange city. A red fog, a huge wave of blood rises and rips the bed from the floor. Bolts moan as they are torn out of the floorboards. The flood turns and hurtles her through the darkness toward the bright room with no walls or ceilings—the room where her sister waits for her, surrounded by a cloud of white butterflies.

Gasping, she comes to, unable to stand up or stay lying down. It has been several days since she could last afford HRT treatment from the street-doc in the Reeperbahn. Her body and brain cry out for the hormone.

She stumbles out of bed. Her eyes avoid the pointy erection, the thing that isn't her and yet is a part of her body. She can't go outside like this; the tight-fitting dress will reveal it immediately, the animal she inhabits. On hands and knees she makes her way to the toilet and tries to pee. Sometimes it helps, but not now. Not a drop comes out. She gets up, ties a scarf around her hair, splashes water on her face, and starts removing her makeup to apply a fresh layer.

Half an hour later she is just about presentable. The bruises to her forehead are barely visible under the foundation. She slips back into the dress. The thing between her legs is still shamelessly drawing attention to itself. She tries one last time to fold it away between her legs, to make it disappear. Her fingers follow the knobbly scars around her scrotum. Finally she bundles up the bedsheet, holds it in front of her and goes outside. There has to be a doctor somewhere, someone who can help.

She is in some sort of alleyway between two long barracks. There are narrow doors on both sides and several bedrooms. Outside an open door diagonally across from her, children sit in a circle playing with a stick and bottle. The moment she closes the door behind her, the first one starts to point with laughter and revulsion. Their parents appear and shout at her in a language she doesn't understand, but she recognizes the tone. She lifts her chin and holds her head high as she sashays between the barracks in her high heels. She smiles to herself when she succeeds, and doesn't start running until the third stone hits her back, knocking the air out of her.

The Red Cross worker at reception is flustered when she appears and can't understand her. It's not until she says the words *Doctor* and *German* that it seems to click. Then she has to wait in the office for hours before the duty doctor arrives. She is sweating and dizzy. The Red Cross worker brings her water, and she drinks a little. The yellow brickwork of the main building blurs into all the other refugee centres in Germany and Denmark. She nods off.

There is a banging sound close to her head. It takes a while before she realizes that this is not part of her dream. Someone has slammed their palm against the table. An older man with black bags under his eyes is leaning over her.

Later he tells her that he initially thought she was a drug addict, that she was looking to score methadone like all the others. But now he understands, and his features soften.

"I can only give you one injection. Normally several sessions with a psychiatrist are required. This isn't something we just hand out, you know, but it's quite obviously what you need. You're lucky I even brought one dose. You need to speak to the resident doctor tomorrow. I'll leave a note for him in his office."

And then he gives her the HRT injection. The foreign body slumps, folding into itself. The testosterone retreats. Serafine lets herself fall, disappearing into the flutter of butterfly wings.

She doesn't feel the stones that hit her as she walks back to her room.

9

"**A**RE YOU READY?" Ulrik placed his hand on the door
handle. "It's twenty-five to."

Merethe Winther-Sørensen wiped her forehead and looked
straight ahead. The low, excited murmur of the journalists could
be heard clearly through the grey door.

"Let's get started."

Lars was standing behind Ulrik and Sanne, leaning against
the wall. Sanne had done everything she could to avoid him
after she had returned from the Institute of Forensic Medicine.

"Are you quite sure it's a good idea to bring her?" It was the
first time Lars had opened his mouth.

"Lars—"

"Wait, Inspector." Merethe Winther-Sørensen turned to Lars.
"Even an ordinary police officer can surely understand that a
minister's presence raises the interest in the press conference

considerably. Hopefully it will lead to more tipoffs from the public, wouldn't you agree?"

Lars ignored Merethe Winther-Sørensen, addressing Ulrik instead. "The case is spectacular enough as it is. And this might sound pompous, but there's something about the separation of powers between the executive and the legislature that isn't quite—"

Merethe Winther-Sørensen took a deep breath.

"If the representative of the executive power could restrict himself to matters he understands, the representative of the legislature promises to do the same."

Ulrik sent Lars a warning glance.

"I think it's time we went inside."

Lars shrugged. If Ulrik was happy to let himself be bossed about by the minister, it was no skin off his back.

The questions began the moment they stepped through the door.

"Do you have a suspect?"

"Do the police have any idea of the motive?"

The journalists were shouting over each other, producing a cacophony of scattered demands. The heat from the squashed bodies combined with the moisture from the exhalations of too many people in not enough space was overwhelming. Ulrik, Merethe Winther-Sørensen, and Sanne reached the podium and sat down, ignoring the questions. A number of cell phones lay on the long table in front of them, ready to record.

Lars positioned himself at the edge of the room and leaned against the wall with his arms across his chest. Ulrik glanced over at him, pointing to the empty chair next to Sanne while pouring water from a carafe into Merethe Winther-Sørensen's glass. Lars shook his head.

A woman's voice cut through the noise.

"How do you think it's going to affect your election campaign, that your son was visited by a prostitute?"

There was total silence. Merethe Winther-Sørensen grabbed her glass and took a sip. Lars looked along the rows and found the journalist who had spoken. She was a skinny, freckled woman of around forty, sitting in the second row. Her hair was partly covered by a blue scarf. It was the same woman who had tried to corner him at the crime scene yesterday.

Merethe Winther-Sørensen leaned forward.

"I'm sorry, I didn't catch your name." Her voice was cool.

"Sandra Kørner, *Ekstra Bladet*." The journalist didn't even bat an eyelid.

"Thank you." Merethe Winther-Sørensen rested her elbows on the table and folded her hands. "According to the police, there was no sexual contact between my son and... the witness. Perhaps we should let the police present the facts before we start speculating?"

Sandra Kørner's pen flew across her notepad.

"Was that the reason he —" she continued, but Merethe Winther-Sørensen cut her off, looking across the assembly.

"I'm available for questions afterward, obviously, but first of all I would like to say that we're all deeply upset by the terrible loss that the Radical Party, our family, and Copenhagen suffered last night. Mogens was a wonderful son, and a rare politician with a remarkable career ahead of him..." She trailed off and reached out for the glass of water in front of her. Her hand was trembling. "My party has issued a press release, which should be with your editors as we speak. It will also be distributed as you leave. I'll now hand you over to Chief Inspector Ulrik Sommer and Sanne Bissen, who is heading the investigation for the police. Go ahead."

Lars caught Sanne's eye. She blinked and looked away, her cheeks flushed. It suited her.

"Thank you." Ulrik coughed. "Sorry. As you'll be aware, Mogens Winther-Sørensen, the mayor of Copenhagen, was found murdered last night at his home in Frederiksberg. A young woman was also found at the crime scene. She arrived from Hamburg yesterday, but we presume she's not German."

An older man shouted from the back: "Is she a suspect? Was it a sex killing?"

Lars shut his eyes. He knew he shouldn't be surprised, but had they really not been listening to a word of what had just been said? Sanne stood up.

"A witness saw the perpetrator escape. But I'd like to turn to another matter: we've just confirmed the murder weapon. Lights off, please." The room went dark.

Sanne tapped her phone and a photograph of the kitchen knife appeared enlarged on the screen behind them. A ruler at the bottom of the photograph indicated its measurements.

"We've found three sets of fingerprints on the knife. Mogens Winther-Sørensen's, the woman with him, and a third person who isn't a family member. We're currently focusing our investigation on this third person."

"The woman... you're saying this wasn't about prostitution?" asked a young man sitting next to Sandra Kørner. "Then what was she doing with the mayor?"

"Like I said, we've found no forensic evidence to indicate sexual contact between the two of them, and—"

"As far as *we*..." Sandra was speaking now. She made a sweeping gesture to include all of the journalists, "Gather, the deceased was found with his pants around his ankles, lying next to this woman." Lars thought about the photograph that had been on the front page of every tabloid newspaper. He cursed himself for not having kept the photographer out of the apartment. Sandra Kørner continued: "Surely it's no wonder that we have some theories about what might have happened?"

Merethe Winther-Sørensen had been stirring restlessly in her chair during the latter part of the press conference. She couldn't restrain herself any longer.

"Please may I?" But she didn't wait for permission before she continued. "Like I said, my son's death is a great loss for the family and for my party. But it's also a great loss for Danish politics, which is why the party and I have decided to issue a reward of a hundred thousand kroner for information leading to the apprehension of my son's killer. You can call the Radical Party in Copenhagen on the number specified in the press release with any information."

Lars closed his eyes. Anything but that. He peered at Ulrik, who was gritting his teeth and staring at the table. The whole thing was spinning out of control. Interns and students would be receiving information from the public and be their first point of contact at the very stage where it was of vital importance that calls were handled by professionals who knew how to listen. And, more importantly, ask the right questions. Merethe Winther-Sørensen had just done everything she possibly could to wreck the investigation. The questions rained down over the podium. The mucky heat made his shirt stick to his back.

OCTOBER 1999

THE RED CROSS worker leads Mogens down the long, yellow corridor. The noise of children outside the sports hall disappears behind them.

"I think Søren is free now, if we're lucky... Yes, it appears so."

Two residents in shabby track suits emerge from a door further down the hall, followed by a stocky Danish man. They exchange a few words in English, but Mogens can't decipher the meaning, and the trio disappear in the opposite direction. The Red Cross worker pops his head around the door, which is decorated with a piece of paper that has DIRECTOR written on it.

"Søren? The new volunteer is here."

There is a grunt from inside the office. The Red Cross worker nods to Mogens, edges around him, and disappears back down the corridor.

The office is narrow and dark and painted yellow like the

corridor outside. There is a desk covered with papers, files, and coffee cups. Two square windows provide a view of a low, grey barrack behind the Margretheholm Refugee Centre. Beyond it is an open area scattered with tufts of grass, wrecked bicycles, and car tires, and the remains of a concrete foundation from a building that was never finished. In the distance, masts from the marina behind Lynetten form a backdrop to the sordid spectacle. Slender trees border the area to the west. A large group of dark-skinned children are using the area as a playground, kicking a ball around under the cold October sun.

"Welcome." Søren gets up from his chair behind the desk, extending his hand. He is a compact man with a barrel chest. He might be in his early fifties; his black, wispy hair has hints of grey.

Mogens sits down.

"Sorry to keep you waiting." Søren rakes his hand through his hair. It sticks up in the air. "I had to deal with some stolen bicycles. Our residents feel safer when a Red Cross worker attends police interviews."

Mogens nods. So the police had been here?

"I gather you're experiencing a rise in the number of refugees?"

"The events in Kosovo have taken us all by surprise. We're building several centres across Denmark, but Margretheholm is the biggest, so we're grateful for all the volunteers we can get. You want to study education?"

"Yes. I was hoping to use this for an assignment, if you'll allow me?"

"I'm sure we can work something out. Have you had the tour?"

"Not yet."

"Our facilities aren't modern, as you can see. This place used to be an old naval base, which explains the wheelhouse on the roof." Søren drums his fingers on the desk and clears his throat. "I have to ask... Your surname?"

Of course, it had to come up. *It always does.*

"Yes, she's my mother." Mogens looks out of the window. He *could* take Kirsten's surname.

"This is the sports hall." Søren points through the dilapidated, brown double doors at their first stop on the tour of the residents' area. The hall echoes with laughter and shouting. Some young Danish men are playing volleyball with far too many boys and girls. "We try to make sure there are lots of things for the kids to do here. Hopefully it'll stop them from dwelling too much on what they've seen and where they've come from."

Mogens nods. Right now it seems to be working.

The tour continues to the centre office, the nurses' station, and the storeroom.

"The residents live in quarters like this one." Søren walks him down a long corridor. Brown chipboard covers the bottom half of the walls on both sides, interrupted only by the blue doors. "Each corridor has its own kitchen where residents can cook. There's also a cafeteria for bigger events, but the bedrooms are small. Excuse us..." Søren greets an older man in sweatpants and a flat cap, who leans his hand on the door handle to one of the rooms while kicking off his plastic sandals. "Could we have a look inside?"

The man steps aside so Mogens and Søren can see in. Bunk beds made of red metal pipes with foam mattresses are lined against both walls; a table under the open, square window is covered by groceries, folded clothing, and books. A young woman sits on one of the lower bunks with her legs pulled under her and an infant in her arms. It is hot, despite the autumn chill outside. It smells of too many people in too little space. Søren smiles at the woman and thanks the man in the flat cap.

They proceed down the corridor.

"Each family is allocated a room similar to the one you've just seen. We also have a number of accompanied unaccompanied children."

Mogens stops.

"Accompanied unaccompanied?"

"Yes—funny term, isn't it?" Søren walks on and Mogens has no choice but to follow him. "Children and teenagers under eighteen who arrive without parents—they might be missing or even dead—but these children aren't necessarily alone either, hence the term *accompanied unaccompanied*. Most come with other family members: uncles, aunts, grandparents. Others have been brought here by neighbours or friends of the family."

"But that's terrible. Do you have many of them?"

"A few. As you know, children are the most vulnerable and always suffer most in a conflict." They stop at the end of the corridor. "Two of them live in here." He knocks on the door frame. "Afërdita?"

The room is similar to the first, only there are no bunk beds here. Two ordinary single beds made from the same red metal pipes are positioned on either side of the window, the brown chipboard covering the bottom half of the walls.

A young girl is sitting on the bed to the right. She has a pretty, elongated face, framed by dark hair that falls in waves over her shoulders. She is wearing a sleeveless dress and reading a magazine. The girl looks up, startled, but her features soften and she flashes them a shy smile once she recognizes it's Søren.

"This is Mogens." Søren leans against the door frame. "Where's your brother?"

"Arbën is out somewhere." The girl retreats a little on the bed. She can be no more than fourteen or fifteen years old, at most.

"Are you telling me that she and her brother arrived alone?" Mogens feels almost sick at the thought.

"They arrived with some family. Their uncles live slightly further down the corridor. Ah, here he is. Hi Arbën." Søren places his hand on the head of a slender boy. He is wearing sequinned running shoes, and presses himself against the wall. A filthy doll trails along the floor behind him.

"How old is he?" Mogens looks down at the boy, whose dark eyes are staring up at him without blinking.

"They say he's eight. But it's hard to know for sure."

"Does he understand English?" Mogens squats down on his haunches.

"Some."

He turns to the boy. "I have a daughter. Sarah is almost five. Do you want to see her picture?"

The boy looks gravely at him. Mogens takes out his wallet and finds the small photograph.

"Here. This is Sarah. Maybe some day you can play with her, eh?"

The boy takes the photograph, studying it.

"I can see that no one has explained the rules to you yet." Søren lowers his voice. "You'll be dismissed if you see the refugees privately. You're not allowed to invite them to your home or give them anything, nor borrow or accept anything from them."

"But . . ." He looks at the boy. Arbën stands holding the photo of Sarah in both hands, completely mesmerized.

"It might sound harsh, but it's actually meant to protect them. They're in a vulnerable situation: they know no one here and nothing about how our society works. It's far too easy for them to end up in a relationship with an unhealthy level of dependency. They might think you can help them obtain asylum if they do favours for you. Many of them would do anything."

Mogens gets up and reaches for the photograph, but Arbën retreats, clutching the small image in his hands.

"You'll have a hard time getting that off him." Søren laughs. "I don't think a small picture of your daughter can do any harm, but you must take extra care, Mogens... with your family, I mean."

WEDNESDAY, SEPTEMBER 25

10

LARS HEADED DOWN the red corridor to the Violent Crime
Unit and opened the green door. A single letter was waiting
for him in his mailbox. He took out the slender, white envelope and checked the sender: *Elena Winkler.* He closed his eyes.
The murder of the mayor had almost made him forget about her,
their unfinished divorce, and the dividing-up of their matrimonial
assets—but only almost.

He had almost managed to forget about Ulrik, too.

Ulrik, with whom Elena now lived; his old friend and boss.
The weasel.

Lars entered his office, tossed the envelope in a drawer, and
slammed it shut. It was time for the morning briefing. The others
would be here any minute.

Lisa was the first to arrive. Her short hair stood right up and
her compact body bristled with energy. She nodded toward the

stack of morning papers on his desk. Every single one had the press conference on the front page with headlines such as **MINISTER: 100,000 KRONER REWARD FOR INFORMATION ABOUT MY SON'S MURDER.**

"The usual garbage." Lars cleared away the pile of papers. "Sit down. There's nothing we can do about the media."

A file folder appeared underneath the newspapers. It contained printouts of the findings from the first batch of calls to the Radical Party's phone line: the result of Merethe Winther-Sørensen's reward.

"We'll get some of our colleagues to trawl through these. Sanne and Allan should be here in a moment." He looked at his watch. Ten past.

The door opened and Sanne entered, followed by Allan, who mopped sweat from his upper lip with a tissue, then placed his briefcase on the floor.

"Good morning." Lars sat down. "Who has interviewed the neighbours?"

"I have. Hang on . . ." Allan rummaged through his bag. "Yes. I got nothing. All the good citizens of Frederiksberg keep to themselves." He sat down. "I also stopped by the Town Hall yesterday, and spoke to one of the building's officials. Serafine met Mogens Winther-Sørensen outside the main entrance. She waited for over an hour before the mayor came out."

"Did she ask about him inside, at reception?" Sanne asked.

"They wouldn't let her in. She looks like . . . well, you know." Allan shrugged his shoulders.

"Are you suggesting that they knew each other?"

"How likely is it that the mayor of Copenhagen would know a random German sex worker?" Allan paused for effect, letting the question sink in. "Not very, is it? Mogens Winther-Sørensen left the Town Hall around five thirty. I've put together some surveillance images . . ." He put his briefcase on his lap, opened it, and produced some still photographs. "Here. They spend a few minutes talking outside the Town Hall. Then they walk to the taxi stand by Burger King and get into a cab. You can see the registration number and everything. It only took me five minutes to find the driver."

"And?" Lars flicked through the photos.

"He drove them straight to the victim's address at Sankt Thomas Plads. They stopped by a pizzeria on the way. According to the driver, they hardly said two words to each other the whole trip."

Lars closed his eyes and leaned back. No such luck, of course.

"But there is one more thing." Allan had something; they could hear it in his voice. "I spoke to a guy at Nets, the online payments company." He took a printout from his briefcase and held it up so everyone could see the list of dates, times, and addresses. "Their records show that Kirsten Winther-Sørensen's debit card was swiped at the Shell gas station at Fredensborgvej 69 in Hillerød..." Allan paused. "At 5:23 p.m. on Monday afternoon."

"She was in Hillerød at 5:23 p.m.?" Sanne made a note. "And how long does it take to drive to Frederiksberg from there? Thirty to forty minutes? Frelsén put the time of death at 6:45 p.m."

"In more than half of murder cases, the spouse is the perpetrator." Allan's upper lip was sweaty again as he looked around.

"Okay." Lars nodded. "You and Sanne go talk to Kirsten and her daughter."

Sanne got up.

"And what are *you* going to do?"

"I've something I need to check."

11

LARS WENT TO the photocopy room to pick up the sizeable pile of paper he had printed out from Infomedia's database: every single article published in the last fifteen years in both national and Copenhagen newspapers about Mogens Winther-Sørensen and his mother.

Back in his office, he dumped the stack on the corner of his desk and shoved the keyboard under the monitor, but his movements were too forceful and he ended up nudging the bottom of the pile so that the top half fell over the edge of the desk and sailed onto the floor, where the papers scattered in an asymmetrical fan.

Lars swore, knelt down, and started gathering up stray sheets of paper. When he had finished he pulled out his chair and sat down to read, not worrying about chronology or whether the articles concerned the deceased or his mother.

He found stories describing how Merethe Winther-Sørensen had wept as she vacated the Ministry of the Interior in favour of her successor when the right-wing coalition had succeeded Poul Nyrup Rasmussen's left-wing coalition government in 2001. He read about Mogens Winther-Sørensen's fight to get parliament to understand that the capital had different needs than the rest of the country. Lars presumed that the family connection must have been of some use in this respect. And there was a lengthy feature about Merethe Winther-Sørensen and her political role model—her grandfather, the Radical foreign minister Holger Winther-Sørensen, who had served under Viggo Kampmann. Lars shuddered as he recalled the sombre portrait in the hall in the imposing house on Amicisvej.

Somewhere in the pile he also found a colourful feature in "Free," the *Berlingske Tidende* supplement, in which Kirsten Winther-Sørensen, *"managing director and head of design for the über-cool Danish clothing brand [Hy:brid],"* invited readers into her home on Sankt Thomas Plads in Frederiksberg. The apartment hadn't changed much in the intervening years, as far he could tell.

However, he failed to find any articles from the time Mogens Winther-Sørensen became mayor of Copenhagen, which was odd. It had been something of a coup for the Radical Party, since the capital had been a staunch Social Democratic bastion for almost one hundred years. Lars assumed it was an event that would have interested most people, and not just those living in Copenhagen.

He went to grab himself some coffee. When he came back to his office, he started organizing the printouts. Arranging hundreds of articles and notes in chronological order was a tedious job and it was late afternoon by the time he was finished. One emerging pattern was definitely clear: Mogens and Merethe Winther-Sørensen had appeared fairly regularly in the media throughout the entire fifteen-year period, but there was a big gap from the middle of September 1999 until just after Christmas that same year.

Lars scribbled down the dates on a pale blue Post-it note before calling Infomedia. A friendly but firm female voice answered.

"Lars Winkler, Copenhagen Police. I've been looking over some articles I found on your website and I just wanted to ensure that you've included every article published in the Danish media. There are several items that ought to be here, but..."

The silence at the other end was deafening.

"Of course." She sounded almost offended when she finally responded.

"I'm just saying—" He wasn't even allowed to finish.

"We stake our reputation on being accurate and comprehensive. It's quite simply not possible for our material to be anything other than complete and exhaustive. Goodbye." The call was terminated. At that moment, Lisa popped her head around the door.

"Ulrik wants a word with you."

12

"ENTER." **ULRIK WAS** sitting behind his desk with his back to the window that overlooked the Tivoli Gardens, the SAS Royal Hotel, and the Axelborg office building. In the white and blue sky, torn clouds were drifting over a restless sea of red and brown leaves. The trees in Tivoli were changing into their winter clothing.

As usual, Ulrik's office smelled of dust, linoleum, and stale sweat.

The chief inspector — Lars's former friend — was in uniform, a tight knot in his tie. His cap lay on the far corner of the desk.

Lars closed the door and took a seat.

"You wanted to see me?"

"It has been more than twenty-four hours since this investigation began." Ulrik moved his fountain pen slightly to the left.

Lars listed the main points from the morning briefing. Ulrik nodded.

"What does Serafine say?"

"I interviewed her yesterday. She still refuses to say anything, but we've heard back from our colleagues in Germany. She applied for asylum in Ilmenau in 1999; Lisa is processing her deportation."

"I would like you to try again, before she's sent back to Germany. We need to solve this case as quickly as possible. The press is all over us, and politically..." Ulrik ran a hand over his forehead. It was deathly pale and sweaty.

"Is it Merethe Winther-Sørensen?" Lars almost felt sorry for him. "She should never have been allowed to attend that press conference."

"It would have gone better without her, I admit that."

"Since we're on the subject... Mogens Winther-Sørensen's parents — what's the deal with them?"

Ulrik folded his hands in front of him on the desk. "Is this relevant, Lars?"

"Merethe Winther-Sørensen can think of nothing but the election, while her husband does jigsaw puzzles. And their son has just been murdered! I did some research on Infomedia. There are plenty of articles about Mogens Winther-Sørensen and his mother, but there's one small gap which is completely blank." Lars pulled out the pale blue Post-it note from his pocket. "Between September seventeenth to just before New Year's in 1999, not a single Danish newspaper mentions the two politicians. Doesn't that strike you as odd?"

Ulrik didn't reply, but he continued to listen.

"I called the Royal Library. They have every single newspaper up to 2009 on microfilm. I can go over later today to view the ones from the latter part of 1999."

"Are you suggesting someone is attempting a cover-up?" Ulrik looked weary. "Promise me you'll be discreet, won't you? I have enough on my plate as it is."

"Uh-huh." Lars looked over the top of Ulrik's head. The wind had gotten hold of a newspaper page outside the window. It rose and fell with the air current until it finally disappeared from his field of vision. "There was a letter in my mailbox this morning from Elena."

Ulrik twitched.

"Yes?"

"It was from some lawyer. He wanted me to sign an agreement to sell the house." The arches of Central Station were visible behind the trees of Tivoli. The Liberty Memorial was hidden, but Lars knew it was there. Somewhere. "I thought all that had been sorted out ages ago?"

"I don't know very much about it, Lars. I try not to interfere in your... in it. But, as far as I understand, the sale can't be completed unless you both sign it."

"Okay." There were more important things than selling houses right now.

"Listen," Ulrik hesitated. "Elena has found a holiday cottage in Dronningmølle, a place she's really quite keen on. You would be doing her—I mean me—a huge favour if you would sign and return that sales agreement as quickly as possible, preferably today. There are other potential buyers, and Elena's share of the money would cover the down payment." A bead of sweat trickled down Ulrik's upper lip and dangled from the corner of his mouth.

Lars got up. Suddenly he wasn't sure that he wanted to sell the house after all.

13

MERETHE WINTHER-SØRENSEN was on the terrace, bent over her flowerpots, when he opened the garden gate. The terrace looked sheltered from the wind, and it caught the sun. Kim turned around, clutching the envelope in his hand. He glanced quickly up and down Amicisvej. Everything was quiet. There were no reporters in sight. The election had been called two weeks ago and the campaign was in full swing. After the murder of the minister's son, everything had spiralled. And yet here she was, tending to her flowers. Impressive.

Her private secretary came out with his cell phone pressed to his ear. Kim couldn't hear what was being said, but the secretary turned around and disappeared back inside the house soon afterward.

Gravel and soil crunched under the soles of his shoes as he climbed the few steps leading up to the terrace.

"Are you a keen gardener?" She was standing with her back to him, still bent over the flowerpots, panting and out of breath.

He stopped at the second step from the top and leaned against the railing.

"Not really."

The minister straightened up, secateurs in hand. Her stripey apron was speckled with soil and patches of old mould.

"It feels good to get your hands dirty. Politics is mentally exhausting. Would you like some coffee?" An Alfi thermos flask and a pair of Royal Copenhagen china cups had been set out on the garden table. The minister sat down on a stool and pulled one of the flowerpots toward her before starting to prune the new shoots.

Kim walked across to the table and poured coffee for them both.

"But one thing I do know about gardening..." He raised the cup to his lips and took a sip. The coffee was lukewarm at best. "Is that you usually prune in the spring."

The minister put down the secateurs for a moment. Her fingers caressed the plant.

"These are British pelargoniums — Bushfires, to be more specific. They must be pruned in the autumn or you risk removing the new shoots and they won't flower. I tend to put them in the greenhouse in the winter. And when it rains... They don't like rain very much. Anyway, that's not why I asked you to come here." She picked up the secateurs again and continued to snip away. The tender shoots rained down around her. "Your former colleague, Lars Winkler—"

The private secretary reappeared. He handed her the phone across the table.

"It's the prime minister's office, they—"

"Not now." Merethe Winther-Sørensen cut him off. "Is it quite impossible to have five minutes of peace?"

The private secretary sent Kim a vitriolic stare and disappeared back inside the house. Merethe Winther-Sørensen put down the secateurs and pulled off her gardening gloves.

"As I was saying: Lars Winkler..."

Kim stared at his saucer, circling the cup around the edge of the dip. A small pool of spilled coffee stained the white china. Discussing a colleague was always a delicate matter, but this one in particular...

"Lars is an incredibly skilled investigator," he began. "One of the best I've worked with."

"But?"

"He's also unorthodox. You can't trust him. He pretty much does whatever he wants. He doesn't care about chains of command or hierarchies. Ulrik Sommer, the chief inspector, is an old friend of his. He lets Lars do his own thing. And..." He trailed off, running his hand over his bald head. "He's an ex-punk rocker."

"I was afraid of that." Merethe Winther-Sørensen looked at her geraniums while the pruning shears snipped holes in the air. "You see, there are certain aspects of this case, certain details... As an intelligence officer, you know that not everything can bear public scrutiny... The public lacks an appreciation of the finer details."

"Precisely. That's why I spoke to Infomedia earlier today. About these." He placed the envelope on the table.

"That's what I like about you, Kim." The minister picked up the envelope and opened it. "You're proactive."

Merethe Winther-Sørensen took her reading glasses from the table and skimmed the printouts of the many articles before handing them back.

"I trust you'll think of something." She finished her coffee and pulled her gloves back on. Then she summoned her private secretary.

"So, what did the prime minister want?"

14

THE BALCONY RAN all the way around the huge hall of Frederiksberg High School. The principal was half-running, half-walking in front of Sanne and Allan. He was a small, portly man whose name Sanne had already forgotten.

Martin had called on the way here, asking if she could come with him to the hospital later today — they'd had a cancellation and were moving his appointment forward. Should she be worried? At the last appointment the doctor had tried to reassure them, saying he didn't think it was serious, but then why reschedule Martin's appointment at all?

She was lagging behind Allan and the principal, and had to run to catch up. Sarah Winther-Sørensen was further ahead, at the rear of a group of girls. The principal had to put his hand on her shoulder before she acknowledged them.

"Sarah." The principal took off his glasses, wheezing. "These people are police officers. They would like to talk to you."

Sarah Winther-Sørensen turned around. She was wearing jeans and a hoodie; her eyes were hidden behind dark sunglasses. She had inherited her mother's features: a broad, olive face and dark, thick hair. She was carrying a knapsack over one shoulder and had earbuds in. The skin on her neck and the top of her chest was still glowing. She must have spent the last summer days on Hornbæk beach. Her holiday had come to an abrupt end.

The other students thronged around them. The principal put his glasses back on his nose and addressed them: "You'll be late for your next class. Off you go."

The girls flicked their hair, then took another look at Sanne and Allan and left.

"Yes, Sarah," Sanne began. "We would like to ask you some questions."

"But..." Sarah gestured to her friends, who were disappearing around the corner.

"It's all right," The principal assured her. "I'll walk you to your next class afterward."

Allan had found his notebook and was flicking back through his notes.

"It's about Monday. Your mother said she was at the holiday cottage in Hornbæk from early that afternoon. Is that correct?"

Sarah's eyes moved from one of them to the other. She was sweating.

"Yes?"

Allan stuck his hand into his bag and found the printout from Nets. Sanne placed her finger on the entry that was underlined in red pen.

"Can you see what it says here?"

The bell went off, announcing the start of the class. Sarah jumped. The last students left the hall. Only a small group working with laptops and notes at a table below remained. Sarah tucked her hair behind her ear and bent over the printout.

"Yes. What is it?"

"It's the number of your mother's debit card. These numbers here represent the date and time of the transaction, and this is the address of the store where the card was used. If you don't recognize the date, I can tell you—"

Sarah looked up. Her eyes narrowed to slits.

"Monday. Do you really think I'll ever forget?"

"Sarah." Allan's voice was low and soft. "We're trying to find out who killed your father." The girl stared at her shoes. Allan continued: "We know it's hard. But this isn't good enough. Your mother didn't spend all afternoon at the cottage, did she?"

Sarah's lower lip started to quiver.

"Right." The principal was practically jumping up and down on the spot, glancing at the group of students congregating at the table. "I think...Why don't we go to my office?"

The light came through the window in a sharp rectangle, falling on a row of hand-carved figures on the bookcase. Apparently the principal had spent time in Greenland. The rest of the office lay in half-light. Sanne waited until Sarah had sat down on the shabby sofa. Then she cleared her throat.

"Sarah?" She paused. "We need your help."

Sarah turned away from them and studied the walrus-tooth figurines. Her jaw was clenched.

"You can't force her to talk. Sarah—"

The girl looked up at the principal and shook her head. Sanne waited. Here it was, that bubbling sensation in her gut just before a breakthrough. So why was she feeling so rotten?

"When did your mother leave?"

And then it all came pouring out, so quickly that Sanne and Allan struggled to keep up.

Kirsten Winther-Sørensen had left the cottage somewhere between 3:30 p.m. and 4:45 p.m., and hadn't returned until eight o'clock in the evening, angry and grim-faced. They'd been eating breakfast the next morning when Merethe Winther-Sørensen called with the terrible news. At this point Sarah started to cry and Sanne suggested a break.

Sarah went to the bathroom while Allan fetched coffee and mineral water from the cafeteria.

"Are you ready?" Sanne poured the coffee. "I'm afraid I have some more questions for you."

Sarah nodded and took a sip of mineral water from the glass in front of her. Then she crossed her legs, wedging her folded hands in between her thighs.

"How was the relationship between your parents?" Allan asked.

"Good. They were happy." Sarah didn't look up. "Why do you ask?"

"Your father wasn't at the cottage. Wasn't he supposed to be with you?"

"The thing is," Sarah chewed her lip. "He had some meetings at the Town Hall that day. He was meant to join us in the evening. He called to say he couldn't make it after all."

"And then your mother got mad?"

Sarah nodded.

"Mom was impossible to be around after that. I went for a walk on the beach and by the time I came back she had left. She hardly said a word when she returned from the city. We had a barbecue that night. I watched TV until I went to bed. Mom just sat there smoking and drinking red wine." Sarah buried her face in her hands.

Sanne and Allan looked at each other.

"Looks like we need to go to Hornbæk." Sanne turned toward the principal. "I'm afraid Sarah will have to miss the rest of her classes today."

15

AN ELDERLY LIBRARIAN wearing designer jeans and a light blue pashmina draped over her shoulders ushered Lars over to the microfilm reader at the Royal Library's East Reading Room. The room was packed, mostly with elderly people and students.

"Here is the Powerscan 2000." The librarian patted the grey and white machine. The computer screen next to the scanner was turned to portrait position, probably in order to replicate the old broadsheet format that most newspapers had now abandoned.

"It's the best investment we've made in a long time," the librarian enthused. Lars was more interested in the box tucked under her arm: microfilms of all national newspapers from the second half of 1999.

She put the box next to the machine, opened it, and took out the first reel of film.

"Allow me."

Lars wasn't watching: he was busy examining the remaining reels of film, one by one. Dates had been written with a felt-tip pen on ageing tape strips stuck to the sides.

"There you are. It's all ready to go." The librarian took a step to the side.

Lars looked up. "Something's missing."

"Impossible."

Lars pointed. He had arranged the reels on the table in chronological order. His fingers ran from August 1, 1999 onward. There was a big gap from October 1 to December 31. The librarian tilted the empty box to get a better look: Lars had included every reel.

"I don't understand." The librarian had to sit down. "This has never..." Disapproving glares cut through the large glass wall that separated the area with the scanners from the reading room itself. An elderly man placed a hushing finger in front of his lips. "I think we had better move." She packed up the film reels into the box, then gestured for Lars to follow her.

A door at the back of the reading room led to a cramped office, which also served as a staff room. The smell of salami and cheese was overpowering. A chubby man in his fifties was sitting behind a low desk piled high with bound books and notes. His whole body quivered as he chuckled.

"These YouTube videos are absolutely hilarious. Come and have a look, Lis." Then he noticed Lars.

"How can I help you?"

Lars introduced himself, explained his problem, and gave him the reference number. The man on the other side of the desk entered the digits into his computer.

"Yes..." He leaned closer to the screen and read. His eyes moved along the lines. "No, that's all we have here." He looked up. Everything about him was bloated, including his eyes.

"You have nothing from October up to and including December 1999?"

"If they're not in the boxes, then I can't help you." He fidgeted with his reading glasses, which were lying next to the keyboard.

"This is a murder inquiry."

The man's gaze flitted sideways, and suddenly Lars realized what had happened. He stuck a cigarette in his mouth without lighting it.

"Now, listen to me. You don't have to say anything, all you have to do is nod." Lars cracked his knuckles, and leaned over the desk and computer. "You and I both know that you have those films. The question is why you won't hand them over to me. My guess is you've had a visit from PET. And PET told you not to. I'm going to give you ten seconds to consider the consequences of it becoming public knowledge that the Royal Library — that you, personally — is preventing Copenhagen Police from accessing information vital to a murder investigation. And I don't think you should count on any help from PET in this instance."

The man opened his mouth. Then he closed it again and nodded.

"Good," Lars continued, holding out his hand. "I'd like the missing films."

"He — he took them. We don't have them here."

Lars was about to say something in a very loud voice when his phone rang.

"It's Ulrik here. Are you on your way to Sandholm?"

"Not yet. First I wanted to —"

"Then get up there, right now. We need to talk to her before she —"

"Is shipped back to Germany. Yes, I get it, but . . . the minister and Kim A —"

"We can talk once you've interviewed the witness. I don't want to hear another word. Get moving. Now." Ulrik hung up.

16

THE TREES SURROUNDING the Sandholm Centre towered over the flat landscape. Red and yellow leaves clung to the half-naked branches. A truck drove past outside on Sandholmgårdsvej, then silence descended on the area. Heavy clouds drifted above Allerød.

Lars showed his badge at the entrance and signed the visitors' register. A Roma family wearing identical, colourful track suits were on their way out. He waited until they had left before he addressed the receptionist.

"We sent you an asylum seeker yesterday named Serafine Haxhi. She's waiting to be returned to Germany."

The receptionist leafed through several papers.

"She's in Room 36. Hang on a second. Carsten?" She yelled over her shoulder. "That prostitute the police brought in last night, didn't she ask to see a doctor?"

Lars was given directions to the medical clinic and walked through the centre, cutting diagonally across the square between the yellow buildings. A Red Cross flag flapped lazily from a flagpole in the light breeze.

The waiting room was crowded with families and elderly people. A tall, dark-skinned man sat right at the back, in the corner below a window. His facial muscles and jaw moved in spasms and tics. His eyes were wild, and thick yellow froth bubbled from the corners of his mouth. The chairs around him were empty. Lars nodded as he entered, but no one made eye contact with him. He walked down the aisle and sat down next to the tall man. The asylum seeker looked at him with what resembled astonishment. Then he wiped his mouth with the back of his hand and continued staring into nothing.

A baby whimpered; its father tried to comfort it. The waiting room smelled of cigarette smoke and solvents.

Serafine's voice coming from inside in the examination room made him snap out of his reverie. It was hoarse and flat, a little too deep, and yet agitated with hysteria.

"Asshole!"

A male voice tried to reassure her. Then the door opened and Serafine emerged, her face a contorted mask. She slammed the door shut behind her, and marched out between the chairs and the waiting patients, who retreated from her.

Lars got up and ran after her. They had already arrived at the square between the yellow buildings when he caught up with her.

"Serafine?" He reached out and got hold of her arm. "Wait."

It took a moment, but then the harshness disappeared from her face and her body slumped. At least she recognized him.

"The doctor...he won't...I need medicine." Then she gave up and staggered toward Lars, who had to take a step back so as not to fall over.

A group of children were playing softball between the buildings.

"There, there."Lars walked her to a bench under a tree and helped her to sit down. "Do you want me to have a word with him?"

Lars didn't knock; he just walked straight into the doctor's examination room.

"Sorry for interrupting. Copenhagen Police." He pulled out his badge and nodded to the young mother, who held her baby tight as she stared at him.

"You can't just barge in like this." The doctor's big hands flapped in the air. Lars ignored him and stuffed the badge back into his pocket.

"It's about that woman who just left. She needs medication."

"If that's a woman, then I'm the prime minister." The doctor laughed. "It's a transsexual. He's trying to blag his way to get hormone treatment."

Lars must have looked astounded because the doctor continued.

"Hormone treatment isn't available on demand. It requires several sessions with a psychiatrist before you *might* be deemed suitable for HRT. It's a very serious intervention."

Lars sat down on a chair. His head was spinning. A transsexual? And none of them had noticed?

"He—she—is our only witness to the murder of Mogens Winther-Sørensen. It would be a great help if you could ignore the rules just this once. In her current state, our chances of getting anything sensible out of her aren't—"

"I'm sorry. I can't do that." The doctor shook his head. "Please excuse me, but I have other patients to see."

It was Lars's turn to slam the door.

Outside the children were still playing softball, but Serafine had disappeared. He tried speaking to them in English, but they just shook their heads and carried on with their game.

Lars looked around. Where could she be?

A group of young men came walking toward the gate; they stopped when Lars called out to them. They pointed behind the buildings.

"Behind that one, third row."

The third row turned out to be a narrow alleyway between two barracks. Young children were playing outside the open doors. A smell of food hung over the area.

Room 36 was roughly halfway down. Men in tank tops and sweatpants, and women with scarves around their heads, appeared in the doorways, watching him.

The door was locked. He knocked, but there was no reply.

"Looking for the whore?" A middle-aged man with a fat belly under his red T-shirt was standing in the doorway behind him. An unlit cigarette dangled from his lips. "Haven't seen her since this morning."

Lars gave up and returned to the front desk.

"She just left." The receptionist looked up from her book.

"Left? What do you mean?"

"This isn't a prison. Visitors have to sign in, but residents can come and go as they please."

"But she was our only witness." Lars had to lean on the desk for support. How could this happen?

"Like I said, it's not prison." The woman shrugged her shoulders.

"She can't have got very far, don't you think?" Lars was already halfway out the door.

"Well, she caught the bus five minutes ago. It was going to Allerød station." She waved her hand to indicate the direction.

Lars ran to his car and sped down Saldholmgårdsvej toward

Allerød. Serafine wouldn't have gotten off yet, not while the bus was winding its way through the residential area or driving through the forest. He parked outside the station, jumped out of the car, and started running just as the back of the E-line train bound for Copenhagen left the platform.

Lars closed his eyes and started counting. He stopped at four and took out his cell.

"Lisa, it's Lars. Where are you?"

"At HQ, enjoying tip-offs from the public. Wasting my time and the taxpayers' money."

"Right." Lars was back at his car, unlocking the door. "Serafine has done a runner. I think she's on the train going to Copenhagen."

"What? From Sandholm?"

"I left her alone for five minutes max. Damn it." Lars kicked the front tire of his car and got in. The sound of Lisa's fingers racing across the keyboard were coming through his cell phone.

"I'll issue a wanted notice immediately."

Lars turned the key in the ignition and reversed out.

"There's more. The doctor up here claims that Serafine isn't a she."

"What do you mean?"

"She's a transsexual. She was trying to get the doctor to give her sex hormones, but he wouldn't. I left her outside and went back to persuade him. I thought she just needed cough medicine or something. And then she ran while I was in there."

Lisa laughed.

"It's all very funny, isn't it?" Lars accelerated, overtaking an old Citroën. "Can't believe we didn't figure it out."

"I'll tell our fellow officers to ignore Skelbækgade and Istedgade. The gay bars are more likely to produce a result."

Lars muttered curses under his breath. He was on the

highway. "I'm heading to HQ. There's just one thing I need to stop off and do on my way."

Lars hung up. The needle was quivering at around 140 kilometres per hour. He hadn't forgotten the stunt Merethe Winther-Sørensen and Kim A had pulled with Infomedia and the Royal Library. They weren't going to get away with it.

17

THE FASHIONABLE SEASIDE town of Hornbæk on a typical
Danish autumn day. A strong wind was blowing from the
Kattegat; leaden clouds were visible through the bare branches
overhanging the road. Sarah, who hadn't uttered one word the
whole trip, leapt out from the back seat, ran up the driveway,
and disappeared into the garden.

Sanne followed the driveway through the gate to the salmon-
pink house. Windswept pines and torn shrubs dominated the
front lawn; the grass was knee-high around the tree trunks.

"What a mess." The lawns in the holiday home area on the
outskirts of Kolding, back where she came from, would be newly
mowed, the bushes and shrubs trimmed into ruler-straight rows.

Sanne opened the gate. Sarah was nowhere to be seen.

"It's meant to look this way." Allan held up his hand, shield-
ing his eyes against a stray sunbeam that sliced through all the

grey. "I would guess a house like this costs over ten million."
Sanne surveyed the cottage and then shook her head. She
was caught off guard and her cheeks grew hot when he asked
the question.

"Tell me, why are you so pissed off with Lars?"

"I don't think I am." *Was it really that obvious?* "Why do you
ask?"

"Oh, I was just wondering... Wait, can you hear that?" Allan
turned his head and sidled up to the house. Now she picked up
on it too: angry voices, the odd word, half-sentences tossed and
turned by the wind.

"You stay away."

"Kirsten, she's also my—"

"That sounds like Merethe Winther-Sørensen, doesn't it?"
Sanne walked through the gate. In the garden, a tall man with
a bald head stood under one of the pine trees, pulling his blazer
tight against the wind. "Kim A?"

"Sanne... Allan." He greeted them. "Sarah went inside."

"Are they fighting?"

Kim shrugged his shoulders and carried on smoking.

Sanne and Allan walked up to the terrace and entered
through the open door. In the kitchen, mother and daughter
were standing in a close embrace. Kirsten Winther-Sørensen
was rubbing her nose against her daughter's hair.

"What do you think you're doing?" She let go of Sarah, who
dried her eyes. "Surely you have no right to talk to her without me being present." Kirsten Winther-Sørensen straightened
her back, but stayed where she was. Merethe Winther-Sørensen
entered the kitchen from the hallway behind Kirsten and Sarah,
and gave Sanne and Allan the ministerial stare.

"What's going on here?"

Sanne glared at Kirsten Winther-Sørensen, pulled out a chair,
and sat down at the dining table.

"Sit down." She smacked her palm on the tabletop in front of a vacant chair. The dirty plates shook.

"What gives you the right to interview my granddaughter?" Merethe Winther-Sørensen folded her arms across her chest. "It's been two days since my son—"

Kirsten Winther-Sørensen looked away.

"Merethe, mind your own business."

Sarah disappeared into the bathroom in the hallway. At that same moment, Kim A entered the room.

"Your meeting with the justice minister... If we're going to be on time, we need to leave now."

Merethe Winther-Sørensen looked hard at Sanne, then at Kirsten, then back at Sanne again. She nodded.

"I expect you to treat my family properly." She raised her voice, calling out toward the bathroom. "Sarah? See you at the meeting this afternoon. You'll put up your hair like we agreed, won't you? It looks better, more serious." Then the minister marched out of the kitchen, followed by Kim A.

Kirsten Winther-Sørensen grimaced and started picking at a napkin. She hugged one shoulder with her other arm. Outside, the noise from a revving engine drowned out the wind for a brief second. Then it disappeared.

"What was all that about?" Sanne spoke in a soft voice.

But Kirsten Winther-Sørensen didn't take the bait.

"What do you want?"

Allan took a seat at the end of the table.

"We wanted to talk to you about Monday afternoon and evening, between three p.m. and eight p.m. specifically."

Kirsten Winther-Sørensen's facial expression didn't change. Sanne produced the printed statement from Nets and placed it on the table.

"At 5:23 p.m. on Monday you used your debit card at the Shell gas station on Fredensborgvej in Hillerød."

There was no reaction.

"Kirsten." Sanne pointed to the printout. "Yesterday you told us that you were here all afternoon and evening."

Kirsten had unfolded the napkin and was tearing little pieces from it, dumping them into a half-empty coffee. The fragments gathered at the bottom of the cup, where they turned into a brown, sticky pulp.

Sanne continued: "Sarah told us that you were gone between three thirty and eight o'clock that night."

Kirsten Winther-Sørensen gathered her cardigan around her. She had finished with the napkin; there was nothing left to tear. Instead, she started picking at the veins in the wood of the table with the nail on her forefinger. Sarah was on her phone in the bathroom. She was sobbing; they couldn't make out individual words.

"You could start by telling us where you were." Allan's chair creaked.

Kirsten Winther-Sørensen rubbed the skin under her nose. She glanced briefly at Sanne, then at the Nets statement.

"I was just driving around. I filled up the car and bought cigarettes in Hillerød and parked down by the marina. I sat staring across the water."

"Was something troubling you?"

"What do you mean?"

Sanne took over.

"Sarah told us that you were angry with Mogens that day. He was supposed to have come up here, but changed his mind at the last minute. How would you describe your relationship with your husband?"

Kirsten Winther-Sørensen started to laugh. It began as hollow, rippling laughter that soon turned into a coughing fit.

"Are you suggesting that Mogens was having an affair?"

"I'm not suggesting anything. I'm asking you." Sanne folded

90

her hands. Now that she had finally made eye contact with Kirsten Winther-Sørensen, she didn't want to let her look away. "I don't think you sat down by the marina staring at the sea on Monday. I think you drove to Copenhagen once you'd filled up your gas tank."

Kirsten Winther-Sørensen reacted for the first time. She pressed her hands over her ears and rocked back and forth. Sanne was about to continue when there was a knock on the French doors.

"Am I disturbing anything important?"

A tall man in his forties with short, mousy hair entered. He was wearing jeans and deck shoes. He took off his sunglasses and stuck them in his shirt pocket.

Kirsten Winther-Sørensen placed her hands on the table.

"Peter. The police are here."

Sanne got up.

"We would like to speak to Kirsten Winther-Sørensen alone, so could you please come back later?"

Sarah rushed into the room and jumped into the arms of the new arrival.

"Peter! Thank God you're here."

Peter hugged Sarah and put her down.

"It's good to see you too." He looked from Sanne and Allan to Kirsten. His smile faded.

"What's going on here?"

"And who are you?" Allan took out his notepad.

"Peter is an old friend." Kirsten got up. "Without him—"

Sarah began to sob, leaning against the table for support. Her hair was a mess.

"I'm going to ask you to leave now." Kirsten Winther-Sørensen put her arm around her daughter.

"We're just trying to do our job," Allan responded.

"What questions do you have for Kirsten?" Peter folded

his arms across his chest. "And Sarah? I understand that you interviewed her too?" He turned to Allan. "By the way, my name is Peter Egethorn. I'm a defence lawyer." He produced a business card from his back pocket and slid it across the table. "Well?"

Sanne studied the card.

"May I?" When Peter Egethorn nodded, Sanne dropped the card into her handbag before summarizing their conversation.

Allan passed the printout across the table. Peter scanned the sheet and then he looked up.

"Do you have any other questions?"

"She said that Mogens was having an affair." Kirsten pointed at Sanne.

"I see." Peter Egethorn placed his hand on her shoulder. Then he turned to Sanne. "On what basis?"

"Sarah told us that Kirsten got angry when Mogens called on Monday to say that he wasn't going to come up here after all."

The lawyer sighed.

"Surely even a police officer would concede that it's normal for people to have marital problems without them killing each other."

Sanne shrugged. "We're trying to find out what happened. It's our job."

Peter nodded.

"I understand. But Kirsten and Sarah have already been through more than anyone should be subjected to. If you don't have anything else to add, I'm going to have to ask you to leave. So either arrest Kirsten, or interview her under caution."

"Peter!" Kirsten's head shot up.

"Easy now." He put his hand over hers. "Everything will be all right."

Sanne opened the door on the driver's side. She looked up just before she got behind the wheel. Peter Egethorn was standing on the terrace with his arm around Sarah, watching them.

18

LARS HALF-RAN UP the stairs to the parliament building in Rigsdagsgården, flashed his badge at an official, and went in. He shared the elevator with a young woman he thought he had seen on TV, a member of the Socialist People's Party. The official at the entrance had told him that the finance minister was in a meeting with her fellow party members. It was impossible to say when it would finish.

Today's events had done nothing to improve his mood. He looked at his watch. It was almost four in the afternoon. He was sorely tempted to kick down the door to the meeting room—not even a minister had the right to obstruct a police investigation. This had to stop. Now.

The Socialist People's Party politician got off on the first floor, and Lars rode alone up to the second. He got off in a red corridor, which led to the parliamentary offices of the Radical Party.

The corridor was crammed with journalists. Parliamentary officials tried in vain to impose some sort of order. Camera crews from TV 2 News and TV Avisen were there, and the printed press was out in full force too. The door to the meeting room could only just be seen through the swarm of reporters. The thick shag carpet on the floor and the numerous bodies in the corridor all helped to absorb the sound waves, but the noise was still deafening. They smelled blood.

A skinny woman separated from the crowd and walked toward him. It wasn't until she started speaking that he recognized her as the pushy journalist from the press conference yesterday.

"Lars Winkler?"

"Might be." Lars tried to keep an eye on the door. "Who wants to know?"

"Sandra Kørner, *Ekstra Bladet*." She held out her hand. Lars ignored it. She let her hand drop and laughed. "You chucked out my photographer from Mogens Winther-Sørensen's apartment on Monday and had him driven halfway to the other side of Amager. Are you aware he's going to file a complaint about you?"

"Let him." Lars continued to stare past her. "He should expect to be summoned for a DNA test within the next few days."

Sandra Kørner scratched her ear.

"I'm just giving you information. I'm not defending him."

"Hmm." Was she actually trying to be friendly? "Do you know when they'll finish?"

"They've been at it for hours." Sandra Kørner turned around and followed Lars's gaze to the door to the meeting room. "Do you have any new leads? Is this why you need to talk to the minister?"

"Listen, we have a press officer who works for our communications department. Try them."

"Oh, come on." Sandra Kørner laughed. "Surely we can help each other out here. For example, I could—"

The door to the meeting room creaked. Lars couldn't see what was happening, but it sounded as if the handle had been pushed down from the inside. The journalists surged toward the door; TV cameras ploughed through the crowd of reporters. A forest of cameras rose from outstretched arms. Sandra Kørner pushed her way to the front.

Lars tried to get an overview. There was no way he would reach the door. It was better to wait until the minister left—but would she turn left or right?

The door opened and the crowd in front grew.

"Hey, hey. Step back, would you?" The minister's distinctive voice cut through the noise. Officials herded the reporters back in an attempt to clear enough space to allow the politicians and the party's press officers to leave.

"Minister, can you tell us what the meeting was about? Did you discuss the situation at the Town Hall?" It was impossible to determine which journalist was asking the questions. Lars didn't care, didn't listen to the minister's reply. Kim A was standing behind her. His bald head mirrored the TV light's glossy reflection in the white woodwork. For a brief moment they locked eyes across the crowd. Then Kim A bent down and whispered in the minister's ear; he nudged her gently, but firmly, in the direction of the nearest exit. Lars followed, hugging the wall, but the reporters formed an aggressive doughnut around the minister. It was impossible to get in close. He rushed after them, following the crowd down the broad staircase, and out through the hall onto Rigsdagsgården where the minister got into her car, which drove off before she had answered a single question. Lars caught a glimpse of her in the back seat, a pair of piercing little eyes staring back into his. Then she was gone.

He pulled out his cigarettes and lit one. Then he closed his eyes as he inhaled—yet another disappointment.

"So you didn't get anything from her either?" He opened his

eyes. Sandra Kørner was standing next to him, watching her fellow journalists disperse toward the waiting cars.

"Can I bum a smoke?" She pointed her pen at his cigarette. Lars produced his pack and Sandra Kørner took one. She used his lit cigarette as a lighter.

"Thank you." She handed it back to him. "Are you sure you don't want to tell me why you're here?"

Lars narrowed his eyes against the smoke. He could tell her about PET and the minister's attempts to block his investigation. He could already imagine the headlines. They wouldn't be welcome in the final stages of the election campaign.

He removed the cigarette from his mouth and tapped off the ash.

"Have a nice day." He started walking to his car.

"Oh, come on." Sandra Kørner followed him. "Just some background. I promise I won't quote you."

"Sorry, no." Lars unlocked his car and got in. "Goodbye."

19

SANNE DUMPED HER handbag on her desk. Allan sat down on the windowsill, dangling his legs.

"What do we do?"

She ran her hands through her hair. They didn't have enough on Kirsten Winther-Sørensen, except a missing alibi and a lie. But there was something. Somewhere, there was a missing piece. If they could only...

"Do you kill your husband because he fails to show up at your holiday home?"

"It could have been the last straw?" Allan's cheeks coloured. "The culmination of years of irritation and anger just waiting for an opportunity to explode. What's the deal with that guy Peter?"

Sanne nodded while rummaging around her handbag.

"Here." She pulled out the business card. "I'll check him out. You go over the surveillance cameras from highways and banks.

Make sure to review all the routes she could have taken from Hillerød and into Copenhagen."

Allan jumped down from the windowsill and smiled. She could feel it, too. They were back on track.

People were walking around outside. Lisa popped her head in.

"How are you two doing?"

"Mogens Winther-Sørensen and his wife had a fight Monday afternoon." Sanne turned her chair to face her. "And we think she's sleeping with her lawyer."

Lisa closed the door behind her.

"Forget about the wife."

Allan sat down again. Sanne blinked.

"What?"

"I've already seen *Ekstra Bladet's* homepage" Lisa said. "It changes nothing."

"*Ekstra Bladet*? What are you talking about?"

"Some genius here at police headquarters leaked the story about Kirsten Winther-Sørensen and her lawyer. It's breaking news right now. But it doesn't change anything. Can you look up her criminal record?"

"Why? That story seems legit. Who could have...?"

"Just do as I say."

Sanne dragged her chair over to the desk and logged on. Lisa was standing with her arms folded across her chest.

"A speed camera caught Kirsten Winther-Sørensen on the Hillerød road going toward Fredensborg at 6:23 p.m on Monday. She exceeded the speed limit by thirty-three percent in an area with a fifty-kilometre limit. That was twenty-two minutes before the time of the murder. This will be one occasion where somebody will be pleased to get demerit points."

"Oh." Sanne let go of the mouse. There really wasn't much to say. "So what do we do now?"

"There's still Serafine." Lisa took a chair and sat down in the middle of the room. "She ran away from the Sandholm Centre."

"Just because she's run away..." Allan started. Sanne nodded. There was something about the wife, something Sanne didn't want to let go of.

Lisa held up a hand and started counting on her fingers. "Number one, Serafine escapes. Then we hear back from the German police: on Sunday night she robbed a Danish businessman at a sex club in Hamburg. It's one of those places with a bit of dancing where you can buy yourself a private session with the performers in the back. The businessman was carrying a copy of *Børsen* with a photograph of him and Mogens Winther-Sørensen on the front page. He said that Serafine asked about the mayor when she saw the photo. The following day she turned up here."

"And what about the knife?" Allan asked.

"Well, she could have chucked it out the window. It was lying some distance away in the courtyard, but a proper throw could have gotten it that far." Lisa shrugged her shoulders. "Allan, you checked buses, trains, and the Metro. Any results?"

Allan chewed his lip and shook his head.

"But..."

"We've dispatched patrol cars to the gay bars. Fortunately, we photographed Serafine on Monday. She's not someone you tend to overlook."

Allan said nothing. His legs had started dangling again.

"The gay bars?" Sanne tossed Peter Egethorn's business card into a drawer.

"Oh, I forgot to mention." Lisa laughed. "Serafine isn't a woman—she's a transsexual."

"A transvestite?" Sanne was nonplussed. Allan stayed silent.

"A transsexual: a man born in a woman's body or—in this case—a woman born in a man's. I read a bit about it after speaking to Lars. They say it's like being born into the wrong body. Don't ask." Lisa got up.

"It sounds..." Sanne didn't know what to say.

"Yes, it does, doesn't it?" Lisa put the chair back. "Allan? Don't nod off. We have a killer to catch." Allan jolted. It seemed as if he had really been asleep. He looked like someone who had just fallen from the moon.

"Where do we start?"

20

"WHAT'S GOING ON?" Ulrik turned his screen so that Lars could see it. The smell of sweat and dust in Ulrik's office was more intrusive than usual. Was it frustration? The chief inspector looked grim. "It's not the article about Kirsten Winther-Sørensen and her lawyer that I'm interested in."

Ekstra Bladet's homepage used a large font, but Lars was no longer a young man. His doctor had muttered something about reading glasses being a good idea the last time he had gone for a checkup. Apparently the rot set in as early as your mid-forties these days. Lars brushed the thought aside and concentrated on the headline:

ELECTION BOMBSHELL: DO POLICE SUSPECT FINANCE MINISTER OF KILLING HER OWN SON?

There was a large photograph from outside the Radical Party's meeting room under the headline. Lars was in the photo, standing at the back by the red wall, and the pack of journalists were pushing against the white door. The picture caption wasn't much better: *Head of investigation, Lars Winkler, tried in vain to interview Finance Minister Merethe Winther-Sørensen after the Radical Party met today. Do the police have new leads? Is the finger pointing at a high-voltage political drama?*

Lars's eyes sought out the byline. Sandra Kørner, of course.

"That's pure speculation."

Ulrik turned the screen back. His mouth was closed, but his cheeks moved as he ground his teeth. Someone had called and pressured him. It wasn't hard to guess who.

"What made you even go there in the first place?" His voice was weary. "It won't be long before every journalist calls for a comment. If I were you, I would switch off my phone." He looked down at the papers on his desk, massaging his temples with his thumbs and forefingers.

"Kim A has access to my email account." Lars sat down. "And I suspect him of bugging my cell phone."

Ulrik looked up. At least he was reacting. Lars continued and told him about his visit to the Royal Library and about the microfilms Kim A had removed.

"They're trying to cover something up." He took a deep breath. "I would like to attend the funeral tomorrow—to see who turns up and takes pictures. I'm going to need the others."

Ulrik thought about it for a long time.

"Is this really relevant? It's my impression that we've just had a breakthrough, even if you did let our prime suspect escape."

"I had absolutely no idea that the centre would just let her go. But, given the way she looks, we'll find her soon."

"Or him."

Lars ignored Ulrik's comment and carried on.

"What about the third set of fingerprints on the murder weapon?"

"It could have been a guest. That print could be days old. Lars—"

"There's something wrong with that family. You saw the minister's husband. Do you think that's normal?"

"I don't know. All I know is that you have to watch your step. We're in the middle of an election. If you're going to continue, promise me you'll be more discreet?"

Lars got up.

"So you're saying it's okay if I go to the funeral?"

"Giving you a slightly longer leash usually pays off, Lars, even if I risk taking a lot of flak afterward. I would appreciate it if you could bear that in mind. Now leave before I change my mind."

Lars was on his way out of the office when Ulrik got up. "The agreement about your old house—Elena asked about it this morning. Please would you...?"

Lars turned around.

"I promise to look at it, all right?"

Then he slammed the door.

Forty-five minutes later, Lars was standing by the coffee maker. He had turned off his cell phone after his meeting with Ulrik and was following the stream of information about the search for Serafine on his computer. She had got off at Nørreport Station; there were nicely sharp surveillance photographs from the S-train and the station itself. From there she'd walked down Frederiksborgade in the direction of Amagertorv, but disappeared after the Round Tower. The last picture they had was of her outside the Marimekko store, holding a pair of running shoes. Lars picked up a plastic cup and filled it with coffee. Proper police coffee: acrid and bitter.

Toke emerged from his office. His blond hair stood out in dishevelled tufts; his pale blue eyes were bleary and drawn.

"You look wiped out." Lars took another cup and filled it for him.

"I need to have all the evidence ready for the prosecutor first thing tomorrow morning. Ukë and Meriton Bukoshi are due in court. We caught them red-handed this time."

"Let's hope so." Lars stared at a stain on the wall. "Listen, Toke. I need some background material, and I'm afraid that PET is trying to block me. Someone has intimidated the staff at Infomedia and the Royal Library. And I can't contact the papers directly without PET finding out. So what's another way of getting hold of old newspaper articles?"

Toke shrugged his shoulders and took the cup Lars had put on the table. He finished it in one gulp and filled it up again.

"Don't you ever get heartburn or indigestion?" Lars raised his cup as a farewell gesture and walked back toward his office.

"After fifteen years with the police?" Toke laughed. "My stomach is lined with Teflon."

Lars shook his head and opened the door.

"Wait." Toke's voice sounded higher than usual, bouncing back and forth in the empty reception area. "DBA."

"Pardon?" Lars turned around.

"Den Blå Avis. People collect the most bizarre things. And what do they do when they get bored of them?"

Lars nodded.

"Sell them through Den Blå Avis. Nice one, Toke."

21

IT **WAS GETTING** dark as Lars drove across the Fredensbro
bridge. A narrow strip of yellow daylight still fell across
the Panum Institute. The blue-black water of Sortedamssøen
reflected the neon light from the Irma advertisement down by
Dronning Louises Bridge. Christine had sounded pleased to hear
from him, but her delight had cooled noticeably when he had
explained the reason for his call.

He turned down Blegdamsvej, passed Amor Park, and pulled
into the parking lot. Rigshospitalet towered over him, perfor-
ated by hundreds of parallel rectangles: yellow lights from the
wards, offices, and corridors glowed in the dark.

Christine was sitting with a cup of coffee in the hospital
reception area next to the 7-Eleven kiosk, checking her iPhone.

"Hi Lars." She got up. "You won't get out of giving me a hug."
She reached up and hugged him. Her embrace was longer than

strictly necessary and her warm lips brushed his earlobe. Her eyes were shining when she released him. Or were they simply reflecting the fluorescent lights?

Lars took off his jacket and sat down. It really was hot in here.

"I hope it's okay to disturb you at work?"

"My shift doesn't start for another thirty minutes. So, what's this about?"

"Our prime witness escaped from the Sandholm Centre. She was last seen in central Copenhagen this afternoon, but since then...nothing, not a peep. But that wasn't what I wanted to ask about. You see, she's not a woman."

"What do you mean?" Christine tucked a lock of hair behind her ear, but she never stopped looking at him.

"She's a transsexual. A man who thinks he's a woman. As a doctor—"

Christine interrupted him.

"Not a transsexual—transgender."

"Same thing, isn't it?"

"Far from it. It's a question about gender identity, not sexuality. A transgender person can be homo-, hetero-, or bisexual. The whole spectrum, so to speak."

"But I thought—"

Christine dragged a finger down his hand.

"There is no such thing as a specific transgender object of desire..." She trailed off, but continued to hold his gaze for a long time. A red flush spread across her cheeks, down her neck. "Come with me."

"In here."

Christine shoved him inside the room, then slipped in behind him. She pushed a cleaning trolley in front of the door, wedging it under the door handle.

"A cleaning cupboard?" Lars pulled off his jacket.

"Shh." Christine fumbled with his belt.

A solitary beam of light from the corridor crept in under the door. The narrow room was filled with shadows. Lars could make out the contours of several other cleaning trolleys, and metal shelves with linen and cleaning agents. The only sounds were their frantic breaths and the throbbing of blood in his temples.

Christine tore off his belt and kissed him with burning lips. Her hands were already inside his pants.

Lars kissed her back. Teeth grated against teeth. His fingers wandered across her white coat, and then gave up. There were too many buttons. He turned her around and pulled her coat and dress over her hips while she wiggled out of her panties.

He parted her buttocks, and guided his penis inside her. He let himself be engulfed by the warmth and wetness. She gasped, thrusting back against his hips while her fingers grabbed sheets and towels. The metal shelving swayed and creaked. The rhythm was awkward at first, but then they found it. He could make out Christine's white butt in the darkness, rotating around his hard, deep thrusts.

"Come!" she moaned, turning her face toward his. Lars reached up inside her coat, seeking the heavy roundness of her breasts. He leaned forward and kissed the corner of her mouth. They were both sweating. The shelving squeaked again. Something fell down, hitting the floor before rolling away noisily.

He stopped and listened. Christine reached back with one hand and pulled him toward her. They could hear footsteps in the corridor, but this time neither of them tried to hold back. There was a tension in his groin, then his balls contracted and let go. He had to bite down on her coat so that he didn't cry out loud.

She pressed against him, everything quivering. They gasped for air as they kissed, tasting each other's lips and tongues.

"Ouch." Christine drew in her leg and whispered. "My back."

"Sorry." He withdrew and pulled up his pants. Christine turned around, fumbling for her panties while she straightened herself out. There were beads of sweat on her forehead.

Lars squinted against the sharp, white light when she opened the door. His eyes began to water. Blurred shadows were coming down the corridor, materializing into the form of a nurse followed by two figures.

"You'll be given an enema before the colonoscopy."

The figures drifted across the veil of tears in his pupils before they came into focus. Finally, he was able to see clearly again.

Sanne and Martin were walking behind the nurse. Sanne had already spotted them and came to a halt, but Martin had yet to notice that anything was amiss and kept following the nurse. His fingers were clutching a folder with information from the hospital. He looked pale.

Christine looked up. Her eyes were shining and her neck and cheeks were flushed.

"Isn't that your colleague?"

Lars nodded, trying to adjust his shirt. He ran a hand through his hair. Sanne stared at him and Christine with a strangely dead expression in her eyes. She flinched. Then she looked away.

"Martin."

Martin turned around. His gaze flitted from Sanne to Lars, ignoring Christine. His face reddened.

"What are you doing here?" Lars nodded at Martin, and took a step forward.

Sanne waved her hand.

"Martin... He has to—we..." Then her hand came to rest on her chest, and she ran past them after the nurse.

Christine tried to catch his eye. "I thought you were both working that case."

Lars looked after Sanne and nodded.

"Well, that'll be fun." Christine gave him a quick squeeze, then glanced at her watch. "Jesus. My shift starts now. Call me soon?"

Then she was gone.

He stopped to put on his jacket by the swinging door that led onto Blegdamsvej. A taxi drove around the fountain, before pulling up to drop off a young man. Lars took out his phone. He had twelve messages on his voicemail. The first two were from the Danish Broadcasting Company and BT. He deleted every single one without listening to them. The 3A bus drove past him on Blegdamsvej.

He stood still for a moment holding his phone, looking at the list of outgoing calls. His thumb hovered over Christine's number. Then he shook his head, pulled up his collar, and left.

OCTOBER 1999

MOGENS PARKS OUTSIDE the fence and walks toward the open, wrought-iron gate to the Margretheholm Centre. The sun is shining, but the temperature has started to drop. He pulls his cardigan tighter around him.

"Moo-genz, Moo-genz!" Arbën comes running toward him, waving the photograph of Sarah. "Sa-rah, Sa-rah!" It has become their ritual.

Mogens shifts his bag to his other hand and ruffles Arbën's hair. Someone has organized a softball tournament on the lawn in front of the centre. The children have been split into teams, and the game is well under way. Folding tables with fruit juice and bread rolls have been set up along the playing field.

"Play, Moo-genz. Play!" Arbën sprints onto the lawn, turning to see if he follows. Mogens laughs. Søren is standing by one of the tables, busy pouring fruit juice.

"Is it okay if I join in?"

"Of course it is. Arbën, why don't you add Mogens to your team?" Søren signals with his hands, and Arbën nods.

The next hours disappear in a confusion of sweat and laughter. It's been a long time since Mogens had this much fun. It is nearly time for lunch; Mogens and Arbën are standing by one of the tables drinking juice and watching the others play.

"You look happy."

Mogens turns around. Arne is standing there, smiling. "Just wanted to see how you were getting on, son." His father has never grown used to his name.

"This is Arbën. Arbën, this is my father, Arne."

"Ar-ne." Arbën pronounces it with equal stress on both syllables and shakes his hand. Arne laughs.

At that moment, a fat man in a track suit appears by the main entrance and shields his eyes with his hand. He peers at them and summons Arbën.

Arbën looks up.

"Later, Moo-genz?"

"Yeah, off you go. I'll see you later."

Arbën waves and sprints across the lawn.

"Looks like you've made a friend." Arne folds his hands behind his back. They start to walk across the grass.

"He came up here with his sister and two uncles. They don't know what happened to their parents."

"How awful. But how about you? You look like you're thriving."

"You have no idea how happy I am. I'm never going back to politics." He pauses. "I'm sorry, I didn't mean to—"

"Relax, son," Arne continues, pulling him alongside the building. "In fact, I'm here to tell you that I think it's great—your decision, I mean. When I was younger, I too had plans." Arne looks toward the trees; his gaze grows distant. "Your mother is a very strong-willed woman. She always gets her own way. You were born, and she became leader of the party." Arne shrugs his shoulders. Suddenly he looks tired and old.

"Is something wrong?" Mogens stops.

"Moo-genz." Arbën comes darting out from behind the centre toward them.

"Nothing, my boy. I'm proud of you. Come." He gestures for Arbën to join them. "Am I allowed to take photographs here?"

"Oh, Dad." Mogens shakes his head. Then he runs onto the grass, picks up a tennis ball, and throws it to Arbën. The boy goes to catch it, but loses his balance and collapses, giggling, on the grass.

"Tomorrow?" Arbën looks up at him. They are warm and sweaty as they walk through the centre. The tournament has lasted most of the day.

"Of course. And tomorrow I'll win." They turn a corner and walk down the stairs to the corridor where Arbën lives with his sister. On the last step the boy stops; his tiny body frozen. The doors to the rooms are closed all the way down the corridor, which is odd—they're usually left open. The corridor should be bustling with residents on their way to the kitchen or the bathroom opposite the room where the siblings live. Children should be playing.

But now it is deserted. There are shoes on the mats of nearly every door, meaning the residents are inside.

"Why are all the doors shut?"

Arbën winces at the question. Then he starts running down the corridor. He turns just before he reaches his room and waves.

"Is everything all right?" Mogens calls out after him. He wants Arbën to stop, but the boy continues and shakes his head. The sound of a door opening behind him causes him to stop. A man mumbles something. Arbën replies in English, but Mogens is too far away to be able to hear what is said.

He turns around and walks softly down the stairs. The door to Arbën and Afërdita's room is closed. The large door at the end of the building is open, and the silhouette of a broad man with a meaty backside fills the frame. The man sticks something in his pocket and turns briefly, staring at Mogens. Then he is gone, closing the door behind him.

"She's asleep now." Mogens rubs his face as he comes down the stairs. Outside, the wind shakes the conifers. The waves pound Hornbæk beach. A gale is blowing tonight.

Kirsten puts the last few items in the dishwasher, but doesn't reply. It is their standard evening ritual. They gave up pretending to be a family after Sarah's bedtime a long time ago. He doesn't know why he even bothers these days. And yet, he starts talking to her back.

"Something strange happened today when I walked Arbën back to his room."

She wrings out the dishcloth over the sink, and doesn't answer. Now that he's started, it feels weird to stop, so he carries on. He talks about the deserted corridor; Arbën hurrying away; and the man coming out of the children's room, leaving through the door at the end of the building. "It looked like he was slipping something in his pocket," he says in closing.

"And?" She doesn't look at him.

"Well, what do you think he was doing?"

"Perhaps they're dealing drugs? How would I know?"

His efforts are futile. She has shut down. He gets up, goes to the bathroom. When he comes back, Kirsten is pouring water into the French press. Her shoulders are tense under the thin, white shirt. His hands long to massage her aching muscles until they are soft and pliable. Instead, he flops down in the chair.

Kirsten puts the lid on the coffee pot and turns around.

"I spoke to Peter today." She looks at him.

Mogens closes his eyes. Here it comes, everything he has been dreading. He doesn't want to hear it. Her footsteps across the bleached floorboards, the sound of a chair being pulled out. She puts the French press on the table and sits down next to him. Her breath is very close, a faint quiver against his skin. It hurts deep inside his chest.

"I've decided to find another lawyer for the company." Her hand settles on top of his, soft and warm. "Did you hear what I said? That I'm going to stop seeing him?"

He opens his eyes. *What did she just say?*

"Why?"

"I had my doubts when you said you were going to quit politics. But these last few weeks . . . You're a totally different person. Sarah can feel it too." She squeezes his hand. Then she takes the coffee cups and fills them. "I've decided that you and I — our family — deserve a second chance."

Everything bubbles up inside him. Kirsten's face starts to swirl before he realizes it is because of the tears welling up in his eyes.

Then she sits in his lap. His hands climb up her back and soon they are everywhere on her skin, ripping open her bra hooks. They writhe naked on the floor in front of the fireplace, their skin glowing in the warmth of its flames. And everything is hands and lips and heavy breathing.

THURSDAY, SEPTEMBER 26

22

IT WAS EARLY morning on Folmer Bendtsens Plads. Bottles were rattling outside the Ring Café. The drilling from the Metro construction drowned out even the S-train on the overhead rail. Raindrops trailed down the window.

Lars rubbed the sleep out of his eyes and turned off the alarm on his phone. He folded his hands behind his head and studied the cracks that branched out from the stucco rose in the centre of the ceiling. Just thinking about yesterday made him hot all over. It had been a long time. But it was more than that.

He rolled onto his stomach. Christine had said something before—about Serafine. Lars got up, made coffee, relieved himself, and took a shower.

The coffee had finished brewing by the time he came out of the bathroom. Lars dried himself off, got dressed, and ate some rolled oats. There had to be a reason why Serafine had come to Copenhagen. Some connection to the mayor maybe?

He went out into the hallway and stuck his hand into the inside pocket of his jacket. It was empty. If he was to have any hope of getting the cogs in his brain to start turning, he needed to smoke.

He walked to the SUPER CORN RSTORE at Folder Bendtsens Plads 4, which was squeezed in behind the front of the building and the fence around the Metro construction site. There were no longer any flowers displayed outside. The thick layer of dust from the construction that had forced its way through cracks in the windows of his apartment had probably killed them off.

The young guy who had been there earlier in the summer was behind the counter. Languorous music swayed through from the back room, which was concealed behind a curtain of green and pink beads. A sweet scent of incense wafted out into the shop.

"Hi." He saluted him with two fingers as he entered. "The usual."

The guy looked puzzled.

"Yeah, I know it's been a while." Lars made a second attempt. "Have you been away travelling?"

"Do I know you?" The young man stared at him, furrowing his brow.

"You could say that." Lars's gaze scanned the adult magazines on the top shelf behind the cashier. "We used to chat last summer; I had just moved in."

"Ah." The boy lit up with a big smile. "That would have been my brother, Alexander. He minds the shop sometimes."

Lars nodded to himself. Twins, of course.

"I live at number two. Your brother used to put two packs of King's Blue on the counter whenever I came in."

The boy took two packs from the shelf behind him.

"There you go. My name is Patrick."

"Lars." He picked up the cigarettes, paid, and made to leave.

"Wait." The boy came out from behind the counter. He wore the same type of grubby track suit as his brother, but the pants were baggy around his thighs. "I remember now. Sander talked about you. You're a cop, aren't you? You tracked down that rapist?"

"Yes. It—"

"I just wanted to say thank you. I know one of the girls. Not well, but—"

"Who? Stine?" Lars peeled the cellophane off one of the packs.

"No, Caroline Størup. She rented my buddy's big brother's apartment last summer."

"Caroline," Lars's fingers stopped. The cellophane stuck to the back of his hand. "She's a friend of my daughter's."

"Do you know how she is?"

"Better. She's in New York. I'm sorry, but I need to get to work." He gestured outside.

"Of course." The boy reversed back behind the counter. "I'll tell Sander you said hi."

Back in his apartment, Lars lit up a King's and closed his eyes while the nicotine kickstarted his system. He was about to pour himself some coffee when he remembered Toke's suggestion. He went into the living room and turned on his computer. Lars went to the DBA website and searched for back issues of *Politiken*, the newspaper that had traditionally supported the Radical Party.

There were several hits, most of them provincial, and practically nothing in Copenhagen. And no one had issues going back fifteen years.

But in Haslev on Midtsjælland someone claimed to have *"almost complete sets from 1995 to 2008."* The guy had probably hoped that the newspapers would one day turn into a collector's item. Now he couldn't even be bothered to suggest a price. Yet another victim of the digital age.

Lars sent a message to the seller: *Could I please visit to have a look at the 1999 issues tomorrow?*

Let Kim A and the minister try to stop him.

23

"**D**ON'T SAY ANYTHING." Lars closed the door behind him and tossed his jacket over the chair. He could tell from the looks on their faces and the big newspaper pile on one table that they had all read Sandra Kørner's article yesterday. Sanne had picked a seat at the back of the room and was sitting with her side to him, pretending to study *Jyllands-Posten*'s "Copenhagen" section. Were those red spots on her cheeks? None of the others seemed to notice anything was amiss.

Ulrik entered just at that moment.

"Good morning. I suggest we get going." He sat down and turned to Lars. "Have you made arrangements for the funeral?"

"Everything should be set to go." Lars had sent a mass email yesterday with detailed instructions for each of them. "The funeral is at noon at Vor Frue Cathedral. If I can have you all at my disposal until two o'clock, I'll be happy."

The others nodded. Ulrik cleared his throat.

"Fine. But until noon and after two o'clock, it's all about Serafine. Sanne? Allan?"

Sanne rose. She started pinning still photographs from various surveillance videos onto the noticeboard. Lars recognized Serafine on Kultorvet by the Round Tower and at the colonnade under Regensen across the street.

"You are all familiar with these images. We've extended our search area and got some of our colleagues to check security cameras from troubled neighbourhoods, but so far it's slim pickings. The gay bars haven't produced any results either."

Ulrik ran his hand across his chin. His stubble grated against his palm.

"Anything else?"

"I visited the Sandholm Centre last night to search her room," Allan said. "The technicians say there's DNA evidence, but there were no notes or photographs. She left practically no trace of herself."

"What about the businessman she robbed in Hamburg?" Ulrik turned to Lisa. "Has anyone talked to him?"

"Not yet. He's still out of the country."

"What are you thinking, Lars?" Allan looked worried.

"All this time we've thought of Serafine as a female prostitute. Now it turns out that she's transgender. No—" he raised his hand when Lisa was about to protest. "Not transsexual... *transgender*."

"Why is that important? I mean, you say *to-may-to*, I say *to-mah-to*?" Sanne had sat down with her newspaper again.

"If she did it—and I simply refuse to believe that she did—she must have had a motive. Why is she here? Why leave Hamburg and go to Copenhagen? Why kill the mayor?"

No one said anything. Lars continued: "Remember, we have a witness who saw a man disappear through the back door. And we have unidentified fingerprints on the knife—"

Allan interrupted him. "Yes, the third man. I interviewed the guy who lives above Winther-Sørensen again yesterday. He's no longer sure that he saw anything. The kitchen floor was covered with blood; it was a mess. You know what witnesses are like. He probably thought that he saw movement. And that turned into the killer."

Ulrik looked at each of them in turn and then slammed his hands on the table.

"Okay. We continue with Serafine. Sanne, Allan, you two will co-ordinate the ongoing review of the security camera footage. Lisa, keep in contact with our colleagues on the street. They've all been issued with her photo; she has to show up sometime."

"What about Lars?" Sanne put the newspaper away.

"What do you mean?" Ulrik had gotten up. Now he sat down again.

"Well, what will he be doing? After all, he was the one who let her get away." There was total silence for a few seconds.

"I've given Lars permission to pursue his own lead."

"Why?"

Ulrik was about to reply, but Lars interrupted him.

"I think we need to explore Mogens and Merethe Winther-Sørensen's past. Something doesn't add up. And that information doesn't leave this room."

24

AFËRDITA. **SHE WAKES** with a start, pain radiating from her back. Her neck is stiff; her teeth furry. Her sister's name echoes through her head. The dream sends a frisson through her body. Together they escaped from the uncles while fleeing through the Czech Republic. Then they bumped into a group of fellow Albanians who took them across the border to Germany. They pretended they were part of their family when they applied for asylum. And when the Red Cross worker asked what her name was and the others hesitated, it was Afërdita who stepped forward and named her Serafine. Even then her sister could see the butterfly.

But rumours spread quickly, even among asylum seekers. Before a few weeks had passed the uncles had tracked them down again and forced them to travel onward.

Sweating, she looks around at the brown walls and bumpy floor. Where is she?

She can only recall fragmented episodes from yesterday: the police officer who left her on the bench in the Red Cross centre; the children who started to shout at her and threw stones. But what happened after that?

She tries to stretch out her neck by lifting up her head, but bangs her forehead against a rough ceiling. Did she sleep under some stairs? Testosterone rages in her once again, but if the years in Hamburg have taught her anything, it's that you pay for relief. More images from the previous day return: the train to Copenhagen; staggering through the city; stealing clothes, jeans, a T-shirt, and running shoes. These are the kind of clothes she hasn't worn for years. She reaches up and touches her hair. The scissors. It'll take years for it to grow long again. After cutting her hair she roams through the city, trying to track down the usual places. Blisters grow and burst on her heels and toes and turn into sores. The only place she knows in Copenhagen is Central Station. She finds a brochure for gay Copenhagen and picks out Café Intime at random.

Her first customer is an older gay man, whom she sucks off in an alleyway for five hundred kroner. The smell of sweat and genitals is overpowering. She tries converting it into euros in her head and figures it must be about €70. She folds the notes, putting them into her makeup bag with the €550 she has left from Hamburg. But she still doesn't know what the street-doc charges for HRT here, so when a somewhat younger man hits on her and invites her home, she accepts.

Her fingers glide across his thigh in the taxi on the way to his apartment. The bulge grows between his legs. Somehow it feels easier when it's not her own. The driver watches them in the rear-view mirror, but says nothing. Up in the apartment the guy is so aroused that he only just manages to get it in before he comes.

As soon as he starts snoring, she checks out his clothes and his apartment. There is cash, a cell phone, and a watch—a Jaeger-LeCoultre. It looks expensive. Her heart is pounding as she scoops it all up. She is too scared to count the money there and just stuffs everything in her makeup bag. She grabs her clothes, finds a jacket in the hall, and lets herself out into the stairwell. She doesn't get dressed until she is outside.

Then she runs out into the street. There is neither time nor energy for regrets or plans.

She doesn't know how she found the stairwell or how long she has been asleep. She is about to count the money when she hears heavy footsteps on the stairs above. Then comes a light, something scratching on the linoleum: a dog or another animal? She can see people passing by on the street outside through the narrow windowpanes in the front door. Serafine presses herself into the corner of the stairwell. And then suddenly he's there—a fat man with suspenders, standing right in front of her. He has an Alsatian on a leash. Its tongue flops out of its jaws.

"What the hell are you doing here?" He spits out the words. "We're fed up with junkies in our building." The dog barks once. Serafine looks away from the dog, trying to disappear into the shadows.

"Get out of here!" He is shouting now. The dog rears up on its hind legs and barks again.

Her legs give way under her out in the street. A sign on the corner says Århusgade. She needs to sit down and have some coffee, and a shower. Her whole body is sticky with sweat and cum.

She disappears into a café; she has no idea how far away she is from the guy she ran away from last night. It is not until she has an overpriced *caffe latte* in front of her that her body starts to calm down and she can breathe normally again.

Various machines are lined up against the wall, with clothes whirling around behind circular windows. People are doing their laundry while having their morning coffee.

Out of the corner of her eye, she sees a pair of narrowed eyes watching her. Is that him? He's out there somewhere, waiting. But no, it's only a father hushing his son.

More than anything she needs something to suppress it—the testosterone—at least until tonight, then she'll see what she can do. There's always someone in the community who knows how much it costs. And if she doesn't have enough money, she'll have to get some more. The guy she was with yesterday mentioned a place near the Town Hall called NeverMind. She must be able to find a street-doc there.

She looks up. A police car passes by the window. That's all it takes for her to be on the run again. Eyes are watching her everywhere, following her.

25

THORVALDSEN'S SCULPTURE OF Christ extended his arms
to receive the surge of murmuring that rose from the aisle.
The grey and white marble statue exuded the gentle authority
required in a situation like a funeral — not that the congregation
would seem to have noticed it. They chatted, adjusted their clothing, and swapped seats. Vor Frue Cathedral was overflowing
with people. And more rubberneckers were waiting outside on
Nørregade and the cobbled Frue Plads between the cathedral
and the university. TV vans were ready to film. The funeral
of Mogens Winther-Sørensen was a proper Copenhagen event.

Lars was standing inside on the left-hand side, between stat-
ues of two of the apostles.

"Is everyone in place?"

"Yes." Allan took up position next to him. Lars checked his
watch. The funeral itself was due to start in five minutes. The

130

body of the mayor was lying in a glossy white coffin in front of the altar. A carpet of flowers led from the plain coffin all the way down the aisle to the entrance.

Sanne was standing under the arch opposite him, scanning the crowd. Their eyes met and locked for a brief second. Then she pulled an indefinable face and looked away. Allan scraped his shoe across a marble tile. It made a faint dragging sound, which was drowned out by the monotonous murmuring.

"What is it with you two?"

"What?"

"You and Sanne? I thought—well, I don't know...You can always tell me to mind my own business."

Lars didn't reply, and scanned the crowd of mourners instead. There were politicians, both from the city council and from parliament, political friends and foes alike. Danish commerce was strongly represented. As for the media, you couldn't hope to keep the fourth estate away.

"She's really got it in for you." Allan shrugged his shoulders. "You'd think—"

Lars interrupted him. "I think you need to take it up with Sanne. I have no idea what you're talking about."

"Okay, okay." Allan held up his hands. "If you don't want to talk about it, fine, but you could at least tell me what you're looking for here."

"I don't know. I just have a hunch that something is wrong."

"Don't you think we ought to use our resources on something else?"

Lars wasn't listening and was craning his neck to look up at the front pew, where the family were sitting, all dressed in black. Arne Winther-Sørensen was wearing a shapeless suit and staring straight into the air. Kirsten Winther-Sørensen was sitting furthest away from them, with Sarah close to her.

"Where's Merethe?" A sudden noise caused Lars to turn his

head toward the entrance. Merethe Winther-Sørensen, wearing a small black hat with a veil, was standing under the arch to the right of the church door, in animated conversation with an older, compact man. Kim A was hovering a short distance away, stony-faced, his hands folded in front of his groin.

"Who is she arguing with?"

"It's difficult to see." Allan narrowed his eyes. "I don't think I recognize him."

At that moment, Merethe Winther-Sørensen turned to Kim A and said something. Kim A took one step forward, grabbed the man by his arm, and dragged him away. The older man gesticulated in protest.

Lars nudged Allan.

"Off you go. Find out who he is."

Allan slipped behind him and ran down the walkway toward the exit. The doors were closing. The sound swelled as the first notes of "The Lord Is My Shepherd" poured out from the enormous organ. Kim A dragged the man outside, just as Allan rounded the corner. The first, tentative voices mixed with the pure note of the cantor. Then the priest stepped in front of the altar and welcomed the congregation.

"Let us pray."

Lars heard footsteps approaching from the colonnade. Without taking his eyes off the mourners, he tilted his head and whispered, "Did you find out who he was?"

"I beg your pardon?" The voice was bright and sharp, so very different from Allan's meaty baritone. Sandra Kørner looked at him quizzically.

"My first reading is taken from the Book of Job." The priest had marked the passage in his Bible with a fraying bookmark. Lars was reminded of his own red bookmark back home in *The Tempest*. Merethe Winther-Sørensen slipped into the seat next to her husband.

"Who is this 'who'?" Sandra Kørner whispered in his ear as the priest's voice boomed through the crackling loudspeakers.

"Do you have any idea how many problems you've caused me with that article?" Lars kept his eyes fixed on Merethe Winther-Sørensen. She was staring straight ahead. The veil hanging from the pillbox hat fluttered slightly when the priest reached a particularly emotive passage.

Sandra Kørner chuckled.

"I'm just doing my job, like you. What are the police doing here?"

The priest asked the congregation to sing "Fairest Lord Jesus."

Sandra Kørner shrugged. "Well, if you won't tell me..."

Lars pretended to be singing along, mouthing the words, but it had been too long since he'd last sung them—he couldn't remember the lyrics. Eventually he gave up and whispered, "I thought this was supposed to be a quiet service for close family only?"

"Oh, please. The minister made a point of listing the time and place in the press release that asked us to respect the family's privacy. So tell me: Do you think the killer is here in the cathedral?"

Lars couldn't help but laugh.

"You don't give up, do you?"

She was about to reply when the priest stepped forward, took a small trowel, and started scattering earth on top of the coffin. Kirsten Winther-Sørensen and Sarah were sobbing loudly. Merethe Winther-Sørensen had bowed her head.

When the last notes of the organ music faded away, an expressionless Arne Winther-Sørensen rose and walked up to the coffin. Five others followed. Together they carried the coffin through the cathedral, along the impressive path of flowers.

"Anyway, I've got work to do. Catch you later." Sandra Kørner slipped out the same way as Allan and left the building.

When Lars finally managed to push his way out, the hearse

with the coffin was about to depart up Nørregade toward Nørreport. The body would be cremated and Lars knew that the internment of the urn, in contrast to the church service, would be exclusively a family affair. Besides, it wasn't as great a photo opportunity.

The colonnade outside was packed with mourners still leaving. Others pushed in the opposite direction, up the broad marble steps from the street and into the colonnade where Merethe Winther-Sørensen was standing with her advisers, Kirsten, and Sarah. There was no sign of Arne Winther-Sørensen. Lars moved across the front of the cathedral, edging his way closer to the minister. Numerous microphones were aimed at her face.

Just as he came within hearing range, Sandra Kørner pushed her way to the front.

"Your political opponents are accusing you of exploiting your son's murder to win the election. Would you care to comment?"

Even the people standing further away fell silent. Merethe Winther-Sørensen bowed her head. Then she looked up.

"Bear them from hence. Our present business is to general woe." She raised her head. "Shakespeare. *King Lear.*" The minister paused briefly to regain control of her voice before she continued: "Today I bury my son. Tomorrow the election campaign continues. I have nothing further to say on the matter. However..." She reached behind her. One of her press officers pushed Sarah Winther-Sørensen forward, gently but firmly. Sarah glanced briefly at her mother, but Merethe Winther-Sørensen claimed her before Kirsten had time to react. "However, I would like to introduce my granddaughter, Sarah Winther-Sørensen. Sarah has just been elected the new chairman — or chairwoman, I should say — of the party's youth branch. She is too upset to make a statement today, but—"

Sandra Kørner interrupted her, thrusting her cell phone at Sarah.

"Congratulations on your election, Sarah. Can you comment on the latest development in the case—the fact that the prostitute who was with your father when he was murdered is a transsexual?"

Sarah Winther-Sørensen's gaze flitted about. Merethe Winther-Sørensen stared hard at Sandra Kørner.

"What do you mean?"

Sandra Kørner addressed the minister: "Was your son gay?"

Noise erupted around the columns—an ear-shattering cacophony. Lars didn't hear the reply and forced his way out through the crowds, desperate to get away.

Allan came through the door to Lars's office, flopped down in the nearest chair, and tried to catch his breath. Beads of sweat stuck to his eyebrows.

"I lost him on Rådhuspladsen. It's a nightmare trying to get through central Copenhagen by car with all that construction work."

"And you didn't manage to get any pictures, either?"

Allan produced a small Sony camera and scrolled through the images.

"This is the best one. Still not good enough." He passed over the camera. The image showed Kim A pushing a man into the passenger seat of the ministerial car. The man had his back to them. He was wearing a grey coat and black shoes, and had short, white hair.

Lars looked around at his colleagues' tired faces. There was no reaction.

"Okay. Let's move to the pictures from the funeral itself. There's one I want to look at."

Lisa looked at a series of photographs on her computer screen, stopping at a picture of the altar and Mogens Winther-Sørensen's coffin. A slim, middle-aged woman in jeans, high-heeled boots, and a short, dark jacket was standing by the coffin. She wore a broad-brimmed black hat; her long hair, streaked with grey, covered her face.

"She stood there, all alone, by the coffin for over a minute. Do you know who she is?"

Allan stared at the picture, then shook his head.

26

LARS FOLLOWED THE Town Hall official down the second storey colonnade, which opened out to a large hall inside the building. Visitors could follow highlights from Copenhagen's history on a frieze on three sides of the foyer, from when Bishop Absalon founded the city in 1167 up until the inauguration of the Town Hall in 1905.

He fiddled with the printout of the photograph from Mogens Winther-Sørensen's funeral in his inside pocket. None of the Radical Party's city councillors had recognized the woman in the picture. But you never knew when politicians were lying. Through her private secretary, Merethe Winther-Sørensen had informed him that she didn't recognize the woman by the coffin either, but Lars knew better than to trust her.

A group of schoolchildren was crossing the granite floor in the foyer. Their happy voices collided and ricocheted between the naked stone walls. Lars stopped. Even if Mogens Winther-Sørensen's mother and his fellow party members were all lying to him, there was always the chance that their political enemies, if such a thing existed in local politics, would love to help him.

"How about Kristian Havholm?" He had to speak loudly to drown out the hard echo of the children's voices. The Town Hall official turned around.

"From the Danish People's Party? Then we need to go back the way we came. I think you might just be in luck."

"Lars Winkler." Kristian Havholm was in shirt sleeves and standing in the middle of his office reading a file. They shook hands. "I caught a glimpse of you at the funeral. Is this still about Mogens's murder?"

Kristian Havholm's secretary was sitting in an armchair with a notepad on her knee. She put her pen and pad aside.

"Would you like...?"

Lars shook his head and produced the photograph.

"I'll be quick. I can see that you're in the middle of something. The woman in this picture." He held up the photo. "Do you know who she is?"

Kristian Havholm studied the picture.

"I'm sorry, I don't. But I haven't been here all that long. She could be a personal friend."

"You're suggesting..."

Kristian Havholm shrugged.

"I've heard nothing to indicate that Mogens had someone on the side, but who knows?"

"Okay." Lars folded up the printout. "Thanks for your time."

The secretary got up and reached for the photograph.

"Please, may I?"

"Edna has been here since the dawn of time." Kristian

Havholm looked almost proud. "If that woman has ever set foot in the Town Hall..." He didn't complete his sentence.

Edna took the photograph from Lars's hand, walked up to the desk, and held it under the lamp.

"No, I don't think...And yet...that nose." She stared at the picture for a few more seconds. Then she straightened up and returned it to him.

"Malene Rørdam."

"Rørdam?" Lars had never heard the name before.

"She was Mogens's head of communications in the first few months of his time as mayor. Then suddenly she quit. There were rumours about an affair...and substance abuse. Prescription drugs, I believe."

27

LARS NIPPED INTO the alleyway between the fence and the front of Folmer Bendtsens Plads 2. He had left work early; it wasn't even five o'clock yet. Construction was continuing on the Metro site — constant hammering and drilling chewed its way through the earth under his feet, and the whole thing was starting to feel strangely familiar. He needed an evening on the couch with the Thai takeout he had picked up at Aroii on Guldbergsgade. He couldn't wait to kick off his shoes and listen to some loud music.

He had asked Lisa to track down Malene Rørdam, the woman by the coffin. She might be able to shed some light on Mogens Winther-Sørensen's past. But Lisa hadn't got back to him yet. The day's only highlight was that the guy from Den Blå Avis with the old newspapers in Haslev had returned his message. Lars was welcome to drop by tomorrow morning and have a good look through.

The stairwell was very quiet; even the drilling and hammering from the construction site outside had stopped. The whole building was holding its breath. Lars put his foot on the last step before the landing and looked up. The door to his apartment was ajar—just a few millimetres, but it was definitely open. He paused with his hand on the banister. Had he forgotten to lock the door this morning? Or had he been burgled? That really would be the last straw. If they had nicked his stereo...He put down the takeout and nudged the door, which swung open slowly. Silence poured out toward him. He bent down, picked up the bag, and was about to enter when a faint hissing noise from inside the apartment made him stop dead in his tracks.

Someone was breathing inside.

He carefully put his foot inside the hallway, praying that the floorboards wouldn't squeak. The hissing sound had disappeared. Had it been all in his mind? He risked another footstep. The hallway was dark; only the shapeless silhouettes of his coats were visible in the afternoon light coming from the kitchen and the living room at the end of the hall.

"Is anyone here?"

An echo was the only response. The hissing returned. Then it disappeared. Lars put down the bag on the floor, closing the door behind him. He tiptoed past the closed door leading to Maria's room. The sound was coming from the living room. Out on the stairwell one of his upstairs neighbours came thundering down, pausing on the landing. Lars held his breath and waited. Then the footsteps continued down and out into the street. He craned his neck, looking around the door frame. The kitchen was empty.

Lars crept further into the apartment. A floorboard squeaked inside the living room on the other side of the wall. The intruder could be armed. It could be a desperate junkie on a bad trip, brandishing a used syringe? He looked around for something that would serve as a weapon. All he found was a small, foldable umbrella. He was probably better off without it. The squeaking from the living room returned. Lars counted to three and took one long leap to the door of the living room.

"What are you doing...?"

He caught a glimpse of a foot wearing a white running shoe disappearing through the door to Maria's room. The door slammed shut. Without thinking, Lars pulled it open and gave chase. At that moment the door to the stairwell closed with a bang.

Lars swore, and ran through Maria's bedroom and out into the hall, tearing open the door. Hasty steps disappeared down the stairs. He only got as far as the landing between the first and second floors when the door to the street slammed shut. Lars leaped down the last few steps and was outside seconds later. The passage was deserted.

He flung open the door to the Ring Café. Fifteen pairs of glazed eyes stared at him from the Pilsner-tinted darkness. The bartender was struggling to focus. The smell of stale hamburgers and cigarette smoke wafted toward Lars. He would bet that none of them had been outside the bar in the last few hours.

Lars went back up to his apartment. He kicked off his shoes in the hall, put the bag with his food on the coffee table, and looked around. Nothing appeared to be missing. Someone had rummaged through a pile of papers and old bills. The letter from the lawyer requesting his signature for the sale of his and Elena's old house was lying separately in the middle of the table. Apart from that, everything looked normal. But the apartment definitely smelled different—a stranger had been in his home.

Lars opened the balcony door, went outside, and lit a cigarette. The nicotine coursed through his veins and started its attack on his pituitary gland. He trailed a finger across the railings, rubbing the white dust from the construction site between his fingers, and coughed. He wouldn't be able to use the balcony for the next few years. He went inside and closed the door.

Lars thought about the white running shoe that had disappeared through the door to Maria's room. It had been significantly cleaner than that of your average junkie, and come to think of it, it had been a long time since he had come across a junkie who could run that fast. Nothing was missing from the apartment and nothing had been interfered with other than the papers on the coffee table. This was definitely not a standard burglary. He decided not to trouble his colleagues by reporting it since there was no need for him to file an insurance claim. Lars stubbed out his cigarette in the ashtray.

He was sorely tempted to go to bed, but it was way too early. His fingers toyed with the phone in his pocket. He couldn't shake off the funeral. He took out his phone and saw a text message from Lisa. It must have arrived while he was chasing the intruder. Lars swore, and opened the laconic message: There is no record of Malene Rørdam's current address at the National Register of Persons.

Lars tossed aside the phone in irritation. Yet another dead end. It was unbelievable. He turned on his computer to search the register. Lisa was quite right—her civil registration number produced no recent hits. Lars drummed his fingers on the edge of the keyboard. Where could she be? Her last recorded address back in December 1999 was Vesterbrogade 44. Since then—nothing. Lars read through her family relationships. Her older brother had lectured at Aarhus University, but had died in 2004. Her father, who had died the year after his son, had just the one sister, who had married a Swede in the 1960s. Since then Malene hadn't been registered in Denmark. Her mother was still alive and living at a care home in Borup. Lars called and spoke to an aide there who was friendly and obliging, but the information he was able to give him was depressing. Malene

Rørdam's mother had severe dementia, and couldn't remember anything at all. And no, they didn't have any information about the daughter either.

He turned off the computer and went to fetch a fork and a glass of water from the kitchen. He sat down to eat green curry with prawns, squid, and jasmine rice, but the food was already cold. *Consolers of the Lonely* by The Raconteurs sounded from the record player.

It was just another evening at Nørrebro Station.

OCTOBER 1999

A **PALE SUN** draws light yellow squares on the grey linoleum in front of the sports hall. The children mill around him, impatient to be let in. They have been waiting all morning and are close to bursting with explosive energy and life. Their nonstop chatter and shouting makes thinking impossible, but he can't shake the image of the man slipping out of the door next to Arbën and Afërdita's room at the end of the building. He has asked the other residents, but all he's received for an answer are evasive replies and downcast eyes. He has watched their corridor, but there have been no more mysterious visitors. However, there is no doubt that his investigations have been noticed.

Mogens fumbles with the keys, pushing his way through the eager children.

"All right, all right, kids. There's plenty of time. How about a game of softball?"

The children's excited screams come to an abrupt end. The squares of sunlight disappear.

"We need to talk, my friend." The hand that lands on his shoulder is heavy and fleshy.

He turns around. The hand belongs to Arbën's uncle, Ukë, the bigger of the two. All jowls and rolls of fat under a grey sweatshirt. His brother, Meriton, is in the doorway behind him.

"Later." He tries to pull his shoulder away to elude the hand, but it is too heavy. "The kids—"

"Talk now." Ukë's hand moves to his neck as he drags him along. He manages to catch a glimpse of Arbën. The boy stares down at the floor as he retreats to a corner. Then they reach a corridor and the noises fade into the distance. His heart is pounding and he starts to sweat, even though he knows they won't dare to harm him—not here.

The brothers shove him into one of the big communal kitchens with cupboards and industrial cookers. Each family has its own locker for plates, cups, utensils, and groceries. The fridges are shared. The kitchen is swimming with light from the broad windows that is reflected in the steel tables.

Meriton flaps his hands, barks something in Albanian, and herds the three women who were in the kitchen out the door.

Ukë pushes him down onto a stool while Meriton fetches tulip-shaped glasses, small saucers, teaspoons, and sugar cubes from a cupboard. A packet of the inevitable apple tea is put on the table and Ukë pours water from an electric kettle.

"Drink the çai. It's good. My brother wants to tell you a story."

Meriton sits down opposite him and folds his hands on the table.

"In our village there was a man named Shpëtim. He was a good man." The brothers exchange a lengthy glance. "Good to his family and good for the village. You could trust him. A man like you."

Mogens looks from one brother to the other. The light pours

in behind Meriton. His upper body is backlit, so it is impossible to make out the expression on his face.

"Shpëtim had a friend who lived further up the mountain. Shpëtim went to see his friend because they were going hunting the next day. The sun was shining and it was spring. But Shpëtim's friend wasn't at home; he had gone to the neighbouring village to buy cartridges. After all, you can't go hunting if you haven't got any cartridges for your rifle, can you?" The brothers smile. Mogens squirms on the stool. Why are they telling him this story?

"It's a long hike up the mountain and it's hot, so when he gets there in the afternoon, he's sweating. He knocks on the door, but there's no reply. It's not a big house: there's a room at the back where the family sleeps, and a room where they cook, eat, and—well—everything else. But he's thirsty, and it's his friend's house, after all, so Shpëtim opens the door. He probably wants to drink some water and wait until his friend returns. But when Shpëtim enters, his friend's wife is washing herself. She has no clothes on, do you understand?" Ukë and Meriton both laugh uproariously. Mogens tries to join in. Then Ukë stops laughing.

"You shouldn't see your friend's wife like that. It's not good. You're not drinking your çai?"

Mogens jolts, raises the glass to his lips, and sips the tea, which has gotten cold in the meantime.

"You're not scared, are you?" Ukë slaps him on the back. "It's just a story."

"Shpëtim goes outside again and sits down," Meriton continues. "And waits until his friend returns with the cartridges. That evening, neither of them mentions what Shpëtim has seen. The next day they hike further up the mountain to go hunting. They shoot mountain goats, and probably some sheep from the village. Shpëtim and his friend set up camp on the mountain, eat roast mutton, and drink raki. But there are bears on the mountain, hungry after hibernating all winter, and they are attracted by the smell of meat. When it has grown dark, a bear comes out from the woods, attacks their camp, and bites Shpëtim's knee. His friend manages to chase it away, but the bear is very hungry, so it comes back." Meriton pauses. "This time Shpëtim's friend can't help him because he can't fire his rifle. Shpëtim is in his way and he doesn't want to shoot his friend. Do you understand? So the bear drags Shpëtim away and kills him."

Ukë gets up, pulling Mogens with him.

"We thought it would be good for you to hear this story. Now, come on, the children are waiting for you."

Mogens is shaking when he leaves the kitchen between the brothers. They frogmarch him down the corridor back to the hallway outside the sports hall. Children are leaning up against the wall and sitting on the floor. They don't look as if they stirred while he was gone.

Mogens drops the keys when he tries to unlock the door to the hall. He looks around for Arbën, but the boy has vanished. The children shuffle through the door and those at the front start to run. The oppressive mood lightens a little.

Meriton pops his head around the door.

"It's good to have friends when you're in trouble." Then the door slams shut.

FRIDAY, SEPTEMBER 27

28

THE KØGE BUGT motorway on a Friday morning; *Sticky Fingers* in the CD player; "Can't You Hear Me Knocking" blasting from the speakers. The clouds were high and flimsy. The traffic was going the opposite way, toward Copenhagen. There were few cars heading south and he could stay close to the speed limit.

Lars turned off the E20 after Køge. The flat landscape in the centre of Zealand flared past. He realized he was singing along to the Stones' version of Freddy McDowell's gospel song "You Gotta Move," with its twelve-string slide guitar and primal bass drum.

Fifteen minutes later, he pulled up outside the farm, parking near what he presumed to be the barn. It looked deserted, but the junk merchant, whose name he had forgotten, had promised that he would be in. Lars walked up to the main door and knocked.

Silence. Lars waited for a short while, then he knocked again, a little harder this time. A little later, the sound of shuffling footsteps was audible from behind the rustic blue door. A key turned, and the squeaky door opened.

"Yes?" The voice was coarse, the face bearded. Suspicious eyes peered out through the narrow gap. Lars caught a glimpse of a staircase, a stone floor, and a chest freezer further inside the house. The rest of the interior lay in darkness.

"Lars Winkler, Copenhagen Police. We spoke yesterday."

The man stared at him without blinking.

"I don't remember."

"We did." Lars shifted his weight from foot to foot on the stone steps outside the front door. "It's about back issues of *Politiken* from the mid-1990s onward. You promised that I could have a look at them?"

"You must have the wrong house." The man spoke quickly, avoiding his eyes.

"But isn't this Sanderhusvej? Number eight?"

"There are no newspapers here. Try next door. I'm busy. I...Goodbye." The door shut. Lars was left alone in the empty farmyard.

He knocked again, but there was no reply. Lars walked back to his car and leaned against the hood. He was sure he had the right address.

There were curtains covering the windows in the main building. One twitched before it settled. Lars returned to the door and knocked again. But there was no response this time, either.

He could always go inside the barn and try to find the newspapers himself, but he had come without a warrant. He got into his car and started the engine. Another wasted morning.

He turned on the radio when he got back on the highway. Lou Reed's voice filled the car with "How Do You Think It

Feels." Then Steve Hunter's guitar took over and the last desperate bends faded into the hourly news update.

"A new Gallup poll predicts that the Radical Party has gained three more seats since last week. The poll was carried out after the murder of Copenhagen's mayor, Mogens Winther-Sørensen. It's still too early to say how Winther-Sørensen's daughter joining the party will impact the election campaign, but observers think she could attract the youth vote. The party is already experiencing a significant surge of support, according to —"

Lars reached out to turn it off. For some reason he started thinking about Christine.

The traffic jam began just before Køge. He took his foot off the accelerator and swore. His phone rang.

"Hello Lars." He recognized that voice. "It's Kim here. I thought we should meet."

They met at Café Apropos on Halmtorvet, by the roundabout opposite Øksnehallen and the Husets Theatre. Kim A had suggested it would be easier for Lars if they met close to police headquarters. How very considerate of him.

Lars opened the door and entered the long room, which was already fairly busy with antenatal groups and pseudo-creative types using the café as their meeting place and office. Kim A's face grinned at him from the back of the room. Lars made a point of ordering himself a double espresso before he walked over to Kim A's table.

"Have you been out for a drive?"

Lars said nothing and sat down. Was Kim A pulling his leg?

"You wanted to talk to me?" The wall behind Kim A was made up of old wine boxes with names and addresses scorched into the wood, including *Taylor's Vintage Port, 1995* and *Bouchard Père & Fils*.

Kim A picked at the label on his bottle of sparkling mineral water.

"You have to stop harassing the minister."

"I'm not harassing anyone; I'm trying to solve the murder of her son."

"Lars. The election is less than two weeks away. Can't you see you risk affecting the outcome? And for what? The minister's past has nothing to do with her son's murder. You're on a wild goose chase."

Lars stirred his espresso. The light brown foam bubbled, drawing spirals on the dark surface.

"I saw you remove an elderly man from the funeral. Who was he?" Kim A didn't reply. Lars continued: "You can't possibly have forgotten how we work, Kim—not that quickly."

"I'm only trying to help you."

"You have a strange way of going about it." Lars looked out the window and took a sip. The coffee was bitter and strong— exactly what he needed.

"Like I said, there's nothing of interest in the minister's past." Kim A leaned back.

"And you know that how?"

Kim A didn't reply. Lars finished his coffee and got up.

"I thought not. I hope you've got a warrant to read my emails. Otherwise..." He paused, tossing fifty kroner on the table. "For the coffee."

He turned to leave without saying goodbye. He was already a few tables away when he heard a soft "enjoy the party" behind him.

29

EVERY MAJOR CITY has an area like the one she needs. Here in Copenhagen she'll find what she wants on the other side of the huge railway station, at the beginning of a long, straight street; Istedgade is Copenhagen's version of the Reeperbahn.

It's neater than the Reeperbahn; not as shabby as back home in Hamburg. There are fewer bars. Cafés and Thai restaurants mix with sex shops and takeout stands. But the girls—they're here, even in the middle of the day. There's no mistaking them.

The first two flap their hands to make her go away before she has even asked a question. The third, a beautiful black girl, looks her up and down with a wistful smile.

"Bukoshi? Why would you want to talk to them, honey?" Serafine offers her a cigarette. The girl shrugs and points down the street. "Abel Cathrines Gade, beyond the church, in the basement of number fourteen. Look for Shqiptarë."

Serafine jolts. *Shqiptarë*—Albania. It's been so long since she last heard the word that even the broken pronunciation doesn't affect her. It's home, but there is no home anymore. Only the uncles remain.

Serafine continues down Istedgade, past the church. People are selling dope outside the fence; the junkies are waiting with their eyes closed. They belong near the central train station, like they do in other cities.

Abel Cathrines Gade cuts diagonally across Istedgade. She turns right and finds number 14. There is light behind the windows, and a scruffy cardboard sign above the basement steps says *Shqiptarë* in large, clumsy, handwritten letters.

The long basement room falls silent when she enters.

"What the hell are you doing here, you faggot?" He speaks in Danish. She doesn't understand the words, but the meaning is clear.

A big guy gets up from a table right inside the door. His eyebrows merge across his nose, which has been broken. Greasy playing cards, cigarettes, and money lie scattered across the circular table. An elderly, withered man with a flat cap and a white beard lights a cigarette and stares at her. Another man enters through a door at the back of the club, zipping up his pants. All three are Albanian. She replies in their shared language.

"I'm looking for Meriton and Ukë, my uncles."

"You're Meriton and Ukë's nephew?" The big guy stares at her, his eyes smouldering with suspicion.

"I've lived in Hamburg since... for many years. Are they here?"

It's the word *Hamburg* that makes him change his attitude.

"They're in prison, but their lawyer says he'll get them out. Give me your number and I'll make sure they call tomorrow." He bares his teeth in something that is probably meant to be a smile. "I'm Valmir."

Prison? That explains why the money stopped coming. Valmir takes out his phone and gets ready to enter her number.

"Well?" He's irritated now. She takes a step backward.

"Tomorrow?" She'll have to manage until then; maybe sleep in a park or stairwell. She can't stay here. "I'll come back tomorrow, then."

She walks back up the basement steps and rushes down the street. *Away.*

30

LARS WALKED UP the stairs, down the long, red corridor, and through the green door to the Violent Crime Unit. No one from his team was there — even Ulrik was gone. They were probably out looking for Serafine. Well, at least he wouldn't have to look at Sanne's sour face.

He poured himself a cup of coffee from the machine in reception, not that he needed it. He could still taste the double espresso from Café Apropos all the way down to his stomach.

He shut the door to his office behind him and kicked his feet up on the desk. Malene Rørdam wasn't listed as deceased, so she had to be alive somewhere. People didn't just disappear — not in a thoroughly regulated country like Denmark. He turned on his computer, and logged onto the National Register of Persons again. Malene Rørdam's details appeared on the screen. Her mother had no siblings, but her father's sister had been married to a Swede — it was probably a shot in the dark, but he might as well try. He dialled the number of Malmö Police.

"Malmö Police, Drottninggaten, Einar Persson speaking." The voice belonged to an elderly man with a lilting Scanian accent. Lars introduced himself, trying to speak slowly and clearly.

"I'm looking for a Danish woman named Malene Rørdam. She might be living in Sweden. Her civil registration number is —"

"Slow down. Civil registration number? I'm not sure what you're talking about."

"Civil registration number — oh, forget it." Of course, the civil registration number would mean nothing to the Swede. And besides, if Malene had moved to Sweden, she would now have the Swedish equivalent of a civil registration number. "Her date of birth is August 17, 1971."

"So she's forty-two years old? Hold on a minute." He could hear very slow typing on a keyboard on the other end, and then a heartfelt sigh. "I'm sorry, I can't —"

Lars tried again.

"Can you try searching for a forty-two-year-old Danish woman whose first name is Malene?"

More single-finger typing.

"Yes. We have a few, with the last names Kristensen, Meisner, Öker…"

"Öker?"

"Yes, it sounds Turkish, doesn't it?" Einar Persson laughed. "But she —"

"Wait." Lars rubbed his forehead. "What was the second surname?"

"Meisner. She works at the City Theatre."

It didn't ring any bells. Lars was about to thank him and hang up when his gaze flitted across his computer monitor: Malene Rørdam's mother's maiden name was Meisner.

"Could I please have her telephone number and address?"

After Lars ended the call, he dialled the number he had been given.

A woman answered the phone. There was a lot of noise in the background: happy voices and the clattering of bottles.

"Malene Meisner? Lars Winkler, Copenhagen Police. Is this a good time? I would like to speak with you."

There was brief hesitation on the other end.

"What is this regarding?" The voice was cautious and croaky. Her Danish had a distinct Swedish accent.

"The murder of Mogens Winther-Sørensen. Would it be possible for you to come to Copenhagen?" Malene Meisner fiddled with the receiver. Then there was silence. Lars waited. When she didn't reply, he continued: "Are you still there?"

"Yes, I'm here. I better... I mean, yes—I can come. We have an opening this evening, so I'd prefer to meet in the afternoon tomorrow. How about two o'clock on Gammel Kongevej, by the planetarium?"

31

THE PROSECUTOR WAS wearing a crisp dress shirt and looked just like all the other snooty Danes, lawyers, and judges—people who thought they were in charge—as he stood in the rust-red courtroom with the high ceiling, a smug expression plastered across his sweaty face. Meriton glanced sideways at Ukë. His brother's body was lumpy under his track suit, spilling out over the tiny chair.

"It's tragic that a project set up to help Albanian asylum seekers find their footing in Denmark has now been reduced to a centre for drug dealing and trafficking. There can be no doubt that the men responsible—"

"Just a minute." Their defence lawyer rose. Meriton almost felt sorry for the prosecutor. "How can we be sure that we are really talking about the same money?"

"Your Honour." The prosecutor appealed to the judge. "We

went over this at the previous hearing. An undercover police officer bought a batch of methamphetamine. The officer explained in his testimony that his team followed the dealer with the money to Shqiptarë, where it was handed over to the accused men. At this point the police intervened to arrest them. I don't see —"

"I repeat my question." The defence lawyer stood up again. "How can we be sure that we are really talking about the same money?"

The prosecutor clutched his head.

"As my learned colleague is perfectly aware, the banknotes had consecutive serial numbers, starting with —"

"Can we please reintroduce this money as evidence?"

"Your Honour. With all due respect, this is a waste of time. The banknotes in question have already been presented to the court."

"Just show us the money so we can move on." The judge folded his hands on the table. He looked weary.

The prosecutor picked up the evidence box from the floor and put it on the table. Then he produced two fat bundles of banknotes and handed them to the defence lawyer.

"Perhaps my learned colleague would like the opportunity to check the money personally?"

"With pleasure." The barrister took the bundles and thumbed through them.

"But these banknotes don't have consecutive serial numbers," He started reading the numbers out loud: "*0466220, 734521, 128975.*" He turned to the judge with a quizzical expression on his face.

"But..." The prosecutor reddened. "I checked them myself the other..."

Meriton closed his eyes. They were free. His brother chuckled with suppressed mirth next to him. The tiny chair was creaking under his weight.

Being remanded in custody could have been a lot worse, but their reputation had preceded them. No one had dared touch them in Vestre Prison. As long as you had money, most things were possible, even in the slammer. Meriton pulled up the hood of his sweatshirt as he ogled a woman crossing Nytorv. Her enormous tits bounced with every step.

Nothing could beat the feeling of freedom and being able to decide when and where to go—almost. He accepted the cigarette Valmir lit for him, and slapped his back. Behind them, Ukë was thanking their lawyer.

"Do call again," the lawyer said as he and Ukë shook hands. "We love repeat business." They both laughed out loud.

Their lawyer disappeared between the columns in front of the court, heading down the marble steps to the taxi waiting for him.

Ukë snorted as the lawyer slammed shut the taxi door. *"Derr!"* Bastard. "He didn't do a thing."

Meriton inhaled, letting the smoke seep out of his mouth. "I was beginning to think our friend had let us down."

"He wouldn't dare." Ukë slapped his stomach; it made a hollow rumble. "I need some grub. You can't eat the crap they gave us in prison."

"Elvir and Labinot have food for you back at the club, *Tavë kosi* and çai *mali*." Valmir lit a cigarette for himself. Meriton's stomach started to rumble as they walked down the steps in front of the courthouse, just thinking about baked lamb with yogurt and mountain tea. It had been a while.

Ukë crossed Nytorv, making a beeline for China House on the corner of Strøget and Nørregade.

"I'll make do with a few spring rolls on the way, then. How's business?"

"The Africans tried to take over our turf. They won't do that again."

"Was it bad?" Meriton stuffed his hands into the pockets of his hoodie. This country was always so damn cold.

Valmir laughed.

"Not for us. By the way, some poof turned up at the club earlier today asking for you. He claimed you were his uncles."

Meriton stopped in his tracks.

"A queer? Young or old? What was his name?" He exchanged a long hard stare with Ukë. If that boy was back in Copenhagen...

32

LARS PARKED HIS car behind Ulrik's silver Audi A4 and turned off the engine. Mist was drifting across the deserted residential road, passing through the white cones of light cast by the street lamps. He had spent thirteen years of his life here, from when Maria was four years old until the middle of this April.

The windows in his and Elena's old house glared at him, black and empty; weeds had grown between the flagstones outside the front door. The grimy for sale sign had been removed from the front yard. The real estate agent had obviously been a little too quick off the mark since, according to Ulrik, the sale couldn't go through until Lars signed the contract.

The party was in full swing at Hannah and Andreas's house further up the street. Coloured lights twinkled in the night. Sheryl Crow's "All I Wanna Do" poured in when he opened the car door. Hits from their tender youth.

He had spent the afternoon searching his apartment from top to bottom, and couldn't shake the image of the white running shoe from the day before. It had been no ordinary break-in. After four hours he had concluded that the apartment was clean, with no hidden microphones or wires. Either he had returned too early and surprised the intruder, or the intruder had merely wanted to snoop through his papers.

Lars got out of the car. He couldn't postpone the moment any longer.

Hannah and Andreas's yellow brick house lay parallel to the street. The light was on in their kitchen window. Lars could see Elena standing inside, arranging flowers. Her dark brown curls framed her face, her dark eyes stared through the night into his.

Andreas opened the door.

"Lars! So great you could make it." He stepped aside to let him in. "How's Maria?"

"Oh, give him a chance to come in first." Hannah kissed Lars on the cheek. "So nice to see you again."

Andreas pulled him aside.

"I hope it's okay that Ulrik is here. We couldn't really..." His voice either faded away or was drowned out by the music.

"It's fine."

Andreas looked relieved, and slapped him on the shoulder.

"So, why are we standing around out here? You need a drink."

Lars followed Andreas into the living room and over to an extravagant buffet. Clearly, things were looking up for architects.

Lars greeted several people he knew from the street, and a few new faces who had arrived since April. A number of Andreas's colleagues were also there. Ulrik stayed close to the wall, glancing furtively at him. But the food was good and the wine plentiful, so Lars soon felt very comfortable indeed.

Half an hour later, someone put their hand on his shoulder.

"Lars, mind if I..." Ulrik was standing behind him with a

glass of whisky in one hand, sweating. "I hope it's not a problem that I'm here?"

Lars stared at him, but said nothing. Ulrik sighed heavily.

"All right then." Elena was watching them from the hall. "Ukë and Meriton Bukoshi were in court today."

"Of course, Toke's big case. Sending them down can only make Copenhagen a better place to live."

"That's the thing. They weren't convicted." Ulrik drained his glass, reached for a bottle, and refilled it. "I don't know how it happened; something about a procedural error in connection with the evidence gathering. The judge released them after thirty minutes."

"What?"

"And now with the mayor's murder, we simply don't have the resources to review their case. For the time being we've had to let them go." There was a stain on Ulrik's yellow silk tie that wasn't whisky. Maybe it was gravy. Ulrik gulped his drink and filled it up again, sending Lars a questioning gaze. Lars shook his head.

"Who was responsible for the error?"

"We don't know yet." Ulrik watched the couples wiggling their way through a Mariah Carey song on the dance floor. "But once I find out..."

Ulrik half-emptied his glass, then wiped his chin with the back of his hand. Elena came gliding through the living room in a pair of her impossibly high heels and tight pants. She looked at Ulrik, then nodded her head in the direction of the kitchen.

"Yes, perhaps a refill is..." Ulrik raised his half-empty glass and bumped into an armchair on his way to the drinks table.

"Lars." She nodded. He accepted the glass she offered him and took a sip.

"Mineral water?"

"With lemon. Alcohol doesn't do you any good."

They clinked their glasses. Then she tilted her head, took the glass from his hand, and put it on a shelf.

"Come, let's dance." Someone had put on Terence Trent D'Arby's "Wishing Well." "Do you remember? This was the only song you could ever be bothered to dance to."

Flashback to a disco in Milan: black-and-white-checkered floor, steel bar, pastel colours—very Memphis Group. People wearing short dresses and sharp suits. Elena—twenty years younger—happy and joyous, dripping with sweat, the heavy drops clinging to her long hair. The whole summer had been one long party. Where had it gone? Lars let himself be dragged out into the middle of the room and followed her confident movements.

"What is this about?"

"Lars, we have a child together. These are our friends. Why can't we just have a good time?" She snapped her fingers over her head and bent at the knees.

"Not if you ask Ulrik." Ulrik was standing behind the sofa, turning his refilled glass between his fingers. He was keeping a close eye on them.

"Ah." She tossed her hair. "No sackcloth and ashes for me."

Lars stopped.

"I've got enough problems with Ulrik as it is. I don't need to get mixed up in yours too."

She moved very close to him and reached up on tiptoes.

"When are you going to sign those papers?" She glanced at Ulrik. "Ulrik has found a holiday cottage in Dronningmølle. A house he has always wanted to own. My share of the money will almost cover the down payment. Lars..." She adjusted his shirt collar. "Please, just sign, will you?"

Lars searched the room. Where did she put his drink?

"I'm afraid I accidentally threw out those papers."

Her mouth contracted.

"You can be a real asshole, you know that?"

Elena turned on her heel and marched into the kitchen. Lars's eyes took in the array of bottles. Terence Trent D'Arby had turned into Talking Heads' "Burning Down the House."

33

CHRISTINE WAS WAITING for him by the fence as he crossed Lundtoftegade. The jukebox was humming inside the Ring Café. The wind was howling through the cables of the overhead railway.

"Lars?" Her red coat was open over a purple dress.

"Christine?" He stuffed his hands in his pockets. "How long have you been standing here?"

"It—" She turned her head and looked toward the Ring Café. "Not very long. I wanted to..." She reached for his arm. Lars hesitated. Then he slowly pulled his hand out of his pocket, letting her hold it. "Please can I come up?"

She was alive and warm; her head tilted slightly to one side.

"I just need to get some cigarettes."

She looked happy, and slipped her arm under his. The fence around the Metro construction site ended at the wall after the entrance to his stairwell. They had to walk all the way around the block, up Lundtoftegade and Nørrebrogade and back into Folmer Bendtsens Plads to get to the store. Neither of them said anything.

Lars opened the door to the SUPER CORN RSTORE.

The same young blond guy was behind the counter, but there was no Persian music playing this time. Instead, they were greeted by the smell of mould and sour milk.

"Hi." The guy leapt up when he saw them.

Lars lingered on the threshold.

"Hi." He scratched his hair. "I was here couple of days ago..."

He trailed off and went up to the counter. Christine picked up a women's magazine and started flicking through it. "Two packs of twenty King's Blue."

Two packets of King's Blue were already waiting on top of a pile of newspapers on the counter. Lars looked from the cigarettes to the guy in the grubby sweatshirt. It took them both a moment to figure everything out.

"Ah, you've met my brother." The guy smiled. "People always get us mixed up. Funny when you think about it. It was me who worked here last summer." He continued talking while Lars gawped at him. "Alexander."

Twins. Lars forced himself to shake his head and laugh.

He unlocked the door, letting Christine enter first. Then he turned on the light in the hallway.

"Well then, here we are."

She flashed him a quick smile and took off her coat. Lars put it on a hanger.

"Do you want something to drink? I think I have a bottle of wine."

"I want you," she purred, pulling him down to her face to kiss him. She started unbuttoning his shirt. He put his arms around her, letting his hands glide across the smooth fabric of her dress and down over her buttocks.

"Wait." He pulled back. "Can we just take it slow?" He attempted a smile.

"Is everything all right?" She followed him into the living room and looked around. Lars tossed the cigarettes on the coffee table next to a pile of bills.

"My ex-wife," he began, sitting down on the sofa. "She's living with my boss now — my best friend . . . my former best friend." He reached for the cigarettes.

Christine sat down beside him and took his hand.

"I thought you had something with that colleague of yours?"

"Nothing ever came of it, which is fine — really, it is. We don't have to talk about it. But Elena, she can be so . . ." He placed a hand on his thigh. "Sometimes I just want to —"

"Maybe now would be a good time for that glass of wine?"

When he returned with the bottle and two glasses, she was crouching down in front of the bookcase. Her finger traced the few books, stopping at a dog-eared paperback: the Signet Classics edition of Shakespeare's final play.

"*The Tempest*?"

Lars froze, the bottle of Ripasso and two glasses left clattering in his hands. It wasn't the book itself that was the problem, but what the red, crocheted bookmark contained, which was something very private — not to mention illegal.

He placed the glasses and the bottle on the coffee table.

"Wine?" He poured for both of them.

Christine got up and took the few steps across to the sofa. She had brought the book with her. Lars tried hard not to look at it.

"Cheers," he said, handing her a glass.

They clinked glasses. Lars rolled the heavy wine around his mouth. On the other hand, she must already know about his little weakness. She had seen his medical records at Rigshospitalet when he was hospitalized after his encounter with John Koes in the summer, and would have noticed the concentration of amphetamine in his blood.

Christine set down her glass and picked up the book again, flicking through it. Lars watched, glancing furtively at her thumb running along the pages. Where was it? He hadn't touched the wrap of speed and the hidden bookmark since the summer, and he was fairly sure that he had returned both items to *The Tempest* afterward. But now there was nothing there: the book was empty.

"You've made a lot of notes." She held up the book, showing him a page with faded, almost thirty-year-old pencil notes between the lines and in the margins.

"I lived with my father in New York for a year in the eighties." Lars took another sip. "If there's one thing they drill into your head at high school over there, it's Shakespeare. We studied *The Tempest.*"

"That's a lot better than Holberg, if you ask me." Christine continued to leaf through the text, before reading a couple of lines out loud.

She loved, not the savour of tar nor of pitch,
Yet a sailor might scratch her where'er she did itch.

"How did your teacher explain that one?"

Lars laughed. He remembered how much fun they'd had with Stephano's drinking song. Their poor teacher, who had just started that year, young and fresh out of college, had struggled to explain the ambiguities of the text.

"He didn't have to. Now it might be that we weren't crazy about Shakespeare, but that side of him we had no problems with at all."

"What a shame that it's not the main theme of the play." Christine studied her glass. Her eyes were shiny. "As far as sex in Shakespeare is concerned, my favourite has always been *Antony and Cleopatra*."

There was silence. Then an S-train pulled out from the station. The construction site below his window lay deserted; the workers must be taking one of their rare days off. Lars thought about Sanne. What was she doing right now?

The letter from his lawyer about the sale of the house was still lying on the coffee table. He reached out to turn it over and and hide it inside the pile of papers when Christine snatched it from his hand.

"You've managed to sell your house? Congratulations!"

Lars glanced at her sideways, then refilled their glasses. Christine drank and carried on reading.

"You need to sign here." Her gaze moved up the page to the letterhead and the date. "This was due several days ago. Why haven't you signed it yet?"

Lars jerked his head, got up, and started pacing up and down the living room.

"I've been thinking about something you said the other day about Serafine being transgender. You said it's about identity, not sexuality."

Christine dropped the letter into her lap.

"Yes?"

"What exactly did you mean?"

"Serafine has the body of a man." Lars nodded, and Christine continued: "But inside, she's a woman. Her entire concept of self is female."

"That sounds very confusing."

"Then imagine how Serafine must feel." Christine took a sip from her glass. "Imagine waking up with an erection every morning, for example. It's quite natural for you as a man. But for a woman? Imagine feeling revulsion at your body, and wanting this thing to disappear. Many transgender people start cutting their genitals as teenagers, even as children, trying to remove their penises or breasts."

Lars looked out the window. That first evening in Mogens Winther-Sørensen's apartment—Serafine had a series of small scars all the way down her forearm.

"What do you think she wants?"

"What do you mean?"

"I mean, what's her motive? What's driving her?"

"To Denmark?" Christine looked into the distance. "Right now she's living in the wrong body, and many transgender people want to become their true physical gender. For Serafine that means becoming a woman. At some point, sooner or later, I imagine she'll want gender reassignment surgery as part of her transition. Here in Denmark, such surgery is performed at Rigshospitalet following a referral from a sexual health clinic."

"And abroad?"

"Thailand, I believe. They're supposed to be really good." Christine drank some more wine, then picked up the letter from the lawyer again. "Why haven't you signed it? After all, you'll get almost half a million kroner."

Lars lit a King's. The police had already issued a description of Serafine; she would be apprehended if she tried to leave the country.

"I don't know." He blew a smoke ring toward Christine. "Elena and Ulrik have found a holiday cottage. They want to use their share for the down payment."

Christine put down her glass and straightened her red spectacles. Her breasts heaved and sank with her breathing.

"Is it to punish her?"

"What? No." He gestured with his hands. The wine sloshed around his glass. "No."

"Lars. This is ridiculous, isn't it?"

He didn't reply, but sucked hard on his cigarette. She took in the whole room with a sweeping movement of her hand.

"Just take a look at how you live. It looks like you've just left home."

He turned his back to her.

"Lars, you're a grown man of how old? Forty? It's time to move on. Free yourself from —"

"I like living like this." It sounded peevish. Even he could hear it.

She got up, came over to him, and put her hand on his cheek. He flinched. Who did she think she was?

"Seriously. The springs on this old sofa almost poke through the covers. You have ladder bookcases, and don't even get me started on that stereo." She looked around again. "Where do you eat your meals?"

He gritted his teeth.

"How I deal with my ex is really none of your business." Talking was becoming difficult.

"It's time to move on."

And then it came: the anger, the red mist. He clenched his fist, but managed to stop just before he shattered the wineglass.

"I think it's best that you leave. Now." His cigarette had gone out. The flame on the lighter trembled as he relit it.

"Lars." Christine tilted her head. "Come on. I thought we were going to . . ."

He couldn't look at her, not now. He inhaled, turned away, and stared out of the window, forcing the words out between his teeth.

"I want you to leave. Now."

"Lars," she said again. There was a pleading quality to her voice. He ignored it.

176

A silence descended upon the room. He shut his eyes and didn't open them until she had taken her coat from the rack in the hallway and shut the door behind her.

34

A**TAXI SWEPT** down Stormgade in the direction of Vesterbro. The street lamps glowed orange-yellow against the sandstone facade of the National Museum. It was late, past two in the morning. Kim opened the heavy door to Rio Bravo and walked through the dark restaurant, passing the polished brass counter where the bar stools were screwed to the floor. In 1983, Helge Dohrmann from the far-right Progress Party had sat here, late on a night just like this. Poul Schlüter, the then prime minister, had called him — and their conversation culminated in what later became known as the "Rio Bravo deal." In those days the bar stools had cowboy saddles. But that was then.

The minister was sitting on her own in a booth in the corner, cutting into a Rio Bravo steak.

"Campaigning is hungry work, Kim." Merethe Winther-Sørensen put down her steak knife and fork. The cutlery clattered against the sizzling platter. "So it's important to eat properly. What would we do without places like this, where the kitchen stays open till four o'clock in the morning?"

He didn't reply, but sat down opposite her.

"I met with Lars Winkler yesterday."

The minister wiped her mouth and summoned the waiter.

"What did he say?"

"It wasn't so much what he said..." Kim leaned across the table and lowered his voice. "Lars is no fool. He knows that we have access to his email and cell phone."

He paused. The waiter arrived to remove the plate and cutlery.

"I trust you enjoyed your meal?"

"It was delicious, Frank. As always."

"Coffee? Or perhaps a digestif?" The minister looked across at Kim and paused. Then she clicked her tongue.

"Two orders of pancakes with ice cream and strawberry jam, please. Yes, Kim," she continued as he was about to protest. "You shouldn't forget to eat when you work late."

Kim let it pass and held back until the waiter disappeared into the kitchen.

"And it's about to get worse. I've just checked your son's Wikipedia page."

"Go on?" The minister finished her draft lager.

"Somebody is tweaking it, making changes to the 1999 section."

"What?' Merethe Winther-Sørensen held her glass frozen in the air above the table.

"Not to worry, I've deleted it. And Wikipedia has a function that allows you to see who's changed or added something to an entry."

"And?"

"He or she is hiding behind several proxy servers abroad."

He stopped when he saw the expression on the minister's face. "A proxy server is a kind of intermediate station... Forget it. It's something that can disguise your identity on the Internet. It doesn't mean that we won't be able to find out who it is, but it's going to take time."

The waiter appeared with their pancakes.

"Here you are. And with chopped hazelnuts and an extra bowl of jam, just like the minister prefers it." The waiter put the plates on the table. "Enjoy."

"Thank you, Frank." The minister picked up her knife and fork. "I trust you, Kim. Just put a stop to it. If Lars gets too close, we'll have to have a word with Ulrik Sommer. Now let's dig in. I hope you haven't got any silver fillings left. Rio Bravo's vanilla ice cream isn't for people with sensitive teeth."

OCTOBER 1999

HE HASN'T SLEPT a wink. Meriton's anecdote about the bear hunt has been spiralling through his brain all night. The story is a thinly veiled threat, there can be no doubt about that. But this is Denmark, and he's the son of a government minister. He tries to laugh it off, and force the faint, nagging fear back in the box.

It is quiet; Margretheholm is deserted today. Staff have arranged a day out for the residents—a proper tourist trip around Copenhagen by bus to visit various historical sites like the Little Mermaid, the parliament building, the Stock Exchange, and the Liberty Memorial. But not all the residents have joined in. Arbën is waiting for him at the entrance.

The boy doesn't come running toward him like he usually does and he doesn't call out his cheerful Moo-genz. His sullen face just stares at the gravel, and he kicks a beer can.

"Arbën." Mogens puts an arm around his shoulder and gives him a squeeze. "How are you?"

Arbën stuffs his hands in his pockets, and doesn't reply. He just follows him to the main entrance.

Mogens stops. "Your uncles... Did they get on the bus?"

The boy nods and peers up at him. Relief washes over him. Today, at least, he is free.

"I'm just running up to the office to fetch the keys. Then I'll be back, okay? Why don't you think about what you want to do today in the meantime?"

Arbën disappears down the corridor. Mogens walks up to the office, which is deserted. He checks the log where his colleagues and the night shift note any incidents. Nothing unusual has happened.

Mogens pops his head into Søren's yellow office.

"I'll try organizing a game of softball for the kids."

Søren is distracted, and stares at his screen without saying anything, bashing the keyboard with his very own two-finger system.

Arbën isn't in the sports hall when he gets back. Mogens walks back up the stairs and down the next flight that leads into the corridor where Arbën lives with his sister. The corridor is empty and deserted again. Only silence can be heard from behind the closed doors. He tiptoes past the uncles' room. It's ridiculous, really. No one is there. For a moment he lingers outside the door to the children's room, unable to make up his mind. Then he knocks.

Afërdita opens.

"Hi Afërdita. Is Arbën here?" Then he notices the bathrobe and the makeup. "Why are you dressed up like that?" The petite, fifteen-year-old girl looks almost like a grown-up.

She shrugs and turns away. A cigarette is burning in the ashtray on the table below the window.

"And you've started smoking?" Mogens walks inside. Her heavy perfume is suffocating in the small room. Afërdita turns, leaning against the edge of the table. She raises the cigarette to her lips.

"Arbën isn't here." She exhales through her nose and looks at him under heavy eyelids. "Maybe outside?"

The whole mood is strange—wrong somehow. He laughs, a small nervous giggle that gets stuck in his throat.

"Afërdita, I've been meaning to ask you something." He might as well get it over and done with. It might be nothing after all. "A few days ago I saw a man leave this room. He put something in his pocket..."

The hand holding the cigarette drops. Afërdita looks down. Then she peels back her dressing gown, revealing her shoulder. She takes a hesitant step forward, reaches up on her toes, and kisses him on the lips. He is far too shocked to react and freezes in the unfamiliar embrace. Her hand fumbles down along his side, finding his hand. She lifts it up and slips it under her bathrobe, pressing it against her breast while she sticks her tongue into his mouth.

Mogens tears himself away, staggering back to the door. Afërdita raises the cigarette to her lips once more and looks at him with empty eyes.

He is back outside her door later that afternoon. He can still taste her lips and feel his hand cupped over the quivering breast. He hesitates, confused at the signals from his body. She's just a child. He doesn't want to, but his body reacts to her touch. Just the image of her... What's wrong with him?

It's time for him to go home—home to Kirsten and Sarah—home to play and cook. But still he lingers.

He can't leave. Not yet. He has to stay. Just a little longer.

SATURDAY, SEPTEMBER 28

35

THE COUGHING WOKE him up. The pain seared through his brain. The blood-red light behind his eyelids.

How much did he smoke yesterday? Lars reached out, rummaging around on the bedside table. He grabbed a crumpled cigarette packet. One left. He'd smoked nineteen then. He opened his eyes, trying to adjust to the light. Flashes of last night returned. The scene with Christine in his living room played out in technicolor in his mind.

He swung his legs over the bed and sat up. The headache almost floored him. He had finished the whole bottle of wine, including the glass he had poured for her, right after she left. Didn't they say you couldn't handle red wine with age? Or had he drunk a second bottle as well? He staggered out into the kitchen. No, thank God.

Half an hour later he'd had a shower and made coffee. The

day had taken a tiny step closer toward being tolerable—but just a tiny one. If only he could focus on his work. He was supposed to meet with Malene Meisner later today.

He sat down in front of his computer with a second cup of coffee and scrolled through the homepages of various newspapers. *Politiken* featured a lengthy interview with Sarah Winther-Sørensen with the headline **DAD IS MY ROLE MODEL**, and a huge colour photograph of her outside Copenhagen Town Hall. Merethe Winther-Sørensen's instinct was spot-on, he had to give her that. Mogens Winther-Sørensen's daughter would be an increasingly valuable asset for the Radical Party: young, female, and pretty. It was almost too good to be true.

Lars sighed and returned to Mogens Winther-Sørensen. He had already searched his name several times, and tried the websites of parliament, the Radical Party, various newspapers, and also blogs—each probably more than once, though it was impossible to keep track of them all. Now he went to Google's homepage and entered *Mogens Winther-Sørensen* in the search field.

The computer pondered his request before it started listing links. The first few, framed in yellow, were for Radical Party sites promoting local council elections later this year. They had yet to remove Mogens from the list of candidates. Then again, they would probably have to find a replacement first. The next link was to Wikipedia. Lars clicked on it and started reading the entry. It was long and written in dense, formal language. It contained details about his education and marriage to Kirsten Winther-Sørensen, along with a passage about his youth. The last few lines of that passage read:

Toward the end of September 1999, Mogens Winther-Sørensen took leave from the city council. This period was supposed to have lasted six months, but at the end of October, only one month later, Mogens Winther-Sørensen returned, as leader of the council and mayor of Copenhagen. The Radical Party fired Mogens Winther-Sørensen's stand-in, who had been promised at least six months' work, immediately afterward.

Lars blinked. He wouldn't go as far as calling it a lead, since the stand-in wasn't named, nor was there any information about what Mogens Winther-Sørensen had been up to during his leave of absence, but it was during the time frame that had been removed both at Infomedia and at the Royal Library.

Lars finished his coffee in one gulp. It was time to go to police headquarters.

Toke sat in his office looking miserable.

"Toke?" Lars closed the door behind him. "You look like you've been hit by a truck. What's the matter?"

Toke turned his head. This minimal movement appeared to cause him physical pain.

"Ukë and Meriton were released yesterday."

"I heard. What happened?"

"The money . . . the banknotes they had in their possession when we arrested them were ours, with consecutive serial numbers starting at twenty-three." Toke pulled hard on his lower lip. "Yesterday in court, the serial numbers didn't match."

"And you're sure that you didn't make a mistake — when you arrested them, I mean?"

"One hundred percent. I checked them myself. That's what's driving me crazy." He tried straightening up. "I don't suppose that's why you're here?"

"Is your computer on?"

Toke turned on his screen without saying a word.

"Please, may I?" Lars stood next to Toke, opened a browser

window, and wrote *Mogens Winther-Sørensen* in the search field. He clicked on the Wikipedia article when the list of links appeared. Toke watched from the side with mild interest.

Lars scrolled down the article, searching for the paragraph about Mogens Winther-Sørensen's youth. There it was, but... what was this?

> *In 1999, the Socialist People's Party and the Conservatives ended their traditional support for the Social Democrats and decided to back the Radical Party's candidate. As a result, Mogens Winther-Sørensen became mayor of Copenhagen. Nearly one hundred years of Social Democratic rule of the capital came to an end.*

Toke read along with him.

"You didn't know?"

Lars straightened up and stared into space.

"Less than one hour ago it said he had taken a leave of absence in 1999 and was represented by a stand-in until he returned to become mayor."

Toke turned the screen back, taking over the mouse.

"Wikipedia is user generated, so someone obviously altered the text. It's usually right... here." Toke clicked *View history* and a new page appeared. "You can see all the changes made to an entry — line by line — displayed and organized chronologically."

Toke used the mouse to point out parts of the screen.

"As you can see, the same two changes are being repeated. "This" — he circled the first passage — "must be what you looked at originally. And this" — again he circled with the mouse, this time below the first passage — "is what it says now. Two users keep editing the same passage back and forth."

Lars's fingers trembled.

"Is it possible to see who the they are?"

Toke continued clicking and reading. He leaned in closer to the screen. Finally, he sat up and let go of the mouse.

"Hmm. There's usually a username connected to any edits. If you don't enter one, Wikipedia will automatically list your IP address next to the change."

"So we know who they are?" Excitement forced him to sit down. Finally he was getting somewhere.

"Sort of. Only in this case, it's a bit more complicated. Neither of them seems very keen on being identified."

"But you just said..."

"Yes, the IP address shows where you are, but there's a way around it, of course. And that's what the two of them are exploiting. I don't think I've ever seen anything like it. Fortunately, our people are good." Toke took a screenshot and looked up. "I'll send this off immediately."

36

A **GROUP OF** ducks glided through the water toward the concrete banks by the planetarium. The pale sun was reflected
in the spray from the fountain behind the birds.

Malene Meisner broke small pieces off her baguette and
tossed them into the water. The ducks darted after the white
bread—they had to be quick or the seagulls would beat them
to it. A pair of swans circled the ducks, their wings majestically
lifted, too aristocratic to mingle with the rabble.

"I rarely come to Copenhagen these days. Too many bad
memories." Malene Meisner pushed her sunglasses on top of her
head and squatted down by the edge of the lake.

Lars remained standing and lit up a King's. They were by
Sankt Jørgen's Lake on the corner of the Tycho Brahe Planetarium
and Gammel Kongevej. He had spent many happy, sweaty even-
ings here in the early 1980s after visiting the long-gone Saltlageret

for concerts by bands like The Birthday Party, Sods, Ballet Mécanique, UCR, and Dead Kennedys. The smell of hairspray and leather still lingered in his nostrils. The music had been wild, loud, razor sharp, and was sorely missed. And now he was back here, a guardian of the bourgeoisie and investigating the murder of the mayor. It wasn't quite where he'd imagined he would be back then.

"Pardon?"

Malene Meisner got up, brushing her long hair away from her face. Up close, her skin looked ravaged. Her eyes were glassy and bloodshot. He would have guessed she was at least ten years older than her actual age of forty-two. To be fair, she'd celebrated an opening night yesterday, but perhaps life really had treated her that badly?

Lars took a drag on his cigarette. Ducks and seagulls fought over the last bits of baguette in the water in front of them.

"Let's walk." She started moving around the planetarium, down toward Gammel Kongevej. Lars followed.

"You want to know about my relationship with Mogens Winther-Sørensen?" Malene Meisner stuffed her hands into the pockets of her coat. She wore jeans and black boots: the same clothes she had worn to the funeral.

Lars crushed the cigarette butt under the tip of his shoe and waited. Malene Meisner looked across the lake and said nothing.

"I thought you must have known him well..." Lars tried catching her eye. "Since you turned up for his funeral after all these years."

"I hated him."

Lars stopped in his tracks, but Malene Meisner continued, forcing him to follow.

"Why?"

They were now a fair distance from the west bank of the lake. She still hadn't answered his question. Lars tried again.

"Something must have happened?"

"My life—what you see now...publicity officer at the City Theatre in Malmö." She gathered up her hair and flipped it over her shoulders. "It wasn't always like that."

They carried on walking for a little while longer. Lars waited, letting her set the pace.

"I graduated as a journalist in 1997 and worked for *Berlingske Tidende* for two years. It was a great job, but when Merethe Winther-Sørensen offered me the position of head of communications for the mayor of Copenhagen..." Another pause. "I obviously couldn't turn it down."

"But what happened? Did you and Mogens have an affair?"

Malene Meisner let out a short, harsh laugh.

"Not in the way you think. Mogens was friendly and helpful. Everything was fine for the first few weeks. It was quite simply a frictionless partnership."

"What was your role?"

"The Danish People's Party had just been voted onto the council and they were questioning every grant given to integration projects, usually vociferously. As I recall it, I was thrown straight into the deep end. But like I said, Mogens was supportive."

Malene Meisner kicked a pebble. It flew across the tarmac in a distorted arc before skipping under the hedge lining the walkway.

"You have to understand that the Radicals see themselves as the perfect political party: we're in charge; we're the king-makers; we make prime ministers and mayors. But that struggle for power also triggers internal rivalries. Every now and then there would be unrest in the party. Don't forget, politics is about power—too many generals, not enough grunts."

They had reached Åboulevarden. The traffic, leaden and relentless, churned past the Lake Pavilion on the way out of the city. Malene Meisner stopped.

"How about a cigarette?"

Lars fished out a King's and lit it for her.

"Thank you." She inhaled, then blew out smoke. "I haven't smoked for years. But sometimes... Sorry, where was I?"

"Too many generals, not enough grunts?"

"Oh, yes. Mogens's family was obviously an asset, but some people hated him for that very reason. I managed to get to know him fairly well in the short time I worked there, and I quickly realized that Mogens did very little out of choice. His whole life—personally and professionally—was stage-managed by his mother. She even picked his wife, did you know that?' She rolled her eyes, tapping the ash off her cigarette. "Kirsten worked at the office of the the party's Copenhagen branch. Rumour has it that she was essentially ordered to marry Mogens. Merethe had plans for everything Mogens did. He used to tell me about the portraits of his grandfather and great-grandfather on the walls of the house on Amicisvej. Merethe always talked about how, one day, his portrait would hang there next to hers."

"I've seen them. They're... unique." They walked for a little while in silence. Malene Meisner looked across the lake. Low clouds drifted in from the west.

"You said earlier that you hated him."

She shrugged.

"To be perfectly honest, I never really found out what happened. We were at a Christmas party and I had gone outside to get some fresh air." She made a face. "Mogens was in the courtyard on the phone to someone, having a heated conversation. I quickly realized that he was talking to Kirsten."

"What were they talking about?"

"I don't know. I could only hear that they were having a fight. Mogens's face changed completely when he noticed me and he hung up straightaway. He was convinced that I had heard every word."

"Did he say anything?"

"I made my excuses, explaining that I should have gone back inside when I saw that he was on the phone, that his personal life was none of my business. But eventually I began to realize they had been talking about more than just personal problems."

"Why?"

"The rumours quickly started in the following days. First, I was supposed to have badmouthed some colleagues at the Christmas party. Then I was an alcoholic. I had no doubt that Merethe Winther-Sørensen orchestrated the whole thing. The first newspaper articles about me being addicted to prescription pills appeared in the days leading up to Christmas. And then I was fired. I got depressed and started drinking heavily. My boyfriend dumped me. I knew I had to get away. My aunt lived in Malmö, so I moved there and took my mother's maiden name."

They were back at the last of the lakes. The diagonally sliced cylinder of the planetarium loomed at the end. Malene Meisner stopped.

"That iron grip Merethe has on the party and her family . . ." She paused and looked at her watch. "It was all a very long time ago, and my head is starting to hurt, so unless you have any more questions . . ."

Lars thanked her. Malene Meisner walked down the steps to Vester Søgade, stopping at the last one.

"And yet I must have been fond of him, since he can make me return to Copenhagen twice in one week."

37

THE LOUDSPEAKER VOICE crackles metallically in the strange, convoluted language. The few phrases she learned as a child are long since forgotten. She has no idea what the voice is saying. Around her people hurry by, keeping their eyes on the floor. Two elderly women are eating their packed lunches on a bench by the wall, with their handbags and plastic bags stacked up around them to guard against strangers. But *they* are the strangers—Romanians, possibly, or Roma. Danes turn up their noses at the women as they rush by.

She sits on a tall stool by the counter with cigarettes and a latte macchiato, the closest she can get to a *Milchkaffee* in this country. How do they refer to Denmark in Germany? Oh yes, *Das Ferienland,* the "holiday country." She still has nightmares from the last time she was here, but she has learned to take care of herself, learned to suffer losses. She knows she can rely only on herself. It's at times like this that self-pity creeps in. Some people have ways of channelling their burdens and can turn weakness into strength. But others go under — too many of her acquaintances from the Reeperbahn have committed suicide, adding to the statistics. It's been years since she decided she wasn't going to be one of them.

Instead, it is yet another night in the city's gay bars. In the last few weeks, since the money from Denmark stopped coming, she has had to get used to selling herself again. She was only thirteen when she learned what you have to do to survive, but that doesn't mean she has to like it. It's degrading and crude.

A man opens a newspaper next to her; a photograph of a smiling young woman takes up most of the front page. She can't read the headline, but she knows the woman with dark hair and broad features. She has seen her somewhere. She opens her mouth even before she remembers the tiny photo, yellow with age, in her makeup bag.

"Sa-rah?"

The man lowers his newspaper. He turns his head and stares at her. She looks down and away, stubbing out her cigarette. She takes the last sips of her macchiato before taking out the photograph.

Moo-genz's daughter. For a brief second she is back in the apartment, with Moo-genz lying on the floor, blood spurting from the cut to his throat and spreading across the kitchen.

She can't see; her eyes are filled with tears. She gets to her feet and pushes her way through the crowd, darting through a kiosk and around an elevator.

She runs and doesn't look back. Her shoes fly across the brown tiles. The uncles must be back now. They are the only family she has left and without her ... without her they wouldn't be where they are now.

She has almost reached the stairs that lead down to the long street, which reminds her of home in Hamburg yet is so different, when she spots him—the big man with the merging eyebrows. He's coming up the stairs. *Valmir.* He has that dead expression in his eyes, seeing yet not seeing at the same time. She dries her tears and greets him.

Confusion and recognition flits across his face. Then he smiles. But just before he does she sees it, the predator gaze, extinguished almost as soon as it has been switched on. And she sees the movement of his right hand. Her adrenaline starts pumping and time stands still even before she sees the light reflected in the blade.

In one gliding movement she turns and swings herself around the man standing behind her by grabbing his shoulder. Valmir pushes people out of the way and chases her. An old woman is knocked over and falls down the steps. Her walking stick clatters, the noise insufferably loud in the narrow stairwell. People scream around them and retreat. One man drops his suitcase.

Then there is only the sound of her feet against the tiles and her heart pounding in her chest. Valmir's heavy breathing comes closer. She has another couple of seconds, no more, before he catches up with her. She doesn't try to work out why. There's no time, she has just one overriding thought: to get away.

Serafine runs past the elevator and the Forex currency bureau. The glass door to 7-Eleven is open and she tugs at a man standing in front of the coffee machine as she passes, hoping the obstruction might slow down Valmir. Boiling-hot coffee splashes over them, but she feels nothing and carries on. Inside the shop she tears down newspaper stands and shelves, anything that might delay her pursuer and give her a tiny advantage. But she has only just made it around the counter when his fingers close around her jacket. She stops. On impulse, she takes a step to the side. Valmir is too heavy and can't brake in time. He continues in forward motion and is forced to let go of her jacket. He swears as he crashes into a shelf of dairy products. A container of strawberry yogurt explodes, splashing across his face, jacket, and pants. She has no time to waste and sprints out of the store, across the narrow passage and into a McDonald's, crashing into the lineup in front of the register.

"What the..." A tall guy in a leather jacket swears, but then falls silent immediately. Valmir has arrived and is now brandishing the knife. He makes no attempt to hide it or his predatory eyes. Serafine throws a tall stool at him, runs out and to the right, around and down the narrow passage behind the shops, then back to the stairs with Valmir still on her heels. The pain in her chest almost causes her to black out. Her lungs are about to give up.

She zigzags in an attempt to dodge the knife dancing in the air behind her. Valmir grunts; his footsteps are heavier now. Serafine's shoe catches a tile and she trips. Valmir reaches her immediately. He grabs her T-shirt and flings her up against the wall, knocking the air out of her. Her back is burning. When she is finally able to open her eyes, all she can see are his eyes under the merged eyebrows and the knife coming toward her with incredible speed. This is the end—she is going to die. She is surprised at how calm she feels. But then something inside her rebels.

She takes a step toward the knife and Valmir, who is moving forward and off balance. He has no time to change direction. As the knife plunges into her T-shirt, stabbing the flesh between two ribs, she knees him in the groin. Valmir buckles with a strangled scream and the knife falls impotently to the ground.

Serafine ignores the burning pain in her side and runs past Valmir, who tries to get back on his feet to continue the chase.

At the end of the narrow passage, a group of seniors are pulling along their suitcases. Serafine musters her last remaining resources and sprints. She leaps as high as she can, over a wheeled suitcase. Valmir, lacking a clear sightline and still groggy from being kneed in the groin, carries on. He has no time to stop or jump, but crashes straight into a suitcase, knocking it and its owner over. He swears, and the case springs open. Pale blue shirts and underwear spill across the floor.

A door labelled POLICE is opened behind the seniors and several officers rush outside.

She can't hear Valmir anymore, so she risks looking over her shoulder for a brief second. He is snarling and trying to disentangle himself from the pile of seniors and suitcases. He has dropped the bloodstained knife, and the police officers are all over him now. A female officer chases after her. Serafine starts running down the stairs and disappears onto a side street.

Several blocks later she dodges into a basement, through the darkness, and up into the courtyard on the other side. She finally stops, pressing herself against a wall behind some garbage bins. She starts hyperventilating, and doesn't know if she is still being chased. She is too scared to examine the cut in her side. All she knows is that she has to hide and get away from the street. Out there, she'll die.

PUPA

[Pupa (from Lat. *puppa*, a variation on *pupa*, "little girl, doll"), last adolescent stage in insects with total transformation. At the pupa stage the adult insect's body is constructed after a major or minor breakdown of the larva body. See also insects and transformation.]

The Great Danish Encyclopedia

SHE BITES, LASHES out. Scratches and screams. Afërdita is gone. The uncles forced her to hold the lamp while they dug her sister's grave. Now Afërdita lies in the cold earth outside their room. Meriton holds her tight, whispering in her ear, and sings songs she has heard since she was born: *Dritë Kosovës, Këmbana e paqes, Xixëllonja, Ëndërrova.* Songs that used to mean security, warmth, and love.

Now there is only emptiness, terror, and the stench of blood. Serafine screams, *"Baba, mami!"* But no one answers. Nothing matters anymore. She stares into space and shuts down.

The following evening she arrives at Hamburg Hauptbahnhof. Five hours earlier Meriton put her on the train with a note around her neck. She doesn't know what it says, but the grown-ups on the train nod when they read it and smile at her. A sweaty ticket inspector with bad breath even pats her on the head.

Meriton promised that someone would meet her, but she has no idea who they are or what they look like. She stands alone in the darkness on the platform, clutching her small cardboard suitcase as the other passengers disappear.

Why couldn't she stay with the uncles? She tries to cry, but there are no more tears left. She ran out of tears long ago.

"Ah. There you are." She jumps and drops the suitcase. The small, bowed man with a flat cap and woollen coat speaks a strange kind of Albanian.

The man looks her up and down and glances briefly at the note around her neck, then tears it off.

"Shame about your sister. Come on." He turns around and starts shuffling down the platform. He doesn't check to see if she follows him.

It has grown dark, the air is cold and damp. Halos of light surround the station's lamps. She tries to pretend that they are butterflies or angels, but she already knows there are no angels. No one is coming to her rescue. She has only herself.

The traffic roars past on the wide road that runs above the railway tracks. The man with the flat cap turns right and walks down a side street, then opens the door to a battered, light brown car. The seats reek of onion and sweat.

"In you get. We've a long way to go."

She slumps inside the car, clinging to her suitcase. While the lamps pass by outside, the heat inside makes her drowsy. Her head lolls, her eyes keep closing, and...

Blood. Blood everywhere. A dark, sticky puddle that stretches from one wall to the other, running from the gashes in Afërdita's body, which is underneath the Dane on the bed. *Afërdita.* Her throat hurts when she shouts her name, but not a sound comes out. Her sister's teeth glisten in the redness of her mouth. Red and black flowers spring up across her small breasts, seeping out onto the filthy white bed linen. The window clatters against the frame on its rusty hinges.

Half-asleep, she lets out a small scream, and kicks out her feet. "Easy, boy. Not long to go now." The man doesn't look at her. He just concentrates on driving.

The car zooms through the night, rattling ominously every time they go over a pothole. They drive through dark streets, under iron bridges and scaffolding, past deserted industrial areas. There are no people on these streets, and the lamps are broken.

"Where are we going?" Her voice is shaking. She has to make an effort even to ask the question.

"Home," is all he says. *Shtëpi*.

When the car stops, he nudges her out, shoving her in between two derelict houses. There is a small, crooked shed at the very back of the last courtyard. It presses up against the wooden fence around a scrapyard behind it. A light flickers behind the small windows. An old woman welcomes her and lifts her up, holding her tight for a long time. And, for a moment, she thinks that yes, this could be home.

But her dream bursts as early as the next morning. The couple's sons came back late at night, and they stare at her with distrust when she gets up from the mattress in the corner and splashes her face with water from the bowl. After a breakfast of tomatoes, olives, Turkish feta, and bread, it is time for her to get dressed. And it is when she takes her doll out of the suitcase that she receives the first slap across her face.

2004
HAMBURG

THEY HAVE TRIED for five long, dark years: castigated, disciplined, abused, and punished her, both at home and at the Albanian school. The teachers, refugees like her, have scratched their heads, boxed her ears—and there was never any shortage of slaps. They have pointed their fingers at her, and tried taunting her when they can think of nothing else to do. The mere fact that she calls herself a *she* is a provocation. It is impossible to conform to their expectations when everything inside her cries out to do the opposite of what they want.

At home, Dora and Bekim and their big sons' contempt slowly turns into indifference and coldness, thrashings and daily humiliations. She is given the heaviest and filthiest work. Only the monthly payments from the uncles in Copenhagen stop them from throwing her out.

At the same time, the enemy within rises. Something is growing inside her, threatening to take control, thrusting itself to the front. She is on her way back from Penny Markt the first time it rears its ugly head. She has taken the bottles to the recycling centre and is clutching the few euros she got in exchange, when a German schoolgirl walks by on the opposite side of the street. The sun shines on her short, blonde hair. Tender breasts strain behind the girl's T-shirt and her gaze is downward.

The fire makes her blood flare up, fuelling fantasies. The useless little spout between her legs twitches. It is all alien, all wrong. She runs off, sobbing, overcome by shame. The next morning when she wakes up, there is a sticky patch on the sheet. Qendrim, the oldest of her new brothers, tears the blanket off her. It's time for her to empty the latrine bucket. When he sees the stain, he doubles up with laughter and dances back and forth between the two little rooms in the shed while waving the sheet in the air in triumph.

Even her own body has betrayed her.

She runs away that same night, weaving through the narrow streets of the suburbs. She rides the U-Bahn without buying a ticket and heads for the city centre. She has been to the main railway station on one occasion since she arrived—with Qendrim.

Once she reaches Hamburg Hauptbahnhof, she asks around. She knows now where she is heading: the Reeperbahn.

When she finally locates the street, it is a shock: women wearing practically nothing hang around outside with busloads of men and tourists. There are old and young people, even children. She finds them further down, on a street with the tantalizing name "Grosse Freiheit." They are everything she can't articulate, but she instinctively knows that she is one of them. She walks up and down the street, too nervous to talk to anyone, hardly daring to look. She puts one foot down on the sidewalk, then the other. She sniffs their perfume and listens while they talk. They are wearing dresses and high heels, and have makeup on and hoarse, deep voices. Her heart flitters in her breast. She is not alone.

Later she finds a bar and goes inside. She has no money, but she knows she needs to get closer. The room is long and narrow, the walls red. The bar runs down one side. A giant mirror hangs behind the bartenders in tank tops, leather caps, elaborate wigs, and heavy makeup. The mood is moist and aroused. But she feels at home for the first time in years. For the first time since she lost Afërdita, she is able to be herself.

Serafine sits down by a table near the wall. A wild party is in progress around her: men kissing men, women kissing women, women kissing men. Everyone is kissing and embracing each other. A group of transvestites are singing cheesy pop songs near the bar. She needs something to drink, something strong. But she doesn't have any money.

A man sits down next to her and says hello. He is big and broad.

"Want a beer?"

He smells nice and freshly washed, not of smoke and sweat. She says yes. Soon he returns with two tall, slim, frothing beer glasses. Lothar is funny and nice, and his smile makes her forget about Dora and Bekim, and Qendrim and his brothers. He grabs more beer. Now she forgets that she is hungry, too. And when he asks if she wants to go for a walk, she forgets to be careful.

She walks with him back across the Reeperbahn, down to the river. Lothar puts his arm around her and squeezes her tight. It is comforting and lovely. The beer sloshes around her stomach, making her head spin.

They dash across the street, laughing as they dodge the few cars driving past much too fast, and reach the port. She is tingling all over. Lothar helps her over the wall, and explains that the smell of fish in the air is coming from the market to their left.

"It's nice here, isn't it?"

The sky is dyed purple from the city lights, except for a few inky spots where the stars peek out. Cranes are silhouetted against neon advertisements, and giant ships pass by on the way in. It smells of tar and oil.

"Yes." She hugs him. She feels so safe and light. She looks up at Lothar. He bends down, kisses her carefully, and she kisses him back, letting him part her lips. His tongue forces its way in and explores, gliding along her teeth. His breathing gets heavier and quickens. The kiss is violent and becomes greedy. His hands are everywhere and hard, pressing into her groin. She tries to push him away, but Lothar—nice, gentle Lothar—holds on.

She pulls back her head.

"Stop."

Lothar pants.

"Come on. You know you want it too. I'll give you fifty euros." He rips off her pants and throws her over a garbage bin in the same quick movement. A cruise ship, a fairy-tale castle, passes silently through the harbour, all lights illuminated. A distant world radiates out into the night as he thrusts into her. Something tears inside her and the pain makes everything spin, disappear, while her screams are drowned out by the hooting of the boat's horn.

Once she can see again, she is alone. She is sitting on the cold ashphalt, her clothes in a pile next to her. The pain is indescribable; something is leaking out of her backside. Her hand squeezes a twenty-euro note.

2006
HAMBURG

THE DARKNESS HANGS over Grosse Freiheit—the horny
mile, the beating heart of St. Pauli and Hamburg. The street
exudes raw, pent-up desire and hungry eyes. Coloured lights and
neon signs span a gaudy canopy across the narrow road. It's a
circus, a freak show. Men and women stroll up and down: standing, posing, chatting or displaying themselves, alone or in small
clusters. Everything is permitted and can be bought or viewed.
Further ahead, at number 36, young people, boys and girls her
own age wearing leather and makeup, are waiting to be admitted to tonight's concert.

There are speed freaks, old queers, and teenagers high on
poppers and vodka-laced apple juice. The cocaine flows freely;
the night is beautiful and terrible.

She sashays down the sidewalk in white stilettos,

power-clicking her heels, moving in and out between the groups, the tourists, and the desperate. She is at ease and confident: this is her turf, her family.

"Serafine?" A six-foot-five drag queen grabs her. They kiss on both cheeks and he offers her a cigarette. "I haven't seen you for ages. Jürgen and I thought you were... well, you know." He laughs, flaring his nostrils, and flicks his long hair.

She waves her cigarette in the air.

"Had to find somewhere else to live. The old place had become too gross."

He touches her dress lightly.

"You look gorgeous. Are you working tonight?" Then he gets excited. "Are you going to Georg's party later? Everyone will be there. It'll be *so* decadent."

Serafine leans closer and whispers, "Might be. Have you seen Doctor Stromberg?"

"The street-doc? But what do you want with him, sweetie?"

She runs her hand across her cheek, the latest acne breakout hidden beneath foundation and powder. She knows it doesn't show, but the thing between her legs rages inside her body, ripping it apart. Soon her voice will break and she'll get hairs everywhere.

"You know—"

"Sera, stay away from that *scheisse*."

She clicks her tongue.

"But have you seen him?"

"Someone came by just now, saying he was backstage. You could always try there." He nods scornfully in that direction, but then he softens and smiles.

They air-kiss and she crosses the street, waltzing under the neon sign with the elephant and into the darkness, where anything could happen. She greets Valeria, the cloakroom attendant, and continues into the twilight. The backstage area is a tangle of stagehands, and topless women wearing makeup and selling cigarettes. Helga and Roxette wave as she enters. They are on shortly. Helga is crawling into the coffin where she will hide until she rises just at the right moment, wrapped in a vampire's cloak. Roxette is playing the grieving widow, dressed all in white — and with deep cleavage. Serafine waves back, mouths *good luck* and blows a kiss, then turns right. She spots Horst, the stage manager, with his shiny bald head and his cheeks glowing red.

In the dressing room, the usual eight to ten women and transsexuals sit in various stages of undress. The room is filled with flesh-coloured underwear, mirrors, cigarettes, alcohol, make-up, and powder — both for the cheeks and the nose. The smell of female sweat and the female sex. Oh, how she's yearning.

The wooden floor creaks under her stilettos. Doctor Stromberg sits in a corner wrapped in his coat, his pale face sweating behind his glasses. Juliana hands him the money; he pushes a small wrapper across the table in return, which immediately disappears into her pants.

"Serafine?" Juliana turns to her. "You're not usually here this early." Juliana is a friend. She took her under her wing the moment she started working here almost a year ago.

"I just want a word with the doctor." She starts to shake. *What if he says no?* She sits down beside Juliana, too scared to look at Doctor Stromberg. Juliana gives her a quick squeeze, and doesn't say anything.

"What do you need?" The doctor's voice is coarse. It doesn't fit his sweaty face and glasses. She raises her head. *He has to...*

"Pills. For—" But she can't even make herself continue. Doctor Stromberg, however, can tell just from looking at her.

"Estrogen? It's not good for you. You know that, don't you?"

"What other way is there? Not taking it?" The rage surprises even her. "Sandra killed herself last week. Angie tried last month." She says nothing more.

"How much, doctor?" Juliana asks the question for her. The other girls have stopped talking, and stare at their reflection in the mirror, pretending they are not there.

"An initial dose for one week is a hundred and fifty. You should probably expect to pay three hundred euros per week later on."

Three hundred euros a week? How will she get that kind of money?

Doctor Stromberg licks his thin lips.

"Or you could always get an appointment with a psychiatrist, who might refer you for public health treatment. After all, that's free."

Her heart sinks. She knows it is not an option. She has lived here in Hamburg illegally for seven years now.

"No, I'll find the money. Here." She opens her makeup bag, taking out the crumpled notes and counts them. "Here's a hundred and fifty. When will I need to increase the dosage?"

Doctor Stromberg opens his bag and takes out a small jar.

Later in the evening, once she has finished, she says goodbye to Juliana and the other girls. The jar with Doctor Stromberg's pills is in her makeup bag. She has already taken the first pill. She can't feel anything yet, but she is on her way. The butterfly wings flutter inside.

The show went like clockwork. She sang old German pop songs but didn't strip. The old gays adore her. But what will happen to her once her voice breaks? Who'll want to listen to her then? And three hundred euros? How will she afford that?

The crowd outside has grown in number, their hunger a bleeding wound in the night. All veils have been dropped. The first drunks have fallen asleep in the gutter. Teenagers ramble about with their arms around each other's necks. Further up the street, near the Reeperbahn, beefy bouncers with icy gazes shovel tourist flesh into the strip joints.

Should she go to Georg's party? The only thing waiting for her at home is a cold, damp room with a tiny window overlooking a lightwell. Her life is confined to seven square metres, filled with a few bottles of rum and tequila. She never gets drunk in public; only at home alone does she dare to let go.

She takes out her cigarettes and lights up. Two country boys stop and stare. They're drunk and unpleasant.

Serafine clicks her tongue, turning away.

"So how about it, hun? How much for a blow job?"

"Are you gay or what?" says the other one. The first one laughs so hard he buckles. This is clearly a change of scenery from the turnip fields.

"Why don't you two assholes go back to the barn and suck each other off? After all, that's what you really want to do." The country boys' heads jerk back. She knows that the contradiction between her high-pitched voice and her language makes most people bridle.

"No need for you to be sassy." The bigger of them steps closer. His gaze has taken on a different hue; the brutality simmers just beneath the surface. It's time to leave. Serafine turns, sashaying away from them as fast as she can in her high heels. She might be able to escape them at the rock club, as long as one of the bouncers she knows is on duty.

A hand lands on her shoulder, forcing her to turn around.

"Don't you—" He gets no further. The bigger of the two freezes halfway through his sentence, then releases his hold on her. Two other faces appear behind the country boys.

It has been a long time, but it's them, there's no doubt. She reverses quickly into the crowd, only just managing to see the country boys pushed out of the way. She catches a glimpse of the black barrel of a gun. Then her uncles are on either side of her, frogmarching her across the street and into Dollhouse Diner.

"Ukë? Meriton?" She looks from one to the other. "What about—"

"Oh, they ran away." Meriton grins and sits down in a booth, placing himself on the outside. Ukë waddles up to the bar. He certainly hasn't lost any weight since she last saw him in Copenhagen.

"What are you doing here?" She tries to look relaxed. *What do they want?*

"Looking for you." Meriton's gaze scans the diner. He doesn't look at her. Ukë returns with Franziskaner vom Fass beers for him and Meriton, and a cola for her.

Meriton and Ukë clink their glasses.

"We thought we had lost you, Arbën." Ukë wipes the froth off his chin. His tiny eyes are fixed on her, blinking. Meriton takes over.

"Dora and Bekim couldn't find you. And then we discover you've been here all along...in the red light district."

Meriton gives her the look. She has brought shame on the family. The blood curdles into frosty lumps in her veins. Anything could happen now, but the odds are that she will be found with her hands tied behind her back in the Elbe River tomorrow morning. She turns her gaze inward and leaves her body, as she has trained herself to do. The same way she did when she ran away from Dora and Bekim.

But they don't hit her. Instead, Ukë hushes Meriton.

"There, *vëlla*. Arbën needs us. And we need him." He turns to her. "If we can find you, so can he. No more performing, do you understand? We need you alive."

"But—"

"No. It'll be like we said."

She clutches her makeup bag and the jar of pills, refusing to back down.

"I need money."

Meriton turns and looks at her for the first time.

"For what? Drugs?" His gaze is contemptuous.

What can she do? Would they understand? She hunches her shoulders and stammers as she begins to explain about her body and the pills. When she has finished, Meriton snorts. Ukë says nothing and twirls his empty glass around and around. Eventually he looks up.

"Three hundred euros? A week? That's a lot of money."

"I don't know how else to get it."

Ukë's eyes narrow again.

"If you agree to stop performing, we'll send you seven hundred euros every week. Then you'll have enough for food. I guess you have rent to pay as well?"

"Are you mad? Seven hundred euros?" Meriton squeezes his glass and stares at the remaining beer at the bottom. His face has gone red.

"Now, now, *vëlla*. It's still a good business. And we won't have to pay Bekim and Dora anymore."

Ukë thrusts his hand into the pocket of his sweatpants, finds a greasy bundle of notes, and counts out seven hundred euros.

"Here. This is for the first week. Remember: no more performing. And you must promise to keep in touch. Meriton, give him the phone and the bank card."

Meriton is still sulking, but pulls out a cell phone and a Commerzbank card, then slides both across the table to her.

"You'll use it only to text the number in the contact list every week when you've withdrawn the cash from the bank. Do you understand?"

HAMBURG—COPENHAGEN

This transaction has been declined.
Please contact your bank.

She scrunches up the receipt printed by the ATM. The staff in the bank stare at her through the glass. She is so used to it now that she hardly notices. She doesn't exist in their world; she has no name and no number, only the bank card for the Commerzbank account from the uncles. She chucks the receipt in the wastebasket beside the ATM and turns around. Perhaps the money will arrive tomorrow? But who is she trying to kid? It should have been here more than a week ago. The last five-euro note lies neatly folded in her makeup bag: the last of Juliana's money. The thought alone makes her feel sick. Juliana let her stay at her place and Serafine thanked her by stealing the money Juliana needed for her daughter's medicine. That's the kind of friend she is. But she needs to eat. And the pills matter more than anything—or anyone—else. She hardens herself. She no longer buys from Doctor Stromberg, fortunately, but that doesn't make the drugs any cheaper. She'll never get a regular job. There is only... The chill spreads from somewhere in her groin. The long nights on the street, the cars, and the customers.

So far she has managed to avoid sex, apart from that one time with Lothar—the one time she couldn't avoid. She has buried the memory in the same darkness that swallowed up the last terrible evening and night in Copenhagen. But just because she has avoided sex doesn't mean that she has escaped the desire. She knows that people want her. She can see it in their eyes on the streets and on the U-Bahn, in the Penny Markt and in Kaisers. And those few times when she can't afford any pills, the desire—the enemy—also ravages her body.

She has obeyed the uncles' ban on performing—so far. But she needs money. Horst has opened a new club, a secret club. It is sleazy, not artistic like Safari. She'll dance and sing, but there are also private rooms in the back where customers can retire with a girl. She closes her eyes. The prospect is better than long nights on the street. And Horst has promised her she can say no if the customers are too disgusting.

But she has one more option before she goes to see Horst: her old foster family—Dora, Bekim, Qendrim and his brothers. Perhaps they have news from Copenhagen?

She takes the U-Bahn to the industrial estate and walks through the old streets, past the dilapidated houses. She hasn't been here since she ran away and hasn't seen them, even though they must have known where to find her. The uncles must have told them to leave her alone.

The place is even more grey and desolate than she remembers; it's a wasteland. Black shadows creep along the house walls.

Dusk is falling when she finally finds the alleyway to the yard where Dora and Bekim's tiny shed stood against the back fence. But now...

She gets to the end of the alleyway and finds herself in an empty yard. There is no house. There is nothing, just a building plot, weeds, and lead-coloured grass growing in holes in the tarmac. Garbage is piled up in the corners. The sound of dripping water comes from somewhere in the darkness.

She lowers her head and turns to leave. But a voice from the shadows calls her back.

"Arbën?"

She peers into the darkness. A figure, lying along a half-demolished wall, flings aside a blanket. Qendrim—it has to be him. He sits up and grins. He is missing three front teeth; the rest are black and rotten. He must be all of twenty-five now.

"What happened?" she asks, but she's not really sure whether she wants to know the answer.

"The council decided to renovate and rebuild. They started knocking everything down. The next year they ran out of money." He shrugs his shoulders and lights a Marlboro. "How about you? You look like you're doing all right."

The place is deserted and no one else is here. More than anything she wants to turn around and leave. But Qendrim was family once. Serafine smooths her skirt at the back and sits down on the brick wall. Qendrim passes her the cigarette.

"I'm okay. Staying with a girlfriend," she lies. Then it dawns on her. He lives here.

Qendrim grins and blows out smoke. Neither of them says anything.

"And Dora and Bekim?"

"They moved back to Pristina and took Iskender. But there's nothing there for me. I've got a future here. There's..." Qendrim inhales, staring out into the darkness. A small animal, likely a rodent, darts across the plot. Something squeaks. Then there is silence.

How would he have any news about her uncles? But now that she has made the long journey out here, she might as well ask him.

"Have you heard anything from my uncles?"

Qendrim shakes his head. She closes her eyes. It means that Horst is her only option. She gets up quietly, glides across the ground, and heads for the street.

"Arbën," Qendrim calls out after her. "Arbën?"

But Serafine walks on — doesn't turn around.

Early morning, two weeks later. The grey daylight falls through the rectangular window. The back room with the black walls and the mirrors is quiet. The Danish businessman is snoring lightly; he has fallen asleep in the armchair with his pants around his ankles. He is drooling slightly. The thing lies limp and white between his hairy thighs.

The exhaustion is overwhelming and her jaw aches. Her throat hurts. She needs to use the bathroom but can't go because of the pain in her backside. Instead, she pours herself a drink from the tequila bottle on the table. She drains the glass, letting the alcohol slosh around, trying to wash away the taste and the smell. There have been so many these past two weeks, many more than she would like to remember.

The newspaper lies folded on the floor next to the armchair with the snoring Dane. There is a colour photograph of him, smiling and shaking hands with another man on the front cover. The Dane had swelled with pride as he showed her that he was on the front page, next to the mayor of Copenhagen. But Serafine only sees Moo-genz, Moo-genz, who has now become the mayor. He must have power and money. If anyone can help her it's him.

There is 963 euros in cash in the customer's wallet: she's counted it. The credit cards are no use to her. But 963 euros is enough for a few days worth of pills, a ticket to Copenhagen, and for her to repay Juliana so she can buy medicine for her daughter. She pours another tequila and stands with the wallet in her hand, weighing up the pros and cons.

Fifteen minutes later she is running down Simon-von-Utrecht Strasse, past St. Pauli — the bar she has never been into — and the laundromat in the basement. She's clutching the 963 euros in her hand. Traffic is busy: the people of Hamburg are on their way to work or taking their children to school. This is where Juliana lives with her daughter, in a damp basement apartment at the back of the building. Up until recently, Serafine lived here too.

She stares at the sidewalk, trying to make herself invisible. It's the easy way to get through the day — to avoid all the normal people and make it to evening. But every now and then she is forced to look up, to dodge bicycles coming toward her on the sidewalk or to check the traffic lights. Right by Möbelheim, when she stops to let a flustered mother with a stroller pass, she looks up — and it feels as if an ice pick is sliding through her.

He is standing in an archway with his hands stuffed in his pockets, his stomach bulging under the polo shirt. Narrow eyes check the street but constantly return to the archway, to number 85: Juliana's building.

Serafine can't move; an icy hand closes around her internal organs, squeezing them. He has tracked her down. The uncles warned her about this. He has come to finish it. She sees her sister's dead body; the sticky pool on the linoleum floor at Margretheholm; his cheek on her sister's chest with the red flowers; a big baby at his mother's breast; a twitch at the corner of his mouth with a little saliva drooling down. He heard her open the door. His eyelids twitched and opened. His narrow eyes looked straight into hers.

The man in the archway freezes, taking one hand half out of his pocket. The icy hand tightens its grip on her inner organs, squeezing a thin sound out between her lips. Then the ice shatters into a thousand pieces and she is free. She starts to run and he chases after her. His heavy footsteps get closer as he accelerates. She can already feel the cold steel of the scissors in her back; she has to get out of here. She flees straight down Simon-von-Utrecht Strasse, passing the low, red factory building on Millerntorplatz, and runs on toward Hamburg Hauptbanhhof.

IMAGO

[Imago (from Lat. *imago*, "image, depiction"), a biology
term for the fully developed, mature insect (plural:
imagoes or imagines). See also transformation.]

The Great Danish Encyclopedia

38

IT IS DARK before she finally dares to venture out. The lights are lit in the windows above the archway. A little girl is skipping on her own in the ash-grey courtyard in front of two large pots with scrawny bushes. The skipping rope drops to the ground. The girl watches, her mouth hanging open, as Serafine emerges from her hideout behind the garbage bins.

They have tried to kill her. The uncles know that she is in Denmark and that she is looking for them. And their only response is that she must die. It can mean nothing else.

There is nowhere she can go for help. She is alone in a strange city. She lifts up her T-shirt and examines the cut to her side. The blood has already congealed and formed a crust on her skin. It is only a flesh wound.

Serafine staggers out of the courtyard, past the girl and out into the street. This is a neighbourhood with cafés, shops, and life. Here, there will be doctors she can go to.

There are coloured lights, royal portraits, and knick-knacks on the shelves of the boudoir-red walls of the Café Intime. Serafine sits at a table at the far back with a cola. There are others like her, but she keeps to herself, drawing circles in the dust on the table. Her thoughts are churning and running amok. Finally, when there are no more places for them to go, she finishes her drink and heads up to the counter. She slides a five-euro note discreetly across the counter and asks a half-whispered question before returning to her seat to wait. Half an hour passes; then an hour; until, finally, the bartender gives her the nod. An older gentleman in a suit jacket and jeans has just entered, and sits down by a round table to the side, a scuffed leather bag on his lap. Someone like her slips along the wall, glides into the chair opposite him, and whispers across the table while looking away. Everything is deftly done; Serafine barely has time to notice the money changing hands. Then the girl gets up, and a jar of pills flashes in her clenched hand. A faint smile on her face. The street-doc has already slammed his bag shut, waiting for the next customer.

Serafine also waits — around fifteen minutes — until there are no more customers left. Then she walks straight over.

"I need a surgeon." She pulls out a chair and sits down opposite him.

The doctor studies her.

"I see."

"Can you help?"

"Can you pay? It's not cheap."

Serafine nods. The doctor takes out a yellow, pre-printed pad that looks like it's for writing prescriptions, and a ballpoint pen. He scribbles down an address, tears off the top sheet, and hands it to her across the table.

"I make no promises. Meet me outside this address at nine o'clock tonight. Do you know where it is?"

"Yes," she lies, and gets up. The doctor reaches out to hold her back.

"Five percent, do you understand?"

She understands. Everybody wants a piece of her. It's just the way it is.

39

"A JAEGER-LECOULTRE... Do you have any idea how much they cost?"

Lars shook his head, and picked up his crumpled pack of King's Blue. Was it all right if he smoked? The man reporting the crime, Aksel Lynge, a thirty-three-year-old banker, flung out his hand and rolled his eyes.

"About ninety thousand kroner. So you can probably guess why I'm exceedingly keen to get it back."

"Take it easy." Lisa closed the door to the enormous kitchen outfitted with black cabinets, dark grey marble flooring and counters, a stone sink, and a specialty coffee machine that probably cost as much as the watch, which Aksel Lynge had made no bones about wanting back.

He had come to the station the day before, but due to the general bureaucracy and chaos of police headquarters, his report hadn't been passed on to them. It wasn't until today that some bright spark had connected the description of the thief as "English-speaking with a German accent" to Serafine and passed the file up to the Violent Crime Unit. Then it had taken another couple of hours for them to contact the victim.

Aksel Lynge sent Lisa a look of despair and raked his hand through his hair. Then he sat down in a designer chair covered with black leather. It didn't look comfortable.

"I knew I should've stayed away from her, but those eyes..."

Lars took his time lighting his cigarette. He inhaled and then expelled a cloud of smoke through the balcony door. The view across Trianglen wasn't half bad, better than his own of the Metro building site. Car headlights swept down Blegdamsvej, neon advertisements glowed on the other side of the street.

"So you met Serafine at Café Intime Wednesday evening. And the two of you agreed to carry on the party back here?"

Aksel Lynge nodded.

"And then?" Lars looked around. The man followed his eyes, and then pointed to an ashtray sitting on a steel grey Montana bookcase by the door. Lars took the ashtray and tapped off the ash.

"Well, we weren't playing tiddlywinks, were we?" Aksel Lynge moved the ashtray a few centimetres closer to Lars. The aggression had vanished from his voice.

"We're aware that this is uncomfortable, but we have to ask." Lisa was making notes and didn't look up.

"Yeah, yeah, I know. We had sex, all right? Afterward I fell asleep. And when I woke up—well, she was gone, and had taken my watch and any cash I had lying around."

Lars took out a photograph from his inside pocket.

"Is this her?" He put the picture on the table in front of him. Aksel Lynge took one look at it.

"Yes, yes! That's her." He pressed the tips of his fingers against his eyelids. His hands were shaking.

"Please look carefully." Lars pushed the photograph closer toward him. The banker sighed and bent over the picture again. The seconds passed.

"Those eyes... You're not likely to forget them in a hurry." He looked up. "It's her, except for the hair and the nails, I mean. She wasn't wearing any makeup either."

Lars nearly dropped his cigarette. Lisa had stopped making notes. "What do you mean?"

"She wasn't dressed up. She looked like the other guys. But I could tell just by looking at her what she was."

Lars closed his eyes. It was obvious now. Serafine had cut her hair, removed her makeup, and changed her clothing. It was so incredibly simple and effective. All their efforts to trace her in the last few days had been in vain. He tapped the ash off his cigarette with an irritated movement.

"So she didn't speak Danish?" He exchanged a brief glance with Lisa.

"No, she spoke English with a German accent, like in those films, you know? But I've already told you this." He rummaged around in his pocket. "Listen, I have the receipt for the watch, but I'll need it back for the insurance. You can't—"

"We'll make a copy. We promise to return it to you." Lisa reviewed her notes.

"Don't get your hopes up." Lars stubbed out his King's. "Your watch is probably already out of the country."

His phone started ringing in his inside pocket.

"Yes? Lars speaking."

Lisa concluded the interview with Aksel Lynge while Lars was on the phone. He didn't hang up until they were out on the stairwell and Lisa had closed the apartment door behind them.

"That was the duty officer." Lars was half-running down the curved staircase. "An Albanian guy tried to stab someone at Central Station. It could be Serafine—without the hair and the makeup."

"Right, so we've got her."

"Unfortunately not. She got away. But the Albanian is back at headquarters."

Lars looked up from the surveillance footage from Copenhagen Central Station as Sanne entered his office. She didn't bother to say hello.

So that was how it was going to be from now on.

He pulled out a chair for her and pointed to the screen. Sanne stared at the chair, about to protest. Then she snorted and sat down, leaning back with her arms folded across her chest.

At that moment, Toke popped his head around the door.

"Lars? I thought you might want an update on the Wikipedia business. I've just spoken to IT. Turns out it's a bit more complicated than they originally thought. Your guy is hiding behind several proxy servers. They've followed the trail to Dubai, but it looks as if there's at least one more."

"Are you telling me my guy is in the Middle East?" Lars spun around in his chair.

"No, no." Toke laughed. "But the proxy server is. He could be sitting next door or in the corner behind you." He winked. Then he was gone.

Lars turned back. Sanne had changed position while he'd been speaking to Toke. Now her head was close to the screen. Her face was open and attentive, lit up by the blue-grey glow from the monitor.

"There." Her finger followed a thin, short-haired figure passing diagonally between the picture frames. "That has to be her. But what happened to her hair?

"She cut it off and removed the makeup." Lars looked at her. Sanne's gaze had cooled once more. So they were back to square one.

40

VALMIR WAS SITTING at the square table in the interview room. A whitish substance had dried on the collar of his leather jacket and the shirt underneath it. The stain had cracked and was emitting the sweet-and-sour smell of yogurt. Lars closed the door and sat down. Sanne looked down at the report with her pen poised.

Lars smiled. "Right, Valmir. That *is* your name, isn't it?"

Valmir swept his longish hair away from his face. "Got any smokes?"

"Sorry, no. Perhaps we can take a cigarette break later. But first we have to get started, don't we? What's your last name?"

Valmir stared out the window. He knew the drill.

"Valmir Shqender." He reeled off an address. Sanne wrote it down. All three of them knew that the address was fake, but none of them said anything.

"Okay, that didn't hurt very much, did it?" Lars folded his hands on the desk. "So what were you doing at the railway station?"

"Meeting someone." Valmir was still sitting with his side to them, staring out of the window. A police officer sat bent over his desk on the other side of the oval courtyard.

"Would that be Serafine?"

"Who's that?"

"Oh, give us a break. The person you chased after with a knife." There was no need to mention her transgender status at this point.

"I don't know what you're talking about."

Lars looked at Sanne, who stared at her notepad with her lips pursed in a smile. What was so funny? Lars leaned back in his chair. If she had any better ideas, he'd like to hear them.

There was a moment of silence. Then Sanne looked up and put down her pen.

"Listen." She took out the knife, which they had found in Valmir's possession, and put it on the table between them. It was a heavy hunting knife with a short, broad blade, wrapped in a transparent plastic bag. "Security footage shows you clearly pulling out the knife the moment you saw Serafine. You're just wasting everybody's time."

Valmir shrugged his shoulders.

"We could always have another look at your residence permit." Sanne had picked up her pen again, but had yet to make any notes.

Lars had another go.

"More than twenty witnesses saw you chase Serafine through the railway station. Four of them are the police officers who arrested you. If you think—"

Sanne interrupted him. "Did your crew pay Serafine to kill Mogens Winther-Sørensen?"

Valmir raised his eyebrows.

"I don't think..." Lars frowned at Sanne. What was she getting at? But Sanne wasn't listening.

"Answer me. Did you pay her for the murder?"

Lars got up.

"Sanne, could I please have a—"

Sanne leaned across the table, locking eyes with Valmir.

"Because that's what happened, isn't it? You paid Serafine to kill the mayor, and now she's an awkward witness you need to get rid of."

"Sanne." Lars opened the door. "Outside. Now."

Sanne rolled her eyes at the ceiling. Then she got up and followed. It was dark and quiet in the reception area. Most people had gone home. Only a strip of light was visible under the door to Ulrik's office — that was it. Lars closed the door behind her.

"What do you think you're doing?"

"Questioning the suspect." Sanne blew a lock of hair away from her face.

"It looks more like an attempt to derail my interview." He tried to keep his voice calm. "We had agreed that you would make notes and I would ask the questions."

"But he isn't going to say anything."

"It can take hours, you know that. He's been here before. The moment he senses that you and I aren't working together—"

"You're obsessed with Merethe Winther-Sørensen." Sanne half-turned away from him, waving her hands. "Why complicate everything?"

"So you think Serafine is an obvious hired killer, do you? I can give you at least five reasons—"

A door squeaked. Lars paused. The strip of light under the door to Ulrik's office widened on the threadbare carpet.

"Sanne, Lars. Can you please step inside for a moment?"

Ulrik was standing with his back to his desk, arms folded across his chest.

"Care to tell me what's going on?" He looked from one to the other.

Lars sat down. "We're questioning Valmir Shqender."

"From where I'm sitting, it sounded more like you were about to start a fight. Sanne?"

Sanne clicked the nails of her thumb and middle fingers. She hesitated. Then out it came: "I think Lars's angle is wrong. All the evidence from the crime scene points to Serafine being the killer. There's no reason to—"

"You're forgetting the fingerprints on the murder weapon." Lars studied his nails.

"Serafine's fingerprints were on it too."

"I interviewed Malene Rørdam earlier today. She overheard a fight between Mogens Winther-Sørensen and his wife at a Christmas party in 1999, during the very period the minister is trying to stop us from investigating. She was fired soon afterward. I—"

Ulrik raised his hand.

"You two are my best people. I—we—can't afford to have you wasting your energy fighting each other. And that guy in there?" He pointed in the direction of the interview room. "Is a waste of time. You'll get nothing out of him. As far as I can tell, we have enough witnesses and security footage to charge him. But Serafine got away—again. Regardless of which one of you is right, she needs to be found."

"Hello?" There was shouting from the reception, someone swore.

"In here." Ulrik got up from the desk.

A uniformed officer appeared in the doorway with a firm grip on Valmir's arm. He had twisted it behind his back in a stranglehold. In the other hand, the officer was holding the hunting knife they had left behind on the desk.

"You need to keep a closer eye on your suspects in here, or somebody might get hurt."

"I think I'm going to retract what I said about you being my best people." Ulrik laughed. The uniformed officer had put Valmir in a cell. "What on earth were you thinking, leaving a suspect alone with a murder weapon?"

Lars and Sanne looked at each other for a long time. There was nothing they could do, except suck it up and leave.

Lars held open the door for Sanne, and then closed it carefully behind them. They couldn't carry on like this. One of them had to make the first move.

He caught up with her halfway across the reception area.

"Is Martin very ill?"

She flinched. Then she carried on walking.

"I saw you at the hospital. Oh, come on. We can't act like this forever. What's wrong with him?"

She stopped. They were now in his office.

"I don't want to talk about it." She grimaced. "What about you and that doctor?"

Lars took Sanne's leather jacket from the chair. She let him hold it for her while she put it on.

"It was a one-time thing." He followed the line of her neck. The fine hairs below her hairline shone in the light from the anglepoise lamp. He could be mistaken, but was that a faint smile on her lips?

Sanne turned around and pulled up her collar.

"I'm going home to get some sleep. Tomorrow..." She chewed her lip. "Tomorrow we'll start over. Okay?"

41

SERAFINE GETS UP from the café chair, stuffs her hands into her pockets, and walks down through Nyhavn. The area looks like Grosse Freiheit and the horny mile, but the attempt at gentrification has failed. A single glance convinces her that this place is just as cheap as back home, only there is no room here for those who don't fit in — the freaks. Only tourists with fat wallets are welcome.

Night has fallen and the first drunks appear on the streets. The neon lights from the tourist traps along the quay reflect in the water. She hurries across the small bridge by the harbour entrance and down Holbergsgade. Cort Adelers Gade lies a little further ahead on her left. A taxi passes in the opposite direction, and Serafine crosses the street.

A silhouette is waiting outside number 17. The glow from his cigarette brightens, lighting up his face for a moment. It has to be him. There is no one else on the street—no life. She can see the wide entrance to the harbour behind the figure.

"Finally." The street-doc tosses aside his cigarette and picks up his bag. "Do you have the money?"

Serafine squeezes the watch in her pocket. It has to be enough.

"Right. Let's go inside." The street-doc rings the bell. They are let into a lobby with white panels and walls the colour of blood. She follows him up to the second-floor landing. He rings another bell, and they wait until a bald, elderly man opens the door. He greets the street-doc briefly, and looks her up and down several times. Then he grunts something in Danish and lets them in. So this is the surgeon who will be performing her operation.

Serafine follows the two men into the consulting room. The surgeon sits down behind the desk and crosses his legs.

"You realize this can be dangerous?"

"Yes." She shudders as she sees a glass cabinet of surgical tools.

The surgeon laughs.

"Relax. The operating room is next door." Then his voice becomes businesslike. "And the money? How will you pay?"

She sticks her hand into her pocket and pulls out the watch. She hasn't had time to check how much it is worth, but she has seen the brand in expensive shops at home on Neuer Wall. It's a Jaeger-LeCoultre. She places it on the desk in front of the surgeon.

The surgeon's eyes narrow. He picks up the watch and examines it, turning it over in his hands. His fingers tremble with excitement as he grabs the magnifying glass in his desk drawer. He holds it up to the back of the watch, rotating it to find the best angle from which to read. Finally he looks up.

"That'll do."

She feels a tingle run up and down her spine, a flutter of butterfly wings. Now. It's about to happen.

Then he says: "I can't operate now." The surgeon gives a light, regretful shrug. "It's impossible to get a nurse at such short notice, but tomorrow afternoon at three o'clock will work. You can eat breakfast, but don't eat or drink anything after that, do you understand? It's dangerous because of the anesthetic."

The street-doc raises an eyebrow. "And my cut?"

Serafine looks down. It has to be enough. She needs the last of the money for clothes and a ticket home.

The surgeon says something in Danish. The street-doc appears to accept it.

"Well then," the surgeon says, getting up. "You can walk down with me. We'll take the back stairs."

Serafine gets up too and reaches out for the watch. The surgeon puts it in the drawer with a sweeping movement.

"That stays here. I'll take good care of it."

She bows her head and forces herself to think about tomorrow. Tomorrow, she will be free.

OCTOBER 1999

"WHAT'S THE MATTER with you, Arbën?" Mogens squats down beside the boy. They are alone in the lower-ground-floor cafeteria that juts out in front of the centre's main building. But the windows overlooking the lawn are huge, and everyone walking past can look in and see them. The boy's small body closes in on itself; he turns his back to him. Arbën hasn't said one word to him all day. Nor did he come running this morning when Mogens turned up for work.

Outside, the wind shakes the trees; the first autumn gale has started blowing. Mogens picks at some breadcrumbs left behind on the table. Søren cornered him when he turned up for work at ten o'clock, asking if he could try to find out what had happened. No one has seen the boy's sister since last night. Could that be what's upsetting him?

Mogens puts his hand on Arbën's shoulder; the touch makes the small body flinch.

"Where is Afërdita?"

Arbën's shoulders start to tremble, but he doesn't make a sound.

Mogens rubs his palms on his pants. Then he gets up and holds out his hand. Kirsten and Sarah are visiting one of Kirsten's old school friends. He has the apartment to himself.

"Come on."

It must be his tone of voice that makes the difference. At any rate, the boy reaches out his hand, and continues to stare at the ground as they walk to the car.

Mogens parks outside number 28 on Frederiksberg Allé.

"This is where I live."

Arbën stares at the tree and the fountain. The autumn sun hangs low and red over Frederiksberg Garden at the end of the avenue. When Mogens opens the car door, the boy jumps out and starts kicking the big piles of yellow leaves.

The leaves fly up, and are carried off by the wind before tumbling down the sidewalk. Arbën chases after them, trying to catch them in the air, and laughs for the first time that day. Then he stops suddenly, the light in his eyes extinguished, and he falls silent.

Upstairs in the apartment, Mogens tries tempting him with chocolate, then Sarah's computer games, but nothing seems to work for more than a few minutes before the boy sinks back into apathy.

Mogens sits down on the sofa next to Arbën. Normally he has a knack for talking to children.

"Are you hungry?" he asks. "Is there something you really fancy? I'll cook it for you."

The boy actually turns his face toward him.

"Pizza?"

Pizza? That's not something he can make right at the moment.

"Know what? We'll just order in."

Twenty minutes later the food arrives. Mogens puts the box on the small kitchen table, takes a bottle of cola from the fridge, and pours Arbën a glass.

"There you go."

But Arbën has never eaten pizza before. He's struggling, unable to hold the long, triangular slices properly. Mogens has to show him how to squeeze the pizza slices together in the middle to stop the melted cheese from dripping.

"Do you know what I really like about Margretheholm?" Mogens says between two mouthfuls. "You. Every day when I wake up, I look forward to seeing you." He presses a finger against Arbën's nose.

The boy looks down.

"I like Moo-genz too."

Now, at least, he is getting through to the boy. Mogens is careful, slipping in the next question casually between two mouthfuls.

"Are there some things you don't like?"

The pizza slice stops halfway between the box and the boy's mouth. The apartment is quiet aside from the faint hiss of carbonated bubbles popping on the surface of Arbën's cola. But Mogens controls himself and waits. He forces himself to chew, pretending that everything is all right.

"I don't like it when *Ungji* Meriton forces Afërdita to work."

Mogens separates a slice for Arbën and helps himself to another. Then, just as he is about to take the first bite, he asks: "What kind of work does Uncle Meriton want her to do?"

Arbën picks up the slice Mogens is offering him and puts it in his mouth.

"Strange men come to see her."

Mogens's throat burns with the taste of undigested pizza and stomach acid on its way up. Only yesterday he was standing outside her door himself.

"Is that why Afërdita has left? Because she doesn't...want the strange men to come and see her?"

Arbën puts down the pizza slice and chews repeatedly. Finally he swallows. It is a big mouthful. Mogens thinks he can almost see the food travel down the boy's throat. His gaze is tuned to infinity. Whatever it was that was opened up a moment ago has been shut down again.

SUNDAY, SEPTEMBER 29

42

IT WAS LATE morning when Lars arrived at police headquarters. Sanne was sitting in his office with Lisa. She looked up when he came in.

"Morning!"

So she had been serious when she suggested starting over. He tossed his coat over his chair.

"Good morning. Any news?"

Sanne reached out, poured him coffee from a thermos flask, and put the cup in front of him.

"Lisa and I have spoken to the police in Hamburg and gotten them to dig around their records. Serafine applied for asylum under the name Serafine Haxhi in 1999, but less than one month later she disappeared, along with her sister, Afërdita, and two people who are known to us—Ukë and Meriton Bukoshi."

Lars whistled.

"So Ukë and Meriton are related to her?"

"Her uncles." Lisa rocked back on her chair.

"Good work. Now all we need to do is find the link between her and the mayor. And work out why Ukë and Meriton want her dead."

"There's more." Lisa now looked uncomfortable. "I made a few calls... That Christmas party Malene Rørdam mentioned? The one where she overheard Mogens argue with Kirsten on the phone? Every Radical member of the city council practically denied they even held a Christmas party that year."

"It could have been a standard case of infidelity," Sanne said. "Or maybe Mogens Winther-Sørensen had a bit too much to drink. Who says it has anything to do with his murder?"

"No one." Lars took a sip. The coffee was lukewarm. How long had they been sitting there waiting for him?

"So what do we do?"

"Right now we carry on looking for Serafine. What does Ulrik say?"

A young man in a crumpled T-shirt popped his head around the door.

"Are you Lars?" It was one of the guys from IT. Lars waved him in. "Toke says you want to know who's behind this IP address?" He held up a yellow Post-it note.

"That's right." Lars asked him to take a seat.

"You gave us something of a challenge." His face was practically beaming. "Most people just hide behind an anonymous proxy server, which hides the user's IP address," he explained. "But your guy used several HAPs."

"What's a HAP?" Lars tried to rein in his impatience. Sanne said nothing.

"A High Anonymity Proxy. It doesn't identify itself as a proxy server, so it can be fairly complicated for the rest of us to work with. This guy took us to one in Dubai, then Manila, and finally

to one in Vladivostok. We've been on something of a road trip."
He placed the Post-it note on the desk in front of Lars.

It was an address written in blue ballpoint pen: *Astersvej 16,
3rd floor, 4000 Roskilde.*

Astersvej 16 in Roskilde turned out to be a modern block of apart-
ments with small, square windows, and a pale yellow facade
decorated with a hopeless grey and green mosaic. Lars parked
behind the building, walked up the tiled steps to the third floor,
and rang the doorbell.

"Yes?" The door opened exactly two centimetres. A broad,
pale face with a receding hairline peered out through the narrow crack.

"Are you Niels Püchert? I'm Lars Winkler, Copenhagen
Police. May I come in?"

"What's this about?" He could smell detergent coming from
inside the apartment.

"I think it's best if I come inside." Lars nudged the door
slightly. The other man hesitated for a moment before he took
a step back.

"Right, if you…"

Niels Püchert showed him into the kitchen, where strict order
and white surfaces reigned supreme. There was a single drying
rack with one plate, one glass, and one set of cutlery. A blue floral
tablecloth on the table below a window with a view of the parking lot was the room's only spot of colour. A local newspaper
was opened to a page with job postings.

"I've just made tea. Would you like a cup?" Niels Püchert
folded the newspaper and threw it in the garbage.

Lars shook his head.

"May I please sit down?"

Niels Püchert didn't reply, pouring tea from a thermos flask.

He held the cup with his slender hands and drank. Lars pulled out the only chair at the table and sat down.

"Why do you keep changing Mogens Winther-Sørensen's Wikipedia entry?"

Niels Püchert looked at the floor and then put the cup on the table.

Lars tried again.

"Does anyone else have access to your computer?"

Niels Püchert looked around the kitchen.

"Does it look like it?"

"So if you didn't...?" Lars let the question linger in the stagnant air. A faint squeaking sound emerged from the lid of the thermos flask.

"I wondered how long it would be before you came."

Lars nodded.

"I'm no expert, but our technicians say you did a good job of hiding."

A wry smile flitted across Niels Püchert's face. He tightened the lid of the thermos flask.

"I used to be an IT consultant with TDC, and I was posted abroad for several years in Dubai and the Philippines. I only returned to Denmark recently."

"You wrote repeatedly that Mogens Winther-Sørensen took leave from the council in..." Lars pulled out his notebook and flicked through it. "October 1999? And said that he was represented by a stand-in?"

Niels Püchert nodded.

"That's correct."

"I've been through practically all the information there is, and I haven't come across a single thing about Mogens Winther-Sørensen being on leave."

"No, of course not."

"What do you mean?"

Niels Püchert said nothing and refilled his cup.

Lars sighed.

"Okay. How do you know that he went on leave?"

"Because I was his stand-in."

Lars raised his eyebrows.

"I used to be a member of the Radical Party," Niels Püchert continued. "Ever since I was a teen, it had been my dream to do something for the common good, to help change society. So when I was asked to be Mogens's deputy... Well, I'm sure you can imagine what that must have felt like."

Lars asked him to continue.

"Mogens was supposed to be on leave for six months, from October to March. As far as I could gather from Mogens, he was hoping this would be a permanent arrangement. He wanted to study education." Niels Püchert lifted his teacup with both hands. "Tell me, do you know who keeps deleting my editorial changes? Every time I update the entry, it takes two hours max before it's changed back."

"Whoever he is, he's more careful than you." Lars made a note. "You said that Mogens's leave might have become a permanent arrangement once the six months were up. What did you mean?"

"What do you think? He didn't want to return to politics. I spoke to him on several occasions before he went on leave. He hated it!"

"So what happened?"

Niels Püchert shrugged his shoulders. The way he did it, his attitude, everything suggested this was something he'd had plenty of practice in.

"Mogens must have discovered he missed politics after all — or he got an offer he couldn't refuse. In any case, he returned as mayor. I wasn't informed, of course. I had to read about it in *Berlingske Tidende* the next day. It was less than a month after I'd started deputizing for him. When I took the liberty of pointing out that my contract was for six months... Well, I was fired and thrown out of the party. That was how they treated me. And then there was the financial aspect. I lost five months' salary."

Lars made another note.

"Do you know what Mogens Winther-Sørensen did during the four weeks he managed to take leave?"

"Oh, yes. He volunteered for the Danish Red Cross."

43

THE SMALL CLICK that sounded when Niels Püchert closed the door behind him echoed down the stairwell. Lars pressed his cell phone to his ear.

"Lisa?" He stepped aside for a young woman lugging four heavy grocery bags. "Could you please check something for me? Niels Püchert claims that Mogens Winther-Sørensen worked for the Danish Red Cross in October 1999. I know today is Sunday, but would you be able find someone from the Red Cross who can confirm it?"

Outside, Lars pulled out his keys and was about to unlock the car when a black Mercedes with tinted windows crept up alongside him.

"Lars. Jump in."

Lars bent down and peered into the car. Kim A was in the passenger seat. A man in a suit with short hair and an earpiece was driving.

"What's this? A spy movie?"

"We just need a quick chat." Kim A gave him an irritated look.

Lars looked across the car park. There was not a soul in sight. The wind tore through the open space.

"Five minutes, Kim." Lars opened the back door.

"Yeah, yeah." Kim A grinned at him in the rear-view mirror. "Drive." The driver revved the engine and drove out between the apartment blocks, turning right to join Astersvej.

"You PET guys have some nice wheels." Lars put on his seatbelt. "But what am I really doing here?"

"It's the ministerial car, if you must know." Kim A turned in his seat. "So I would appreciate it if you could refrain from smoking."

Lars let go of the cigarette packet, took his hand out from his inside pocket, and let his head rest against the seat.

"The two of us have had our differences." Kim A attempted to smile, except it ended up looking like a bizarre grimace. "But you know I've always had great professional respect for you and your work."

If that were true, Kim A had a funny way of showing it.

The car drove through Roskilde. Outside the window, low apartment blocks similar to the one he had just left replaced residential areas.

Kim A continued talking: "To cut to the chase." He licked his lips. "The general election is in nine days. The last time we spoke I tried to appeal to your better nature, but it seems you didn't listen."

The car returned to Astersvej. It appeared Kim A meant to keep his promise.

"I'm telling you this because I'm your friend. If you keep sticking your nose into things that have nothing to do with you — and which you've already been told are of no relevance to your murder investigation—then be prepared to face the consequences. There are people out there with information that could harm you. Information they won't hesitate to make public, if you persist. Do you understand?"

The driver stopped the car. The tremble from the idling engine made Kim A's cheeks quiver.

Lars opened the door without replying and got out. His own car was a few hundred metres away. Kim A opened the window.

"Think about it, Lars. It's for your own good." Then he gestured to the driver and the Mercedes accelerated away. Lars watched until it had disappeared around the corner.

Once he was back at police headquarters, he only just had time to take off his jacket before Lisa dragged him through the maze-like corridors to an empty office in a remote part of the building.

"I managed to get hold of someone at the Red Cross. She went through all of their records and even searched their payroll system. They never employed anyone named Mogens Winther-Sørensen. On an unrelated note, I think I have something else that might be of interest to you: our colleagues arrested a doctor this morning for selling banned steroids and hormones used by bodybuilders and the like."

"What does that have to do with us?" Lars tried to keep up.

"He risks losing his licence, so he's very keen to do a deal. I'll give you three guesses as to what he's selling? Oh, we're here." Lisa knocked on a door and opened it without waiting for a reply.

Sanne and two officers, whose names Lars couldn't remember, were sitting in the narrow room along with an older man in a blazer and a stained shirt. The man was sweating.

Lisa shut the door behind them.

"Tell my colleague here what you just told us."

The man moistened his lips; his gaze flitted around the room.

"But that's—" He stopped talking.

"You were the one who wanted to make a deal." Sanne sent Lars a weary look.

"Right, late afternoon yesterday..." The man hesitated. "We agree that I won't be prosecuted for anything I'm about to say, correct?"

"Just get on with it."

"It's true that I sell these drugs—only for personal consumption, mind you. But yesterday I met someone whose needs were a little more sophisticated."

44

"WELCOME, MY FRIEND." Meriton stood up from the radio in the corner and took off the headset. Calls from patrol cars and police codes crackled out into the room. He signalled to Elvir to take over.

The lawyer had entered behind Valmir. He and Meriton shook hands.

"Thanks for your help."

"Don't mention it." The lawyer took out a packet of Craven "A" and lit one. "But I'm afraid he won't get away with a slap on the wrist."

A big frying pan was simmering on the stove at the back of the room. The smell of onion and fried meat drifted through the club.

While Goran divvied up the food, Meriton pulled out a chair and asked the lawyer to sit down. Valmir had already taken a seat. Meriton brought over a bottle of clear liquid, and poured about three to four fingers' worth into tall, slim glasses. A splash of water from a jug gave the liquid a cloudy, milky appearance. Meriton handed glasses to Valmir and the lawyer.

"Raki—lion's milk. It's good for the heart. Drink."

They raised their glasses, toasted, and drank. The lawyer spluttered, red-faced.

"Well, I must say, that's...special," he gasped.

Valmir and Meriton roared with laughter. Goran came over with three steaming plates of fried mince and onion. A dish of white flatbreads sat in the middle of the table.

"Eat."

They ate in silence, tearing off chunks of bread, which they used to scoop up the meat and onion, before shoving the whole thing into their mouths. After a few bites, Meriton wiped meat and fat from his chin with the back of his hand, and finished chewing. It was good to have Valmir back, but an error was an error. Valmir ought to know that.

Valmir understood, and put his glass down on the table, bowing his head.

"What do you want me to do?"

"Hey, before we go any further..." The lawyer mouthed *bugs*.

Meriton laughed. "We got it sorted. We never leave this place unattended."

The lawyer looked around the room and lowered his voice.

"I had a client once. Police got access to the neighbouring apartment, drilled holes in the wall, and placed microphones at the end of them. He got twelve years for murder and blackmail."

Meriton turned around.

"Goran, put on some music." Goran put on a CD and turned up the volume. A clarinet wrapped itself plaintively around a blanket of jumping percussion. In the background, someone was picking a Spanish guitar.

"Better?" Meriton leaned across the table. The lawyer smiled, picking up his cigarette from the foil ashtray, and glanced at his raki.

"I think I had better leave so you can talk business. I'll send you my bill."

When the lawyer had left, Meriton moved his seat closer to Valmir. The song finished and Meriton waited until the next track began. It was faster and more hypnotic than the previous. He started talking again.

"Having Arbën in Denmark is a risk. If the police catch him again, he could cause us a lot of trouble. It's important, do you understand?"

The door opened and a cold draft swept along the floor. Ukë squeezed himself into the club. A fat hand landed on Valmir's shoulders.

"Having a party, are we? Good to see you." He sat down and turned to Meriton. "I've just gotten word from our guy inside." The chair groaned underneath him.

Meriton spat into his plate. *"Derr."* That bastard. "It's about time. Does he have anything for us?"

"Tonight—the usual place."

45

SERAFINE THROWS THE cigarette on the sidewalk and squashes it under her foot. The street is empty. It is mid-afternoon. Grey waves pass by briskly out in the windy harbour. Perhaps she should be nervous or procrastinate, but she doesn't want to wait any longer. The time has come. Her transformation is about to begin.

Serafine rings the bell and enters, leaving the animal, the alien, behind on the street.

"Welcome." A middle-aged woman in green scrubs meets her on the first floor and ushers her into what must be the operating room. "Have you eaten anything?"

Serafine shakes her head. Hunger gnaws at her insides, but it means nothing compared to what is about to happen.

"Good. You can undress in there. The doctor will be with you in a moment." The woman points to a curtain in the corner. Serafine walks behind it, takes off her jacket, pants, T-shirt, and underwear, and puts everything in a pile on the small stool. She carefully avoids touching the thing between her legs. She has no desire to say goodbye to it. There is a bathrobe on a peg in the wall. She tries to put it on, but her hands and arms are shaking. The nerves are kicking in now. Everything spins. She reaches out and grabs hold of the curtain to stop herself from falling.

"There, there. Come here." The woman is supporting her weight. "Everything will be all right." She puts an arm around her shoulder. "Most people are nervous at this stage; sometimes they have doubts. Are you sure you want to go through with it? Once it's done, there's no going back, you know that."

Serafine leans against the woman, hips against hers. Her scent, her breasts, and the soft curves of her body. She yearns for it, so much that it hurts.

"I want to!" She reaches out and grabs hold of the nurse's green scrubs.

The woman laughs. And Serafine laughs with her. Everything spins. She is so relieved. She looks at the operating table, the windows, and the herringbone parquet floor. Then the flutter starts: butterfly wings carry her forward, welcoming her. *Yes,* she whispers. *I'm coming.*

"Well." The woman smiles at her. "Come on then." She walks her to the operating table and helps her climb onto it. "Now I'm going to put in an IV." She sterilizes Serafine's wrist with a cotton ball. Serafine looks away while the nurse finds a vein and inserts the needle. The woman attaches the IV to her wrist with surgical tape, then she takes a small syringe with no needle and connects . it to the hole in the green plastic drop. "This is morphine—it'll relax you. Afterward you'll be anesthetized. Are you ready?"

Serafine sinks back into the pillow and closes her eyes. A wave of warmth and well-being washes over her, rocking her with soft movements. The butterflies are everywhere now, welcoming her. Time and place disappear.

She has no idea how long she has been lying like this when a series of violent crashes wakes her up, pulling her back. The butterflies fade and fly away, one by one. She is back on the operating table, sweating. What's happening?

The woman is still there; she looks at the door, then the window. Her gaze flits around the operating room.

Where is the surgeon?

Now she can hear voices from the hallway. She recognizes the surgeon's from yesterday, but there are others and they are coming closer. Suddenly the room is awash with strangers. Two uniformed police officers open the door and burst in, followed immediately by the surgeon, who tries to stop them. Then a man and a woman she recognizes from the apartment where Moo-genz was killed.

They argue in Danish, but she doesn't need to know the language to understand that today won't be the day it happens either. Serafine closes her eyes, shutting out the voices. Someone helps her down from the operating table and puts the bathrobe on her. She opens her eyes. The man she recognizes from Moo-genz's apartment and one of the uniformed officers have gone into the adjacent room with the surgeon. Their loud voices can be heard through the door.

The woman and the other officer have stayed behind in the operating room with her and the nurse. The woman finds her clothes behind the curtain.

"You can change in here." She pulls aside the curtain for her. Serafine staggers across the room. She ought to be shaken, terrified, and completely knocked out. Her dream lies in ruins. But the morphine courses through her veins — she is numb. Nothing really matters.

She changes back into her jeans and T-shirt behind the

curtain and puts on her shoes. They start to argue on the other side of the curtain. The nurse is angry and shouts. Something crashes onto the floor. There is upheaval and she hears the sound of bodies rolling around.

Serafine pulls the curtain aside and peers out. The two police officers are busy subduing the nurse. The door to the hall is open.

She tiptoes out into the hallway and looks around, listening to the agitated voices and the sound of the scuffle in the operating room. In a moment, the officers currently talking to the surgeon will rush to the aid of their colleagues. Then they will realize that she has escaped. The main staircase is the first place they will look, so she goes the other way, back into the apartment, and runs quietly down the long, red corridor, passing room after room until she reaches the kitchen. The morphine makes her dizzy, and she bumps into walls and side tables along the way, hurting herself. She prays they don't hear her.

They start to shout, slamming doors in the hallway. Serafine opens the kitchen door, sneaks out onto the back stairs, and pulls the door closed behind her.

She flees down the dark stairs and out into the courtyard, sticking close to the wall. It's the same route she walked with the surgeon and the doctor yesterday.

Twilight. She creeps along the wall until she reaches the entrance to a stairwell, gasping for air. The street is swimming before her eyes, with flashes of neon light. Car headlights sweep past. She can't go on. She is broken by hunger, exhaustion, and the morphine circulating in her body.

And the flutter has fallen silent.

She has no idea where she is. People rush past the spot where she is curled up, giving her a wide berth.

She ran out into the street to hail a cab as soon as she escaped from the operating room. But the tension, the disappointment, and the last few days was all too much for her—she threw up thin, green bile across the dashboard. She didn't understand what the driver was shouting, but the meaning was clear when he pulled up to the curb and pushed her out.

She doesn't feel hungry anymore, only a pleasant, spinning lightness in her body. The glow from the street lamps and the cars come together in an all-embracing radiance. Afërdita is waiting for her in the bright room. Her sister smiles.

My Seraph. Afërdita strokes her cheek. *My angel.* The scissors in her throat quiver. *You've grown so beautiful, Serafine.*

Serafine reaches out and tries to catch her, but her sister's figure flickers and disappears. The white room dissolves into darkness. A single candle burns in the distance, the flame swaying in an invisible draft. And suddenly the fluttering returns.

The sound continues to rise and a moth flies past her. It dances in spirals, approaching the candle in ever-decreasing circles. Mesmerized, Serafine follows its course, closer and closer to the fire. She reaches out to swat the insect away. But it is too late. A final circle leads it directly into the flame. Tongues of fire lick the wings, the body contorting in agony. The moth perishes with a horrible splutter. Serafine closes her eyes and holds her breath while its screams reverberate in her ears.

She sits up with a jolt. She is back on the whirling street. There's only one place left—one place she can go.

46

A **SOLITARY STREET** lamp glowed in the car park behind the Metro superstore in Sydhavnen, casting a yellow oval across the cracked sidewalk. A red Taurus was parked near the wire mesh fence in a corner of the lot.

The cone of light had sharp edges and bounced off the bronze paint on the brothers' Suzuki Grand Vitara. The new apartment blocks by the harbour glowed in the distance. The steep, glass walls of the telecommunications companies flared up in the dying sun.

"When is he coming?" Ukë chewed on his gum and scratched his neck. He had gotten a rash under his chins while he was in custody. Meriton rolled an unlit cigarette back and forth between his fingers, peering out into the darkness.

"Oh, relax, *vëlla*."

He pressed the cigarette lighter in. Ukë muttered something

Meriton didn't catch. The sound of his brother's scratching drowned out his voice.

"Eh?"

"He had better get a move on. I'm starting to get fed up with him."

"Easy now. He got us out, didn't he? And he knows he's a dead man if he tries to pull any tricks."

A shadow dashed across the rear-view mirror. Was that movement behind the Taurus over by the distant fence? Meriton straightened up in his seat, and moved his head in order to get a better look. "What the...?"

The scratching next to him had ceased. Ukë had seen it too.

"Is that him? I swear..."

A dark figure crossed the car park and headed toward their car. A long jacket flapped in the wind. They both followed it in the rear-view mirror.

"Do you think Valmir has fixed it yet?" Ukë whispered.

"Don't know. We'll call him later. Right, there he is."

The dark figure was now standing alongside their car. It knocked on the passenger-side window. Meriton stuck the cigarette in his mouth and pressed a button. The electric windows rolled down with a low hum.

"About time." He took the lighter, held it up to his cigarette, and inhaled. The tobacco started to glow. Ukë snorted next to him. Something shiny and black was sticking through the window.

"Goodbye, assholes."

Meriton didn't have time to hear the gunshot—he only caught a glimpse of the flash before his face was ripped to pieces, torn off his skull by hundreds of small pellets.

Ukë swore; a bubbling sound came from the open wound to his neck where part of the load, which had missed Meriton's face, had hit him. He fumbled with the door lock, blood pouring down his grey sweatshirt. The shotgun turned, pointing straight at him.

"Sorry." The voice behind the weapon rasped in the wind. "But it's time to clean up. They're getting too close."

Ukë held up his free hand, trying to shield himself. His gaze darted to the side. A plastic bag tumbled across the empty parking lot, carried along by the wind. The other barrel fired. Pain. Then — nothing.

47

"SO WE'RE BACK to square one." Lars flopped down into his chair. Right now, all he wanted to do was put his feet up on the desk and close his eyes. Sanne shut the door behind them, and leaned against the filing cabinet. Lisa had been sitting on the windowsill when they came in. She had already heard.

They had closed off the whole area between the Royal Theatre, Nyhavn, the Port of Copenhagen, and the National Bank, and searched every stairwell and courtyard. Ulrik had even deployed a helicopter, all to no avail. Serafine seemed to have vanished into thin air. Dogs had followed her trail through the apartment, down the back stairs, across the courtyard, and out onto Holbergsgade, where the scent disappeared in the middle of the street. They hadn't been able to pick it up again.

However, they had learned something new in the last two days. Serafine was related to Ukë and Meriton. She had seen

Mogens's photograph in a newspaper in Hamburg and decided to travel to Denmark to get him to help her with her surgery. The two of them must have known each other, so why would Serafine want to kill the very man she was hoping would come to her rescue? And, more importantly, there was still the question of the third, unidentified set of fingerprints on the murder weapon.

The process of elimination was continuing. The fingerprints didn't belong to the victim's family or acquaintances, or anyone else who had been in the apartment by Sankt Thomas Plads in the week leading up to the murder. The investigation now needed to focus on this third person.

It had started to rain outside, which was exactly what they needed right now.

The surgeon, who was supposed to have carried out the operation, didn't know anything, having only met Serafine the day before. He claimed it had been a completely innocent appointment regarding a urinary tract infection. Now, it was remarkable that a surgeon like him who specialized in obstetrics would offer urinary tract treatment to a man, but he had taken his Hippocratic oath and so forth...

They had confiscated the Jaeger-LeCoultre watch that Serafine had used as payment. At least it could now be returned to its rightful owner.

Sanne sat down opposite Lars.

"I know it's my fault, and—"

"Don't." Lars opened his eyes. "She also got away from me up at Sandholm. We all thought she would be so high on morphine she wouldn't be able to think, let alone avoid capture." He scratched his stubble. "We just have to move on."

These were just platitudes, stock phrases you used in situations like this. There was nothing to do but to move on.

His cell phone rang. It was the duty officer.

"Hey Lars. Listen, we've just received a tip—anonymously, of course—but I thought I had better tell you just in case."

"Fire away.'"

"Caller was an elderly man. He claims someone made a complaint that Mogens Winther-Sørensen was a pedophile."

"And?"

"Well, that was pretty much all he said."

Sanne raised her eyebrows. Lars held up two fingers.

"No year or location? Nothing?"

"Sadly no. I've checked the records without success. But I thought you ought to know."

Once Lars had repeated the conversation to her, Sanne started flicking through a file. "It sounds a bit feeble."

Lisa nodded at Lars, who was still holding his phone. "Do we do anything with it?"

Lars stuffed the cell phone in his pocket.

"Right now I think—"

There was a knock at the half-open door. Toke popped his head in.

"You may want to sit down. We've just had a call from Café Intime."

Lars opened the door for Sanne. The café was quiet; it was still too early for the Sunday crowds. A transvestite in high heels and a tight blue dress was standing next to the piano, singing:

Someday I'll wish upon a star
And wake up where the clouds are far behind me.
Where troubles melt like lemon drops,
High above the chimney tops,
That's where you'll find me.
Somewhere over the rainbow

Blue birds fly
Birds fly over the rainbow
Why then, oh why can't I?
If happy little bluebirds fly beyond the rainbow
Why, oh why can't I?

Serafine was sitting in a corner, staring at the table. Her jeans were filthy, ripped across her knees and thighs. One sleeve of her jacket was coming apart at the shoulder where the stitches had been torn. Aksel Lynge, the man who had reported his watch stolen the day before, was sitting opposite her. He was scowling; his arms were folded across his chest. He also had a nasty cut on his cheek. Two bartenders were keeping guard.

Aksel Lynge was the first to spot them. He knocked over his chair as he got up.

"I only wanted my watch back. Tell—"

"Sit down, man." One of the bartenders pushed him back into the chair.

Serafine looked around with a panicked expression, desperate for a way out. Lars walked straight across the bar and put his hand on her shoulder.

"Serafine?"

"Five minutes?" She looked ravaged and exhausted. "Please?" Lars looked around. Why was she so keen to wait five minutes?

Serafine's hands fluttered across the table. The transvestite by the piano sang the last line of the song, received her applause, and walked away. The pianist continued to play on alone.

"Come on," he began, but she wasn't listening. Her eyes shifted from side to side, scanning the room every few seconds.

"What's the problem?" Lars was addressing the nearer of the two bartenders.

"Something about a watch." The bartender shrugged. "Fortunately, we managed to separate them before anyone got seriously hurt. To be honest, I don't know who to believe."

Lars stuck his hand into his pocket and placed the watch on the table in front of Aksel Lynge.

"I'll need you to sign for this."

Lynge snatched the watch and raised it up to his lips.

"Thank you. You don't know how happy you've made me."

Aksel Lynge had barely crossed the threshold before Serafine started to murmur. She half-rose, then fell back into the chair.

"There he is!" she exclaimed.

Lars looked over his shoulder. An elderly man walked in, wearing a shabby suit jacket and jeans and carrying a bag. It was the same man they had interviewed earlier. The doctor had yet to notice them.

Sanne got up and walked across the room.

"Good evening." She grabbed the doctor's arm and marched him over to the table where Serafine was sitting.

"Good eve—" The doctor's face lost all colour. "What the...? Since when is it a crime to pop in for a drink?"

"Sit down, doctor." Lars pointed to the chair Aksel Lynge had just vacated. The doctor sat down with a surprised thud. "We're willing to accept that you just came in for a drink, aren't we?" He looked at Sanne, who nodded.

The doctor wiped his forehead.

"But then—"

"As long as," Lars continued, "you give her what she needs. Now."

The doctor gawped at him, clutching his bag. A strand of white hair fell onto his forehead. Then he nodded, opened the bag, and put a small jar of tablets on the table in front of Serafine.

"That's all I've got."

Serafine grabbed the jar and took out some pills—Lars couldn't see exactly how many, more than two and less than seven—and shoved them into her mouth.

"Lucrative sideline you've got there," Lars said before pointing to the door.

The doctor jumped up and knocked over the chair as he fled. Lars turned to Serafine, who was washing down the pills with a gulp of her cosmopolitan. Her hands stopped flapping; the frantic expression disappeared.

"Perhaps we can go now?"

Sanne was already outside on the steps when Serafine stopped, balancing with her foot on the threshold. Her posture had stiffened. Lars nudged her from behind.

"Come on. It's no use."

Serafine shuddered, then she started moving and they walked out into the street. A gay couple was sitting at a table outside in the September evening, smoking and holding hands. Allan and Lisa were waiting by the corner of Frederiksberg Bredegade.

Lisa looked at Serafine, who was struggling to stay upright between Lars and Sanne. "You won't get anything out of her tonight. She's completely out of it."

"I'll drive her up to Sandholm." Sanne unlocked her car. "We'll interview her tomorrow when the morphine has worn off. Everyone else can go home. We're done here."

"She's bound to run away again," Allan said. "She needs to go to Ellebæk, the secure unit right next to the Sandholm Centre. Why don't I take her." Allan started walking toward his car.

"It's okay, I don't mind."

"Are you sure? Do you want me to come with you?"

"There's no need. We won't have any problems, will we?"

Serafine shook her head, but kept her eyes on the sidewalk.

OCTOBER 1999

THE TRAFFIC ON the Helsingør motorway is at a complete standstill. The wipers sweep across the windshield; the rain batters against the roof. Mogens drums his fingers on the steering wheel. He turns on the radio, then turns it off again. Now that he has made up his mind, he just wants it over and done with immediately. But instead he is sitting here, stuck in a traffic jam by Gammel Holte.

When they had finished eating their pizza, he drove Arbën back to the centre and walked the boy to his room. It was very quiet, the corridors were dark and deserted. He put the boy to bed and went up to the office to say hello to the night watchman, pretending he was looking for a missing wallet. Then he drove to Hornbæk, but found it impossible to think in the dark cottage. Instead, he went down to the beach and let the salty wind shake him up. His clothes still bear the scent of seaweed and sand.

The question was simple: Should he keep quiet or speak up? Would he be able to live with himself if he didn't?

He had spent most of the night going over the arguments for and against, and hadn't fallen asleep until three o'clock in the morning, on the sofa.

The backlog in front of him finally stirs, and the long snake of traffic edges forward at last. The clock on his dashboard shows 8:11 a.m.

It's 9:10 a.m. by the time he parks outside the centre. The rain has eased off now, and is down to a quiet trickle. He half-runs through the puddles, ignoring the splashes that stain his pants.

Mogens takes the stairs two at a time. His side hurts as he runs down the yellow corridor to Søren's office. He bursts in without looking left or right.

But Søren isn't alone.

The director is standing by the window with his hands in his pockets. He's staring into the distance, his attention far away. Three people sit in front of his desk. Arbën looks down when Mogens enters. Merton and Ukë are sitting on either side of him, smiling.

Mogens wheezes and leans against the door frame for support.

"Søren—I have...I know what happened. I—"

"Sit down, Mogens."

"But..." He points at the brothers. "It's them. They rent out Afërdita—they sell their own niece. That's why she's run away. Call the police."

Søren leans across his desk and rests on his palms.

"Sit down, Mogens."

Mogens wipes his hand across his face, which is wet from the rain. He understands nothing. Why is the boy so scared? He pulls out the chair at the end of the desk and sits down.

"Is it correct that you took Arbën to your home yesterday?" Søren's diction is clear.

Oh, is that it? Mogens laughs.

"You told me to find out what was wrong with him yourself. He refused to say anything, so I thought..."

Søren suddenly looks very tired.

"We have one inviolable rule here at the centre, at all Red Cross centres—a rule with absolutely no exceptions. I made it clear to you when you started working here that you must never enter into a dependent relationship with a resident. Do not borrow or accept anything from them and do not meet with them outside the centre. And never, ever take them to your home."

Meriton and Ukë say nothing. They just sit there, either side of the boy, with inscrutable smiles.

Søren straightens up and resumes staring out of the window. Everything is wet outside. Mogens follows his gaze. The water splashes over the rim of the gutter on the low barrack. A couple of children are jumping in puddles.

"Arbën says that you touched him." Søren's voice is devoid of expression.

The boy jolts. *So he understands what is being said?*

"What?!"

Søren turns around. His voice is louder now.

"He says that you took off his clothes and took off your own clothes, and touched his genitals and made him touch you."

No. Everything drains of colour. He feels leaden inside and tries to straighten up in the chair.

"But that's..." He can barely speak. The uncles are grinning from ear to ear. "But they're making him say that. Can't you see? So you won't believe that they're running a brothel."

Søren sits down, defeated and resigned.

"I need you to hand over your ID card and your keys. You're

banned from the centre until we've investigated the matter thoroughly."

Everything happens in slow motion. Mogens reaches down for the leather briefcase he has put on the floor containing his ID card and keys. It's so heavy he can't even lift it.

MONDAY, SEPTEMBER 30

48

LARS MADE COFFEE and took a long shower. He was still mulling over yesterday's meeting with Niels Püchert. The Red Cross continued to deny that Mogens Winther-Sørensen had ever worked for them, but then why would Niels Püchert waste so much time editing the Wikipedia entry again and again?

Lars turned off the shower, dried himself, and got dressed. Then he went outside onto the balcony with a cup of coffee and the day's first cigarette, and watched the Metro workers who had started work below. They were not fumbling around blindly; they had their fixed routines, their tried-and-tested procedures.

Lars took a last drag on the cigarette and squashed it on the balcony. No way he was going to let them get away with this.

He closed the balcony door behind him to reduce the noise and looked up the telephone number online. To his enormous surprise, he was put straight through.

"Lars Winkler?" Merethe Winther-Sørensen's voice was cool. "I thought I had made my position perfectly clear."

"Don't worry. I had no trouble understanding Kim A yesterday." Lars took a sip from his coffee cup and made a point of slurping. "I just have one question. Did Mogens work for the Danish Red Cross when he went on leave in 1999?"

The slight hesitation before her answer was barely noticeable, but it was there.

"You would have to speak to the Red Cross about that. I have more important things to do."

"Surely nothing is more important than finding Mogens's killer?"

But he received no reply. Merethe Winther-Sørensen had already hung up.

Lars returned to the kitchen to refill his coffee cup. So Mogens Winther-Sørensen did have some sort of connection to the Red Cross. But what exactly? It was time he spoke to the mayor's father, the eccentric Arne Winther-Sørensen.

Lars made another call.

"Lisa? You're the one who interviewed Arne Winther-Sørensen, weren't you?"

"Hang on..." Lisa's voice grew faint. She was speaking to someone at the office. "Toke, there you go. Please take..." Then she was back. "We're a bit busy right now. Ukë and Meriton Bukoshi were found murdered a couple of hours ago. Shotgun wounds."

"What?" Everything was starting to happen a little too quickly.

"Out in Sydhavnen, in front of the Metro superstore. Toke says it looks like a professional hit." Lisa broke off to answer a question. "Okay then... Now, Lars, what did you want...? Arne, yes, I spoke to him—to the extent that was possible."

"What do you mean?" Lars was sitting down on the sofa with his coffee, pen and notepad ready.

"Arne Winther-Sørensen is one of those absentminded-professor types. You know, super intelligent within their subject, but has the social skills of a five-year-old. And it wasn't just his social skills that were an issue; practically every other form of human interaction seemed stunted. I could barely get a word out of him. He just sat there in front of one of those giant jigsaw puzzles. It was a German castle, I believe."

"He was working on it when we told him and his wife about their son's death." Lars made notes. To be fair, there were many different ways to deal with such news.

"So you got nothing out of him?"

Lisa shuffled some papers.

"I don't think that he and his son were close. It seemed almost as if Arne Winther-Sørensen had repudiated him."

Lars put his notepad down on the sofa.

"Did he mention the Danish Red Cross?"

49

THE ROYAL LIBRARY'S black glass facade sparkled in competition with the harbour basin every time the autumn sun peeked out from behind the grey clouds. Down on the water, two kayakers were battling their way through the waves to Knippel Bridge.

Lars walked past the basin in front of the library entrance and entered through the swinging door.

"Arne Winther-Sørensen?"

"Down to the basement and turn left." The woman behind the counter pointed to an elevator on her right. "Go down as far as you can. Hey, wait." She stepped out from behind the counter, hurrying after him with short, stiff strides. "You're not allowed to go down there unaccompanied."

The elevator opened with a small ping and they stepped inside. Lars let the woman press the button marked *Basement*.

"Do you know if he's in yet?"

The lift started moving with a lengthy sigh.

"Arne? I can't remember the last time he was ill." She lowered her voice as the elevator came to a halt. "Is this about his son?" The doors opened, and they stepped out and turned left. "It's a terrible business. Right, here we are." She knocked.

"I'm afraid I'm not at liberty to say."

A grunt came from behind the door. Lars pushed down the handle. "Thanks for your help."

Arne Winther-Sørensen sat hunched over his desk in the low-ceilinged office. He was peering through an illuminated magnifying glass at a confusion of ageing paper. Behind him, several yards of shelving was filled with stacks of paper, magazine holders, and ring binders. In the far corner at the top, boxes of old jigsaws were squeezed in between the shelf and the ceiling. There was a noticeboard above the desk. A jumble of notes, scraps of paper, and letters covered the cork surface.

"Arne?" Lars shut the door behind him. "Lars Winkler, Copenhagen Police. I would like—" Arne Winther-Sørensen looked up. An expression of disgust crossed his face. "Have you got a few minutes?" Lars took a step forward. The heat was suffocating.

Arne Winther-Sørensen muttered something that could be either yes or no.

"We've been told that Mogens worked for the Danish Red Cross back in—"

Arne got up and shuffled to the far corner of a bookshelf. He found a folder, removed it from the shelf, and carried it with him back to his desk. He opened it and started studying the densely written notes as if no one else were present.

"Perhaps we could go upstairs to the café? I'll buy you a cup of coffee."

Arne Winther-Sørensen merely hunched even further over his work.

Lars changed tack.

"What are you working on?"

Arne Winther-Sørensen looked up. His face gained colour and his eyes lit up.

"This is a draft of a letter from Council President D. G. Monrad to the king of Sweden suggesting a Nordic union by way of a royal marriage." Lars must have looked at him with a blank expression, because Arne Winther-Sørensen continued with mild irritation. "Monrad, the one from the Battle of Dybbøl. The letter to the king of Sweden was written after the armistice and before Denmark's war with the Germans had flared up again. I guess he was seeking support from the Swedes for the ongoing war effort. According to the Swedes, their king couldn't make up his mind if Monrad's letter was a joke,or should be taken seriously."

Lars knew absolutely nothing about it, and yet he nodded.

"The draft has been torn up. It'll be interesting to see if there are shifts in meaning between that and the final letter. I already think—"

"That sounds fascinating.But I'm here to talk about your son."

The spark in Arne Winther-Sørensen's eyes extinguished, and he turned his attention back to the magnifying glass and the papers underneath.

Lars continued: "We've been told that Mogens worked for the Danish Red Cross back in 1999. Is that correct?"

If possible, Arne Winther-Sørensen immersed himself even further into his work, trying to shut Lars out with his hunched back.

"This is about your son's murder." Lars leaned across the desk. The archivist pushed him away with a sudden and violent movement.

"Go away. You'll only ruin..." At last he looked up. A shadow of the revulsion returned. "Ask Merethe."

"We can either do this here, or I can bring you in. It's your choice."

Arne Winther-Sørensen pushed back his chair and got up.

"Mogens has been dead to me for more than ten years. I..." He stared at Lars with wild eyes before he stormed out of the office. The door slammed shut.

Lars looked after him, mystified. What was wrong with this family?

He took in the magnifying glass and the scraps of paper on the desk. The bookshelves behind the desk sagged with papers and looked close to collapsing under the weight. The desk itself was also covered with piles of paper and leather-bound books. A tall jar with rolled-up posters stood by the door. And then there was the noticeboard. Lars got up, and skimmed the invitations to openings and the internal memos. There was a menu from a pizzeria on Strøget, and photos of people he presumed to be Arne Winther-Sørensen's colleagues.

He reviewed the papers on the noticeboard, then his gaze moved across the piles on the desk. So many papers, holding memories from a whole life. He went behind the desk and sat down, leafing through trays and stacks, carefully avoiding the sheet with the torn pieces of D. G. Monrad's draft letter. The desk contained nothing but work-related documents, but he wondered about the drawer unit that had been pushed under the desk. Lars wheeled it out and opened the top drawer: nothing but pens, paper clips, Post-it notes, erasers, and a hole punch. The bottom was stained dark from ink.

The door opened behind him. He had just enough time to catch a glimpse of Arne Winther-Sørensen's face before it closed again. Apparently he was checking up on him. Lars took a step toward the door, then changed his mind. Arne Winther-Sørensen had clearly indicated that he didn't want to contribute to the investigation.

He returned to the desk and examined the other drawers one by one. The second and third drawer contained papers, printouts of emails, and handwritten letters from the 1970s. Should he call in the technicians? Lars tried the bottom drawer, but it was locked. He swore, yanking the drawer, but it refused to budge. He had no search warrant, but surely he couldn't give up now? A drop of sweat trickled from his hairline down across his forehead to his nose, and dripped onto his thigh. The boiler room had to be close by. He opened the top drawer, pulled out a paper clip, straightened it, and bent down.

It took him only a few seconds to pick the lock.

The bottom drawer contained a number of suspension files, each one labelled with the year. They contained handwritten minutes from meetings, organized chronologically. The meticulous order in the drawer was in stark contrast to the rest of Arne Winther-Sørensen's office, but there was nothing of interest to the investigation. Lars swore again, slamming shut the drawer. The metal framework rattled. Something skated back and forth inside, across the bottom. Lars opened the drawer again, flicking through the files. Everything looked the same. Then he tilted the drawer upward, pulling it out of its tracks and placing it on his lap. He could see the bottom of the drawer when he pressed the files together. Something was glittering in the darkness at the front. Lars stuck his hand inside. His fingertips fumbled across a knobbly surface that had once been smooth. It was a photograph. Lars pulled it out and held it up. A younger version of Mogens Winther-Sørensen was throwing a tennis ball to a dark-skinned boy who looked about eight years old, on a lawn. They were both laughing and looked happy. A table with bread rolls and jugs of fruit juice was in the background. The Red Cross flag was flying from a flagpole. Lars put the drawer on the floor and held the photograph under the magnifying glass. There was something familiar about the boy's face. Lars moved the picture back and forth under the lens to achieve the maximum enlargement.

The grinning boy, who was gazing up at Mogens Winther-Sørensen, could only be a younger version of Serafine.

50

THE GRAVEL CRUNCHED under the winter tires.

"We've arrived." Kim drove the car up the driveway and parked along the row of yew trees behind the red Toyota. The light inside the bungalow was on. "Don't forget you're due to visit a factory in less than an hour. *News* will be there, and—"

"But that factory is here in Nærum, isn't it? We have plenty of time." Merethe Winther-Sørensen produced a fat envelope from her bag. "I would appreciate it if you dealt with this, Kim."

"You won't be joining me?" He placed his left arm on the steering wheel and the right on the back of his seat as he turned around.

"You'll manage fine on your own." She handed him the envelope. "Now, this is what I want you to do."

Søren Gjerding opened the door before Kim had even pressed his finger to the bell. The man, whom he had escorted away from Mogens's funeral, was in his late fifties and had once been stocky and broad across the shoulders, but the years had shrunk him. He slumped as he leaned against the door, waiting passively.

"You?"

Kim nodded. The man cast stolen glances over Kim's shoulder toward the ministerial car in the driveway. Kim followed his gaze. The minister was staring at them from the back seat. He turned back again just in time to see the small tic by Søren Gjerding's right eyelid. The man was terrified.

Kim took a step forward and entered. Søren Gjerding wavered, shifting his weight from foot to foot, still staring at the car. Then he closed the door and followed Kim inside.

Søren Gjerding's wife served coffee and biscuits in the living room. Kim had to force himself to eat the stale shortbread, but the coffee was good.

Kim finished chewing. "The minister sends her regards. She thinks you're doing well.'"

"I've been lucky." Søren Gjerding looked glum.

"Yes, that job at Blegdamsvej came in very handy."

Søren Gjerding stared into his cup. "I don't believe it was solely to my advantage."

Kim set his coffee down on the smoked-glass table.

"There are certain... unforeseen events we've been forced to deal with."

51

SANNE OPENED THE door to her office a crack. Sarah Winther-Sørensen was sitting by the desk, picking at the seam of her pale green cigarette pants. She had swapped out the dark top for a white shirt.

"Poor girl." Lisa looked over Sanne's shoulder. "First she loses her father, and now this."

Sanne leaned against the door frame: the shit had really hit the fan.

OLD PEDO CHARGE MOTIVE FOR MAYOR MURDER?
SOURCE AT POLICE HQ CONFIRMS EXISTENCE OF OLD CASE

The article—written by Sandra Kørner again—had sent shock waves through the whole establishment from the justice minister down. Everyone in the department was under huge pressure, and Sanne felt they had no choice but to bring Sarah in for an interview.

"If I ever get hold of the idiot who leaked this," Lisa hissed.

"Calm down." Sanne pushed open the door and entered. "We'll deal with it later. Hi Sarah." She closed the door behind Lisa. "Would you like some coffee? Tea?"

Sarah shook her head and continued to pick at her pants.

"I want Peter here."

"We've called him and he's on his way, but he'll be a while, okay?" Sanne opened a bottle of mineral water and pushed it toward Sarah.

"You know why we want to talk to you, don't you?" Lisa put her pen and notepad on the desk and sat down.

"Someone in my year showed me the article on her phone," Sarah whispered.

Sanne chewed her lip. She had to get something out of the girl before the lawyer arrived. Once he was in the room, she would get nothing.

"You're almost an adult, so you understand why we have to ask." She hesitated. "Did your father ever, well...you know?"

Sarah closed her eyes; her face was white. Her hand shook as she reached out for the bottle of mineral water. There was a knock on the door and Allan's head popped around.

"Lars is on the phone in my office. I thought you would want to hear what he has to say."

"We'll be back shortly." Sanne got up and left. Lisa followed.

"I'm going to the washroom. You two go ahead." Allan pointed to his office and disappeared.

Allan's desk was overflowing with papers and reports. Lisa moved a small pile, which had Allan's cell phone on top of it, and sat down. Sanne picked up the landline.

"Lars? I'm going to put you on speaker. Lisa is here as well." She pressed the speaker button.

"Hey Lars." Lisa flexed her foot up and down. "What's happening?"

He sounded agitated; his voice was well above his normal pitch.

"I've figured out how Mogens Winther-Sørensen and Serafine knew each other." Pause. The sound of traffic in the background was perfectly audible. He was probably driving. "I've just left Arne Winther-Sørensen's office."

"We've brought in his granddaughter. Remember that anonymous call we got about the pedophile story yesterday? It's breaking news on *Ekstra Bladet* now."

"They don't waste any time, do they? Hang on . . ." Lars swore. "Okay, I'm back. Arne Winther-Sørensen wouldn't tell me anything, but I found an old photo in his office of Mogens with a boy who looked roughly eight years old. That boy can only be Serafine. You can see a Red Cross flag in the background."

"So Mogens did work for the Danish Red Cross? But then why did they insist they had never heard of him when I contacted them yesterday?" asked Lisa.

"I'm on my way to their main office on Blegdamsvej now. I'll give you a call when I'm done."

Sanne hung up. Allan's phone pinged to signal the arrival of a text message. Sanne tilted her head to read it.

The text consisted of one word: *Thanks!* The sender was Sandra Kørner.

She turned the phone so Lisa could read it as well.

"That . . ." Lisa stared at the phone and jumped up, her small body like a coiled spring.

"How long do you think he's been feeding her information?" Sanne picked up the phone and tried to unlock it, but it had a passcode. "We have to wait until we . . . Hi Allan." Allan was standing just outside the office.

"Yes?" He looked from one of them to the other.

"Can you explain this?" Sanne held up his cell phone.

He narrowed his eyes and stepped closer.

"That's . . ." Then he spotted the text, and opened and closed his mouth. "Listen, I haven't . . ." But the time for denial had passed. He sat down on the windowsill and buried his face in his hands. He rocked back and forth for a long time before he started to speak.

"I didn't tell her anything she didn't already know — she just wanted confirmation on the pedophile story." He looked up. "She kept pushing me . . . Do you know how much they're willing to pay? I've got the mortgage on the apartment, and . . ."

Lisa closed the door of the office and looked at Sanne for a long time. What should they do?

"I think . . ." Sanne tried to buy time. "First, I want you to unlock your phone right now. We want to be quite sure that you didn't give her any other information. Here . . ." She tossed Allan the cell phone.

He caught it and entered his passcode.

"There's nothing else — see for yourself."

Lisa snatched it from his hand.

"Hmm. There's just the one text message." She scrolled to outgoing calls. "Although you spoke to her a couple of times this morning. Apart from that there are no other calls to or from her number, but that doesn't prove —"

Someone started to scream. They could hear the sound of fighting, and chairs and tables being knocked over.

"What's going on?" Sanne rushed outside. The reception area was a battlefield: chairs and tables were lying helter-skelter. Someone had knocked over the table with the coffee maker, and brown liquid was splashed high up the wallpaper. Three of her colleagues were on the floor, pinning down Sarah Winther-Sørensen. She was no longer screaming, but sobbing. Her hair and makeup were a mess and the collar of her white shirt was half torn.

At that very moment, Peter Egethorn stepped through the green door to the Violent Crime Unit. It took him less than one second to take in the scene. Three long strides later, he had reached the tangled knot of police officers, freed Sarah, and helped her to her feet. Then he looked furiously at Sanne.

"What the hell is going on here?"

52

THE LOW, MUSTARD-COLOURED main office of the Danish Red Cross was located at Blegdamsvej 27, squeezed in between the imposing temple of the Freemasons and a 1970s, seven-storey college built of concrete and glass. Lars signalled and turned into the parking lot. A Jay-Z song was playing on the radio; he hadn't caught the title and hoped never to hear it again. The music faded the moment Lars found an empty parking spot, and the announcer took over.

"The Danish Meteorological Institute has issued a weather alert for torrential rain in eastern parts of the country. And tonight, DR will show the first live televised debate leading up to the general election. Every party leader will be in the studio to debate the three major themes for this election: the financial crisis..."

Lars sighed, paid for parking, and entered the building. It had already started to drizzle.

"Mogens Winther-Sørensen, you say? The mayor?" Agnete Thomsen took off her tortoiseshell glasses and looked at him. The head of the asylum section was a slim woman in her late fifties. "No, he never worked for us."

Lars shifted in the Børge Mogensen chair. The pale wicker seat cut into one of his buttocks.

"My colleague who phoned you yesterday was told the same thing." He took out the photograph of Mogens Winther-Sørensen and eight-year-old Serafine from his inside pocket. "But then I found this."

Agnete Thomsen studied the picture.

"Yes, that's the mayor — and that looks like a centre for asylum seekers. Hang on . . . It must be the Margretheholm Centre." She gave him back the photograph.

"Where is that?"

"The Margretheholm Centre? It's here in Copenhagen, on one of the Holmen Islands. The navy used the buildings for educational purposes. From 1999 and for some years after that, we took over the facilities to house asylum seekers, primarily Kosovo Albanians, but later refugees from Iran and Nigeria."

Lars drummed his pen on his notepad. Kosovo Albanians would certainly fit with the Bukoshi family.

"So what would Mogens Winther-Sørensen have been doing out there if he wasn't an employee?"

"He could have been visiting? It's the most likely explanation. In those days, visitors were free to come and go practically as they pleased."

"But to be so friendly with a refugee child . . . Is that possible from a single visit? I would think those children would be fairly shy. Just look at it — the two of them obviously hit it off."

"It's difficult to tell, it's just a snapshot." Agnete Thomsen put her glasses back on. "The old director of Margretheholm would surely know, don't you think?"

Agnete Thomsen found a contact list in a desk drawer, flicked through a couple of pages, and entered a number on her phone. Thirty seconds later she hung up.

"Right, we'll try his cell." She entered a new number and raised her phone to her ear. "His name is Søren Gjerding. He was my predecessor here, incidentally. He retired five years ago." But she had no luck with his cell number either.

"How odd. He almost always picks up. Just a moment." She got up and walked briskly across the office. She opened a door and stuck out her head to speak to a secretary.

"Would you please check if anyone knows how to track down my predecessor? Thank you."

She turned around in the doorway.

"This could take some time. Would you like some coffee? We've got one of these latte makers." Lars got up and followed her.

A machine was flashing and hissing in a niche in the wall beside the elevator. Lars stared at it.

Agnete Thomsen laughed. "They claim it makes regular coffee as well."

"Am I being that obvious?" Lars took an IKEA mug from the stack, put it into the machine, and pressed the button marked *Black Coffee*.

"Why are you so keen to know if Mogens Winther-Sørensen ever worked for the Red Cross?"

"I'm afraid I'm not allowed to discuss the investigation."

"Of course. I understand." Agnete Thomsen furrowed her brow, which was almost concealed by clouds of steam rising from the chrome coffee machine. "Only it's just—your case . . . It won't be good for the Red Cross to be dragged into a murder investigation, especially one involving the mayor, of all people. The last thing this organization needs is something that could damage our fundraising. Our financial assistance means the difference between life and death for a lot of people across the world—"

"Nobody wants to put the Red Cross in a bad light." Lars took the mug, which was now full of coffee. "Why don't we ask your secretary if she's found him?"

He followed her back down the corridor to her office. The coffee tasted acidic and chemical. They passed a shelf with information about the work of the Red Cross. Lars left his mug behind a stand of leaflets about fundraising for Congolese refugees.

Agnete Thomsen stopped. "Signe." They had reached her secretary, who was sitting with the telephone pressed to her ear.

A few seconds passed before Signe finished the call.

"Søren Gjerding was supposed to give a presentation at a conference in this building half an hour ago—only he never arrived."

53

"**HOW AM I** supposed to remember one argument I might
have had with my husband, what...fourteen years
ago?" Kirsten Winther-Sørensen had arrived less than ten minutes after Peter Egethorn. And if he had been furious, she was
incandescent. But once Kirsten had been given the opportunity
to speak with Sarah and Peter in private, Sanne had managed to
talk her down somewhat. Now she and Sanne were sitting alone
in Sanne's office. But although Kirsten seemed calmer now, she
was by no means in a forgiving mood.

"Malene Meisner." Sanne kept her voice controlled. "Ring any
bells? Or Malene Rørdam? That would have been the name you
knew her by. For a very brief period she was Mogens's head of
communications, just after he was elected mayor."

"I kept as far away from politics as possible." Kirsten Winther-
Sørensen turned her gaze inward. "Now, please may I—"

But Sanne pressed her. "Malene Meisner was fired after a Christmas party in 1999. Allegedly after a smear campaign orchestrated by Merethe Winther-Sørensen. Still not recalling that fight?"

"What's wrong with you people? My daughter just lost her father. She's falling apart, and you..." Kirsten Winther-Sørensen looked away. "You don't give a crap. You're just like Merethe. All she cares about is getting Sarah into the party's line of succession. Surely you can see..." she said, trailing off.

Kirsten Winther-Sørensen left police headquarters with her daughter, without answering any more questions. In light of the situation, Sanne didn't feel she could detain them any longer. Now she and Lisa were sitting in Sanne's office. Peter Egethorn sat on a chair on the other side of the desk with his face in his hands.

"I've tried to convince Kirsten to be frank with you." He exhaled slowly. "But she refuses."

Lisa was ready with pen and paper. Sanne stared at Peter's fingers.

"Then perhaps it's time you start telling us what you know."

The lawyer took a deep breath and took his hands off his face.

"You can never be sure about the Winther-Sørensen family. But I knew Mogens. There was never anything inappropriate between him and Sarah."

Sanne nodded.

"What's your relationship with Kirsten Winther-Sørensen?"

Peter Egethorn took a sip from the glass of water Lisa had put in front of him. Today's edition of *Ekstra Bladet* had been tossed in the wastebasket. He glanced at it.

"It was all over the front page..."

"Perhaps that makes it even more important to tell the truth?"

Peter Egethorn nodded. Slowly.

"Kirsten was thinking of leaving Mogens. That's why she went for a drive last Monday when he was... We had spoken on the phone a couple of times during that afternoon and evening. My advice to her was to wait until after the election. They had been together for years, and it would be damaging to the party if..." He paused. "If she left Mogens in the middle of the election... Merethe would destroy us."

"How long have the two of you been seeing each other?"

"Kirsten and I... We've been together since high school. When she started her company, I took care of the legal side, patents, that sort of thing. Her father was a Conservative member of Gentofte Council, so politics is in her blood. Only she picked the wrong party." Peter Egethorn's mouth took on a bitter expression. "Merethe Winther-Sørensen spotted her in the Copenhagen branch of the Radical Party in the mid-1990s and decided that she would be perfect for her son. And what Merethe Winther-Sørensen wants, she gets. I never heard it from Kirsten herself—the minister's private secretary took me aside and explained the situation to me."

"And you just accepted it?" Lisa made a note.

"You don't understand—it wasn't like I had a choice. And at the time, I believed it was what Kirsten wanted. But a few months later, she started calling me again."

"And you've been together ever since?"

"More or less."

"So Mogens and Kirsten...?" Sanne tried to catch his eye, but Peter Egethorn avoided her.

"Well, they have Sarah. But apart from that..." He shrugged his shoulders.

"There is a period of time we've been unable to shed any light on. It's the autumn of 1999. Can you help us?"

"Yes—1999... At some point during that autumn, probably

late September or early October, Kirsten told me she wanted to end our relationship. She was going to give Mogens another chance. He had changed." Peter Egethorn fell silent and stared into space. "There's still a lot I don't know. Please understand, we had a tacit agreement: we never discussed her life with Mogens. Ever. So I didn't see her for about a month, and I guess I thought it really was over. But then suddenly—it must have been early November—she called me out of the blue. She was in a state and said things between her and Mogens were worse than ever. It was just after he had been elected mayor."

54

THE SUN IS high over the main building. The air quivers inside the narrow room between the urine-coloured walls. She lies in the bed with the blanket pulled right up to her nose, sweating in the cool room.

She has been given a single room at Ellebæk, the secure unit next to Sandholm—in a ward for single men. Because now they know, the staff—know what she is.

The residents know it too. They watch her. They prowl up and down the corridor, on the other side of the window, casting long glances at her.

She rolls over and curls up. Hunger gnaws at her stomach. She turned down the food the female police officer tried to give her. She has not eaten since the night the street-doc introduced her to the surgeon. That was Saturday. She's gone almost two days without food. She weighs so little that the slightest gust of wind threatens to carry her away.

The jar of pills she got yesterday is empty. She took the last ones early this morning. Zits have started erupting; her face is covered with infected craters. And hairs—she has hairs everywhere. The beast rears its head inside her and roars.

Outside, the men wander back and forth outside her window.

She hallucinates from hunger. From time to time she drifts off, her body releasing its hold on her. The room dissolves and she is elsewhere—in the bright room, a space with no walls or ceilings. She doesn't feel hungry. She has no acne. Only white butterflies everywhere. She sees her sister's figure between the butterfly wings. Afërdita glances over her shoulder, then turns her back on her.

And then the hunger returns, eating her up. She is back in the narrow bedroom. She clings to the dream, and tries to contain it in the bed under the blanket, every muscle locked in spasm. She tries to hold on to it, but it slips away and dissolves. What remains is a void demanding to be filled. She is dripping with sweat. She checks her cell phone. Yes, it is time. Dinner is being served in the cafeteria. She untangles herself from the blanket, staggers out into the bathroom, and splashes some water on her face. Her makeup is smeared; her face streaked. But that can't be helped right now. She needs something in her stomach before she disappears completely.

They grab her as she turns the corner, right before the open square of the cafeteria. Hands yank her into the darkness between two barracks. Their excited voices in the alleyway. She knows what comes next even before they tear off her clothes: hands on her, dicks inside her. It is the alien body they take— yet her they take it from.

She has no idea how much time has passed. It is not until the voices ebb away that she becomes aware of the damp ground underneath her, the grass tickling her left ear. Her mouth is sticky; something oozes out of her backside. The pain is everywhere.

Small clouds drift across the blue sky, high up between the roofs. The sun is shining. She lies gasping for a long time, trying to touch it, but every time she reaches out, it retreats—the sun is rejecting her, too. She closes her eyes, waiting only to disappear.

It is not until the hunger becomes unbearable that she forces herself to get up and lean against the wall for support. She tries wiping herself down with handfuls of grass and washes her mouth and chin with saliva.

The sun bounces off something in the grass near the building at the end of the alleyway. Some kids have thrown stones at it. Perhaps one of the residents got drunk and smashed it against the corner of the house—the shards of a broken glass bottle. But it's her way out, to the bright room and to Afërdita.

OCTOBER 1999

THE KEY IS in the ignition, but he has yet to start the engine. The wheelhouse on the roof of the old naval base is almost hidden in the fog. A resident passes; their eyes meet. Then the man disappears, swallowed up by the grey mist. Mogens leans over the steering wheel and closes his eyes. His grip around the steering wheel is so hard that it hurts. The wheel is his only point of reference—without it he will be dragged down into the maelstrom that has opened up beneath him. How long will it be before Søren calls the police? Perhaps he is talking to them at this very moment. Everything is floating, falling apart, except for Kirsten and Sarah. Kirsten has to listen to him—she must.

Mogens starts the car and pulls out onto Forlandet. His thoughts turn to Kirsten, but all the way through Holmen and the city of Copenhagen, he can't shake the image of Arbën's terrified face.

"Where have you been?" Kirsten shoots up from the chair when he enters her office. Her dark hair is a mess and the bags under her eyes speak volumes, but anger simmers under the thin varnish of concern.

A garment rack with spring's must-haves stands in a corner. A petrol blue, A-line blouse lies across the desk on top of fashion magazines and catalogues. The rich silk shimmers in the glow from concealed spotlights. There is a single gladiolus in a glass vase next to the telephone.

Mogens flops into the armchair in front of the desk and buries his face in his hands.

"Hornbæk—the cottage. Kirsten..." Everything is spinning and it is impossible to think straight. "It's all so horrible."

Kirsten folds her arms across her chest and stares at him for long, terrible seconds. He can imagine only too vividly what she must be thinking. Then she turns around, rummages in a cupboard behind her, and takes out a bottle. She pours a few fingers' worth of the amber liquid into a glass and pushes it across the desk.

"Here. Drink."

Mogens drinks, clutching the glass with both hands. Southern Comfort, the excessively sweet liqueur, burns all the way down to his stomach. He sets down the glass, letting Kirsten refill it.

"I kept calling..." She puts down the bottle and takes a seat. "Do you have any idea how worried I've been?"

"I needed time to think. It's all so messed up." He looks down at his wet clothes. And then the words pour out. He tells her about the scene at Søren's office, the accusation, and the uncles' triumphant smiles.

Kirsten lets him talk without interrupting. Once he's finished, she perches on the edge of the desk and takes his hand.

"Do you think Søren will call the police?"

"It sounded as if they would carry out an internal investigation first...before..." Mogens rubs his temples with his forefingers. "You should never have brought that boy to the apartment." "I would have never got him to talk otherwise." He leans his head back and stares up at the ceiling. "But you're right, of course."

Kirsten tries again. "You say that his sister is missing?" "The other day I went to their room to fetch Arbën. He wasn't there. Do you remember the man I told you about? The one I saw leaving their room? You thought they were dealing drugs. But they weren't." Mogens buried his face in his hands. "I asked Afërdita who he was. And then she started to kiss me."

"Kiss you? But she's just a child."

"She was totally dolled up. She looked..." His fingers scrunch up the pattern on the A-line blouse. The thin white paper crackles against the fabric.

Kirsten makes a strange sound. Then she pours herself a double.

"So they're pimping their own niece." She gulps down almost all the liqueur. "Christ almighty."

"Kirsten?" A young assistant in a very short skirt opens the door without knocking. "I've got the Danish Design Centre on the phone. They would like to confirm that booking." The assistant, whose name Mogens has forgotten, looks from one of them to the other.

Kirsten ushers her out with a well-placed "later."

"Well, you haven't done anything." Kirsten puts the cap back on the bottle and returns it to the cupboard. Mogens desperately wants to rip it from her hands and chug it back in one long gulp. But he controls himself. He needs a clear head. And then he can't keep it in any longer; the words just spill out of his mouth.

"When I was about to leave the other day, I suddenly found myself standing outside her door. I tried to leave, but..." The words almost choke him, but he cannot suppress them any longer. "I'm not like that, but my body. It...Kirsten, you know me...I didn't do anything!"

There is silence, broken only by the static crackling of Kirsten's shoes as she glides across the carpet, away from him.

"What are you saying? That you wanted to...?"

Then she explodes. She snatches his glass and smashes it at his feet. "You sick—" The other glass is ready in her hand, but he ducks in time. It hits the wall behind him and shatters. The rest of the Southern Comfort and the shards of glass slide down the white wall. The smell of sugar and alcohol stings his nose and throat.

"Kirsten..." He hides behind the armchair. "But I didn't go into her room."

"You bastard. You'll never see Sarah again!"

She spits at him, then turns on her heel and marches out of the office. Out in the corridor he catches a glimpse of her staff's terrified faces, before she slams the door shut. The vase holding the long gladiolus is knocked over, a dark stain spreads across the silk blouse.

Then his phone rings.

"It's your mother. We have quite a lot to talk about. Why don't you come by. After midnight, okay?"

55

"YOU JUST NEED to sign here, then you can take him with you." The Red Cross worker pointed to a dotted line on the document. Sanne scribbled something illegible and pushed the form back across the counter.

After interviewing Peter Egethorn, she had told Ulrik about Allan leaking information to *Ekstra Bladet*. Ulrik had been livid and summoned Allan immediately. After a tongue-lashing that could be heard throughout the whole department, he had been escorted out of the building; his cell phone and computer sent to IT. Ulrik wanted to make absolutely sure that Allan hadn't leaked anything else. Shortly afterward, they got a call from Ellebæk. Serafine had tried to kill herself.

Now Serafine was slumped against the counter next to her. She had yet to say a word. Her left hand was resting on the countertop, hidden under a thick bandage. She looked exhausted and wasn't wearing any makeup. Her skin was grey and pale, almost transparent. Her dress was practically reduced to threads below the waist.

"Do you know how it happened?"

The Red Cross worker, a well-upholstered guy in a charcoal-grey T-shirt and black jeans, took the form with Sanne's signature and filed it in a ring binder, which he then put back on the shelf.

"Sorry, no. One of the cafeteria workers found him outside the door to his room. He had lost quite a lot of blood. If you're referring to the dress..." He shrugged his shoulders. "I guess he fell or something."

They had reached the Hillerød highway. Serafine leaned her head against the window and gazed out at the rush-hour traffic. Sanne chewed her lip.

Serafine had blinked once when Sanne repeated the conversation with the Red Cross worker, but said nothing. Sanne continued: "And do you know what he said? That you must have fallen. If you want me to help you, you have to tell me what really happened."

Serafine turned her head. Was she smiling? If so it was a strange, lost smile.

"No one can help me. It was already too late, many, many years ago." It was the longest sentence Sanne had heard escape from Serafine's lips. Was she finally lowering her guard?

"There's always someone who can help," she tried to explain. "No one should be alone."

"Do you take me for an idiot?" Serafine's voice was so sharp in the little car that Sanne's hands yanked at the steering wheel out of sheer fright. The car skidded. She straightened out, forcing herself to concentrate on her driving. Serafine continue shouting with her eyes closed. A spray of saliva coated the inside of the windshield. "People like me, we're killed and raped. And those of us who survive commit suicide—half of us before we turn twenty." She sat back in the seat and smoothed out the remains of her dress. Her voice settled into a calmer tone. "And I've tried all three."

Sanne forced herself to breathe deeply and slowly. She was getting somewhere. She tried reviewing all the bits of information they had gathered in the last few days over in her head. She rubbed her face with one of her hands.

"You've been to Denmark before—with your uncles, Meriton and Ukë, and your sister. Am I right?"

Serafine didn't react. She appeared to have said all she wanted to on the matter; now she just stared at the Ring 3 beltway.

"Oh, come on. If you won't help yourself, then at least help me. Mogens Winther-Sørensen practically died in your arms. What happened?"

Serafine gave her a quick look, a slight twitch at the corner of her mouth. She was on the verge of loosening up and letting go. Then her gaze died, and she looked away.

Sanne had to try to tempt her and reel her in. They drove past Utterslev Mose park and overtook a silver Škoda.

"We know that you and Mogens met at Margretheholm."

Serafine closed her eyes.

Sanne was getting desperate. She sifted through the information yet another time.

"Okay, you said you had tried all three. You've just tried to kill yourself. There has to be a reason why you slit your wrist." She paused when she realized what she had just said. "They raped you."

Sanne shuddered. The traffic enclosed them and she was forced to reduce her speed.

"They raped you," she repeated. "At the centre. And nobody did anything?"

56

"THE PARTY LEADER debate?" The receptionist looked briefly at his badge before letting him in. "You want Studio 6. It's through the gate at the end, then go left."

Lars half-ran through DR's headquarters. The debate would be going live in ten minutes. Hopefully he'd made it in time.

He dashed through the gate and down a high-ceilinged corridor with concrete walls and floors. It resembled a factory more than anything else. Staff, politicians, and press officers were standing or wandering around in small groups, moving toward the studio. A host from a TV show whose name he couldn't remember started walking in his direction with a cup of coffee in his hand. Lars narrowly avoided bumping into him, but knocked over the paper cup. Half the contents splashed over the man's shirt.

"Look where you're going, moron."

Lars ignored him and carried on toward Studio 6. Kim A was standing outside the entrance wearing a black suit and an earpiece. Lars's ex-colleague took a step forward and held up his hand when he spotted him.

"And that's as far as you go."

"Kim A." Lars stopped. "So, tell me, does your jurisdiction extend to lying in a murder investigation?" The words came out louder than strictly necessary. It fell silent around them. Makeup artists and press officers from various parties stared at them. A young Social Democrat—a tall, blonde girl—gave Lars a terrified look before slipping behind Kim A and through the black door to the studio.

"You watch your mouth," Kim A hissed before coming right up to him, but he was intercepted by the minister who was walking toward them.

"Kim. Let me talk to him."

Kim A blinked twice, then stepped aside.

Merethe Winther-Sørensen took Lars by the arm and dragged him down toward the washrooms by the glass wall at the end of the corridor.

"What on earth do you think you're doing?" She kept her voice low and neutral. "Are you aware that you're only one phone call away from being fired?"

Lars said nothing, and slipped his hand inside his jacket to produce the picture of Mogens Winther-Sørensen and Serafine as a child.

"Does this ring any bells?"

Merethe Winther-Sørensen glanced at the photograph.

"My son playing with a ball?" She didn't move a muscle.

"I have repeatedly asked you about your son's past, and every time you've either denied knowing anything or prevented me from finding the information I need. This photograph was taken at a Danish Red Cross centre called Margretheholm back in

1999. Do you deny that Mogens worked there for a month before he became mayor? That he met Serafine there? Are you sure there's nothing you want to tell me? About him being accused of pedophilia, perhaps?"

The minister was more than a head shorter than him, but that didn't appear to bother her. She lowered her voice.

"If I were you, I wouldn't be quite so loud. Something about a red bookmark containing a small wrap? Its contents aren't standard equipment for a police officer, I believe. It could very easily find its way into the wrong hands."

A producer came toward them holding up two fingers.

"Two minutes. You're on now."

"Please excuse me." Merethe Winther-Sørensen turned and walked away. "I'm going to be on TV."

Lars was still shaking when he returned to his car. He sat on the hood and lit a King's as he looked out across West Amager. He had read somewhere that nicotine affects the same pleasure centres in the brain as cocaine—and music. Right now, he was prepared to believe it. His heart rate settled, and the hand holding the cigarette stopped shaking. It was growing dark; projectors lit up the blue canvas that surrounded the cube-shaped Concert Hall. Inside, the minister—along with the leaders from the other parties represented in parliament—were about to hold a debate that would make absolutely no difference to the election.

He took out his phone. Lisa had called him twice within the last ten minutes.

"Lisa, what's happening?" He took a drag of his cigarette. The wind snatched away the smoke the moment he exhaled it through his nose.

"Serafine tried to kill herself."

"What?" He nearly choked.

"Are you sick?"

"It's just smoke." Lars finished coughing. "When?"

"A couple of hours ago. I think she's all right. Sanne went up there to bring her back so we could interview her. I think Sanne felt that Serafine shouldn't be left alone. And another thing: we got a call from the airport. You told them to be on the lookout for a Søren Gjerding?"

"A-ha?" Lars took one last drag, and then squashed the cigarette on the tarmac with the sole of his shoe.

"Airport police are holding him right now. He was on his way to Thailand with his wife."

57

SANNE UNLOCKED THE door. The apartment was dark and empty. Thank God Martin was working late at the office again.

"So this is where I live. Make yourself at home." She put her handbag on the chest of drawers. Serafine said nothing, but looked around. She stayed close to Sanne, following her into the kitchen.

It was early evening now and growing dark outside. Sanne opened the freezer and pulled out a couple of ready meals.

"You can choose between lasagna and lasagna." Sanne flashed Serafine a cautious smile as she put the trays in the microwave. They stood for some minutes in silence while the food heated up. Then Sanne plated their dinners and carried them into the living room. She lit a candle and opened a bottle of red wine. Serafine still had not said anything, but she was smiling—or it looked that way, at least.

There was a beep from her handbag. Sanne returned to the hallway, Serafine following at her heels. Not a surprise that she didn't want to be alone.

Sanne found the cell phone in her bag. Hi, Sanne. Lisa says you've picked up Serafine? Am on my way to the airport. Call me when you can. It's starting to make sense. Lars

Typical Lars. No information but an order. What use was that? She dropped the phone back into her bag. On the other hand, it was good to hear from him. That soft tingle in the pit of her stomach returned.

They went back to the living room. Sanne pulled out a chair and hung her handbag over it. She signalled to Serafine to sit down.

"Dig in." She poured some wine and pushed a plate toward Serafine, then cut a corner off her own lasagna and tipped it onto her fork.

"Are you sure you don't want to report them? We can drive to Rigshospitalet immediately if..."

Serafine cut into her lasagna. Minced beef, béchamel sauce, and diced tomatoes oozed out over the plate. Steam rose up. She shook her head and smiled that wistful smile again.

"It doesn't matter."

"I mean, I believe you." Sanne put down her fork.

"You're sweet." There it was again—that smile. It was so sad, it trickled down the walls.

Serafine placed a small piece of lasagna on her fork and put it in her mouth.

"What was it about? The text message? You didn't look happy. But at the same time, you kind of did."

Sanne placed her hand on her chest and took a deep breath in.

"Oh, it was just a colleague. We had...a thing once. It's over now."

"Men are bastards." Serafine chewed with her front teeth and stared into the candlelight, losing herself in the flame that was dancing in the breeze from the window. Then she straightened up and looked directly at Sanne. "I was only eight years old. We lived here in Copenhagen at the Margretheholm Centre: my sister Afërdita, me, and our two uncles. One night..." Serafine fell silent and gulped. Then she pushed her plate away. She took the glass of red wine, drained it in one go, and held it out for more. Sanne took the bottle and filled up the glass, too scared to say anything for fear of breaking the spell. "Our uncles forced Afërdita to be with men. You know..." She waved her hand in the air as she emptied her glass a second time. "For money. Men from the centre and local Danes. They had usually finished by the time I came back. But one day..." Serafine broke off. This time she filled the glass herself. "When I opened the door, there was blood all over the floor. He had stabbed her to death with a pair of scissors."

"Oh, Serafine..." Sanne clasped a hand over her mouth. Serafine stared into space. Her wistful expression had not changed.

"He was lying naked on top of her. I watched him open his eyes and look straight at me." Serafine paused again, scratching her scarred forearm. Sanne tried to stop her, but Serafine wiggled free and held up her arms.

"No, I want..." She rubbed her eyes. "Do you have any cigarettes?"

Sanne reached for her bag and found a packet of Princes. Serafine took one and lit it from the candle. Sanne picked up the pack. Her hand shook as she took out a cigarette for herself. She had so many questions, so many things she wanted to know, but first she had to let Serafine tell the story in her own time.

"I got to know Moo-genz at Margretheholm. He was nice — gave me a photograph of his daughter. He tried to help." She sucked hard on the cigarette. "But it went... wrong. After my sister... My uncles sent me to Hamburg. Last Sunday I saw his picture in a newspaper and heard that he had become... What do you call it? *Bürgermeister?*"

"Mayor."

"Exactly. I thought he might be able to help me with my... condition. So I came here, tracked him down, and went with him to his apartment." The smoke seeped out of the corner of her mouth and her face disappeared in the grey fog.

Sanne tried to make sense of it all.

"Who..." She cleared her throat. "Are you telling me that the same man killed Mogens *and* your sister? Can you describe him? Would you be able to recognize him?"

"I've seen him here—with you." Serafine's face was frozen in an expressionless mask.

There was a tiny sound from the stairwell; Serafine jumped and curled up on the chair.

"There's someone there," she whispered. "By the door."

Sanne turned her head and listened. A sudden draft blew out the candle flame, the wick hissing in the melted wax. They heard shouting in the street, a child crying. Music was playing. Was someone really there?

Sanne got up.

"Don't." Serafine reached out her hand, tried to stop her, but Sanne was already in the hallway opening the door.

Darkness there and nothing more. Sanne shut the door and returned to her chair.

"There's nobody here. You can relax." She sat down and poured more wine for both of them. "You were telling me about the killer?"

Serafine stared at her. Her fear slowly ebbed away, only to be replaced with resignation. Her black pupils looked straight through Sanne. She shrugged and stubbed out the cigarette in the remains of the lasagna on her plate.

"After I found my sister..." She reached out for the cigarettes, which Sanne had left on the table between them, then took Sanne's cigarette from her hand and lit her own before handing it back. "The next thing I remember is my uncles coming into our room, talking to him and helping him get dressed. Then they forced both of us to bury her outside the centre. They ordered me to hold the flashlight so they could see. While they..."

Sanne was quiet for a long time, breathing through the cigarette.

"They forced you to bury your own sister?"

Serafine nodded, fixing her gaze on her. Sanne extinguished her cigarette next to Serafine's.

"Can you show me where?"

58

LARS PUSHED HIS way up the escalator to airport security, past the business people, regular tourists, and families with children on their last holiday before the melancholy of winter set in.

An officer from Copenhagen Airport Police met him just before passport control, then guided him around the line and through the shopping area's glittering mix of high street, luxury brands, and empty calories, to the airport police office by Gate C.

"They had already gone through security, but we managed to stop them at passport control." The big airport officer was sweating in his uniform as he pushed his glasses back in place with his forefinger.

"Has he said anything?" Lars peered through the small window in the door at the couple sitting at a white, laminated square table. They looked pale and weren't talking. He had seen the man before—it was the same man Kim A had led away from the cathedral during Mogens Winther-Sørensen's funeral. His colleague shrugged.

"The usual. He says that it must be some kind of mix-up. His wife is mostly worried that they'll miss their flight."

"I think they can forget about that. Can I go in?" Lars left the door open behind him. "Søren Gjerding?" The elderly man did not look up. His face was hidden in his hands and his elbows were resting on the table. The retired director of the Margretheholm Refugee Centre and former head of the Danish Red Cross's asylum section had once been an imposing man, but age and the usual physical decay had caused him to slump, as fat replaced muscle. He was wearing a short-sleeved, checked shirt and had a Skagen watch on his left wrist. A small, brown-leather bag was lying on the table in front of him. Lars guessed it contained a Canon camera more sophisticated than Søren Gjerding knew how to operate and a wallet that was probably full. The wife fiddled with her fingers and looked up hastily as Lars entered the room.

"What's the point of keeping us here? We'll miss our flight." She got up and stood with her hand on the back of the chair, ready to leave.

"Would you please follow my colleague?" Lars gestured behind him to the airport officer filling the doorway. "I would like to speak to your husband alone."

"Out of the question, we demand—"

"Just do as he says." Søren Gjerding didn't look up. His wife fell silent and looked from the officer by the door to her husband. Then she pushed the chair back under the table with a slam and left.

Lars pulled out a chair and sat down opposite the former Red Cross director.

"Lars Winkler, Copenhagen Police. You look like you know why we're here."

Søren Gjerding shook his head, but he still didn't look up.

"It's about the murder of Mogens Winther-Sørensen."

The other man started scratching his hair in short, manic jerks. Lars took off his jacket.

"He used to work for you, at the Margretheholm Centre."

Søren Gjerding's large and wrinkled hands fell to the table.

"I have no idea what you're talking about." For the first time, he raised his head and looked straight at Lars. His eyes were grey and watery, the bags below dragging his whole face toward his chin.

"I think you do." Lars fiddled with the cigarette packet in his pocket. "Mogens Winther-Sørensen took leave from the city council in October 1999, just before he returned as mayor. The original plan was that he would work for the Red Cross for at least six months, but it turned out to be just one month. Why?"

Søren Gjerding shook his head, then hid his face in his hands again.

Lars produced a photograph from his inside pocket.

"I want you to look at this picture." He raised his voice when the other man did not react. "It was taken at the Margretheholm Centre."

Søren Gjerding removed his hands from his face and studied the photograph with a resigned expression.

"That's Mogens Winther-Sørensen and Serafine—our main witness—as a child."

Søren Gjerding stared at the image for a long time. Then he picked it up with trembling fingers.

"It...I think..." His shoulders slumped and he dropped the photo. "It's no use. It's too late."

"It's never too late." Lars pushed the picture to the middle of the table and turned it toward the former centre director. "To tell the truth."

Søren Gjerding fixed his eyes on the yellowing colour

photograph and made a few false starts before he found his words.

"Mogens Winther-Sørensen started working with us as a volunteer—1999 sounds about right." He pulled at his cheeks. "The boy, whom you call Serafine, was known as Arbën back then. He came up here with his older sister and two uncles, Meriton and—"

"Ukë. Thanks, we know. They won't bother anyone anymore."

Søren Gjerding gulped.

"The boy grew very fond of Mogens, and Mogens of him. Arbën's sister disappeared after Mogens had been with us about a month. Obviously we were all upset, but I think Mogens might have taken it the worst. The following day Mogens broke an inviolable rule and invited Arbën back to his apartment. Arbën told him that his uncles forced his sister to prostitute herself. After the boy returned, his uncles must have made him repeat what he told Mogens, because the next morning they were in my office, accusing Mogens of sexually abusing him."

"And had he?"

Søren Gjerding shook his head.

"I really don't think so. It was an attempt by the uncles to protect their business. And it worked." He closed his eyes. "You must understand the whole thing was incredibly sensitive. One word to the media, and the entire Danish Red Cross would have been dragged through the mud. Our work with refugees would have suffered. I had no choice. I suspended Mogens, and I was going to report him to the police—to you."

"But you never did?"

"No." His hands began to shake. "The finance minister called."

"Ah?" Now this was getting interesting.

Søren Gjerding doodled in the dust on the table with his pinky finger.

"Well, I might as well…now that I've started…" He peered at the picture. Lars waited. Suddenly, Søren Gjerding straightened up with surprising agility. "She offered me a deal that would make me director of the asylum section of the Red Cross. It was a big move up. She also promised to secure an extra one hundred million kroner for refugee work in the next year's budget. That money was badly needed, I can assure you." Søren Gjerding put his hand on the photo and pulled it toward him.

"In return for you forgetting all about the uncles' accusation." Lars reached out, took the picture, and stuck it in his inside pocket. "Then what happened?"

"I was going to get the boy an appointment with a psychologist, but he disappeared that same evening, just like his sister."

"Disappeared? Where did he go?"

"I don't know. It's normal for both children and adults to disappear from asylum centres if their application for asylum is turned down. But neither Arbën nor his sister had been refused."

Lars drummed his fingers on the table and looked out through the small window behind Søren Gjerding. So that's what Merethe Winther-Sørensen had been trying to hide. There was no doubt the story would be toxic for her party during the election, but to go as far as sabotaging the investigation into the murder of her own son?

Outside the window, a Lufthansa aircraft taxied to the runway. Its lights reflected in the wet tarmac. It had already started to drizzle.

Lars's attention returned to the stuffy office.

"And now you're on your way to Thailand. Why now?"

Søren Gjerding looked down at the table.

"The minister…"

"She wanted you out of the way until the election was over? Until things had settled down?"

Søren Gjerding stared at the plane now roaring down the runway.

"She gave us money and the address of a remote farmhouse in Sweden. We weren't supposed to come back until after Christmas."

"But you preferred Thailand. Let me guess: your wife doesn't like the cold?"

Søren Gjerding nodded. Lars got up.

"I'll get an officer to drive you to police headquarters so we can get a written statement from you. I don't think you'll be going to Phuket this year."

59

SANNE TURNED HER white Fiat 500 onto Kløvermarksvej. To her right were football pitches, wet and deserted in the autumn darkness; to her left, rows upon rows of empty community gardens. Serafine was sitting in the passenger seat, biting her nails.

"Do you think you'll be able to find it again?" Sanne kept her eyes on the road and reduced her speed as the car followed the bend around to the left. She accelerated again up Forlandet and along Lynetten. "We'll be there in a sec."

Serafine shook her head, pressing herself back into the seat. They weren't good memories.

Sanne had called the duty officer to request a dog and handler to meet them once they got there. Unfortunately he was not due to arrive for another fifteen minutes. She suddenly realized how dark and quiet it was out here.

The road turned. The hangar, which was part of Margretheholm, appeared in the darkness to her right. But the GPS told her to carry on, past a cluster of trees and bushes, before turning right onto Luftmarinegade and pulling up in front of the ruins of the old naval station. Sanne turned off the engine and got out. The wind was tearing at the reeds along the embankment, shaking the treetops above their heads. There was rain in the air. On the other side of the road was a row of newly built, dark-wood terraced houses. The light was on in a few of the houses furthest away. The old B&W shipyard loomed large and ominous behind the marina.

She bent down and stuck her head inside the car.

"Are you coming?"

Serafine opened the passenger door and got out.

"Our room was in there." She pointed to the end of a graffiti-covered building. Bushes, weeds, even small trees had pushed through the stony ground along the wall. An iron door swung in the wind on rusty hinges. A sigh reverberated through the building.

Sanne went over to the passenger side and put her arm around Serafine.

"Come on. The dog handler will be here in a moment. Could you please show me where you buried her?"

Serafine walked away from the building, toward the tree-clad mound that sloped down to the road.

"It was around here. We didn't walk very far."

A car drove past but didn't stop. Its headlights disappeared between the trees. Sanne followed Serafine in between the bushes, turning on her flashlight. The beam danced over garbage, beer cans, used condoms, and cigarette butts. Even the remains of a packet of minced beef had found its way out here.

Sanne's cell phone rang in her handbag, which she had left in the car.

"Hang on." Sanne turned back.

"Don't leave me." Serafine reached out for her, but Sanne was already by the car, opening the door.

"Yes?"

"Hi, it's Lars. Did you get my text? We've got a lot to do."

"I'm out at Margretheholm — with Serafine." Lars didn't sound surprised.

"What has she told you?"

"It's a long story. Just come out here, will you?"

They both hung up. Sanne stuffed her cell phone in her pocket and turned around. Serafine was standing right behind her, wide-eyed, staring out into the night.

"There's someone . . ."

Sanne said nothing and listened.

"It's nothing. Come on." She reached a hand into her bag. "I'll take this. Will that make you feel better?" Sanne showed her the small pepper spray and stuffed it into her pocket.

Serafine grabbed her arm. She was panting. The wind in the trees, the rustling of the reeds, and the hum of traffic coming from the city.

And now she too can hear it. A faint rustling sound in the foliage that is out of sync with the wind.

"He's coming." Serafine grabs a hold of her, hyperventilating.

"Nonsense." Sanne tries to free herself, fumbling with the flashlight. "It's just a cat." She turns on the light.

In the pale cone coming from the flashlight, they both see a running shoe disappearing back into the darkness.

60

LARS TOSSED HIS cell phone onto the passenger seat, glanced quickly over his shoulder, and forced the steering wheel round to the left. The oncoming cars honked their horns and braked. He didn't care, and made a big U-turn before heading back along H. C. Andersens Boulevard toward Amager. Sanne had sounded agitated, as if she had made a breakthrough with Serafine. He sped past Tivoli, the Glyptoteket museum, and the old Royal Danish Music Conservatory.

On the radio, the debate was well under way. By now the leaders had pitched their most important themes for the election and outlined how their party intended to deal with the nation's problems.

"And thank you to Britta Gårdbo from the Liberal Alliance." The host rattled his cue cards. *"This concludes the first round of debate. Before we move on to the second, I'm sure viewers would like to hear*

Finance Minister Merethe Winther-Sørensen address the speculations that were published today about the pedophilia allegations involving her son, the late mayor of Copenhagen." Lars crossed Langebro bridge. The lights from Fisketorvet shopping centre glittered nervously in the black surface of the harbour basin to the south.

There was a collective gasp from the car radio; every participant in the debate held their breath—except one.

"Mogens's death is a terrible loss for me—his mother—and for his wife and daughter—indeed for the whole family." Merethe Winther-Sørensen's voice was calm, and tinged with a suitable hint of melancholy. *"But also for the party and the country. He was an unparalleled political talent. Who knows what he would have achieved if he had been allowed to continue his political work? Fortunately, his daughter, Sarah Winther-Sørensen, has decided to carry on from where he was so tragically forced to stop."* She cleared her throat and her voice rose three whole tones: tritonus, a diminished fifth—the devil's interval. *"At the same time I'm glad that you have given me the opportunity to comment on this rumour."* Lars was impressed. She actually sounded as if she meant it. *"Because I can assure everyone, both here and the people at home, that it's nothing more than that—a rumour. My son was never involved in any abuse case."*

"Can you comment on the accusations that you used your political influence to suppress the case?"

Merethe Winther-Sørensen snorted.

"We live in Denmark, not some banana republic. I can—"

Lars turned off the radio. His hands were shaking on the steering wheel. Did she really think that she could get away with it? His blood was boiling; he moved the car over to the left and into the next lane, unable to drive on.

He signalled, pulled up on the sidewalk outside the SAS Royal Hotel, and grabbed a newly purchased packet of King's Blue from his inside pocket. He tore off the cellophane and lit a cigarette. The smoke unfurled in his lungs, rushing with the blood flow to his brain, where the nicotine built a bridge between his synapses. His heartbeat returned to a normal pulse. Think, he had to think.

They had nearly all the evidence they needed. And if Sanne really had convinced Serafine to open up, the last few links might soon be in place.

However, there was no way they could put together a prosecution file before the election. Merethe Winther-Sørensen and her party would undeniably reap many sympathy votes because of the death of her son; votes she would very likely not receive if they were able to prove the allegations she had just denied in public. He inhaled, letting the glow eat its way through the paper.

If other people could do it, surely so could he? He picked up his cell phone from the passenger seat and dialled the number he'd found online.

"Sandra Kørner? This is Lars Winkler, Copenhagen Police. Are you watching the leader debate?"

"Lars?" Sandra Kørner chuckled. "Well, there's a surprise; I hadn't expected to hear from you. I'm busy writing, but yes, the debate is on a widescreen TV here at the editorial office. Why?"

"Did you hear what Merethe Winther-Sørensen just said about your story?"

"Well, what else would she say? I'm used to it by now."

Lars rolled down the window, took one last drag, and tossed the butt out on the street.

"I have something that I think you might be interested in seeing."

61

"HE'S COMING." SERAFINE** is close to panicking and is
clinging to Sanne's jacket.

Sanne looks around. Light from the street lamps on Forlandet
filters through trees and bushes. The flashlight beam leaps across
the shrubs. There is no one else here; the night is empty. Was
it all in her mind?

Sanne takes a step forward. Then they both hear the foliage
rustle: the sound of a body pushing its way through the shrubs
toward them.

Sanne shoves Serafine to force her to move, then runs after
her toward the rusty door at the end of the old refugee centre.
Serafine gasps as she runs up the three concrete steps. Sanne is
right behind her.

They're hit with an acrid stench of rot and damp, urine and
excrement. Water is dripping somewhere in the darkness. There

are urgent footsteps on the gravel. Sanne pushes Serafine inside and slams the door shut behind them. The bang echoes through the empty building.

She tries to get her bearings in the darkness. The echo, which answers even the tiniest sound, makes it impossible to determine direction or distance. Where should they go? The flashlight shines down a long corridor, illuminating graffiti across the walls and on the floor, and puddles of water and garbage. Dark doorways lead into small rooms on both sides. There is a stack of cardboard boxes about halfway to their left. She shakes; her mind has gone blank. Her fear pumps paralyzing apathy around her body.

Serafine presses herself against the wall by the door. The metal frame rattles, the handle moves. He is outside, trying to get in.

Finally, Serafine reacts and jumps into action. She lunges forward, grabbing Sanne's hand, and bangs her head against the wall, stumbling as she gets to her feet while pulling Sanne down the corridor. The door opens behind them, and a beam of light from the night outside catches them.

"Come with me," Serafine whispers. She's panting. "There's an exit further..." She doesn't finish the sentence and starts to run. Sanne stays right behind her. Her heart is pumping an insane, syncopated dance in her chest. The door is now fully open behind them. She glances over her shoulder. A shadow fills the doorway and slips inside.

They reach a large room. Corridors open out in different directions, with broad glass doors to the right. The moonlight enters, drawing slanted squares on the filthy linoleum floor. Serafine stands backlit and pulls at the doors, swearing.

"It's locked, come on." She drags Sanne with her, up some stone steps, onward to the next set of stairs. A dense figure moves in the moonlight below, looking up. He is wearing a balaclava.

The light reflects in his black pupils. Then he follows them up the stairs.

At the top Serafine drags her to the left, ducking into yet another corridor.

"Step down," Serafine whispers, pulling Sanne into the darkness. She would have stumbled into nothing, breaking her neck, if Serafine hadn't warned her. Sanne counts ten to twelve steps, then they turn and race down yet another staircase. It is a total maze. Above them, their pursuer has started his descent. The sound of his footsteps roars in her ears.

She is sweating. Terror courses through her body, making it impossible to think. All she can do is follow. As they reach the foot of the stairs, Serafine makes a sharp right, slamming a door shut behind them. Sanne points the flashlight at her, and in its pale light sees the chain hanging limply down by the door frame. Sanne reaches up and grabs it. She tries to secure the chain across the door, but can't get it into the track. The metal rattles. He must be able to hear what she is doing out there on the other side. They both wedge their shoulders against the door. The handle moves, then the chain slides into place and tightens as he presses open the door. The chain is stretched to its maximum extension, marking the space between them. They get a brief glimpse of narrow, grey eyes under the balaclava.

"Come." Serafine tries to pull her along, back down the same corridor they first entered. But Sanne stays put. She presses her feet against the floor, pushing her back against the door. One single thought is going through her mind: if she moves, he will get through. The taut chain quivers. A strong hand reaches through the gap, fumbling to get in. Nails scratch the skin of her chest. The blood starts trickling in long lines. He grabs hold of her shirt collar and yanks her violently against the door. His acrid and powerful smell, which wafts through the gap, is paralyzing. Pheromones engulf her. This is communication on a primal level. *All resistance is useless*, they scream. *You're already dead.*

She retaliates out of pure instinct, sinks her teeth into the soft flesh below his thumb, biting until the skin breaks. Warm blood pours out and the taste of iron sticks to the roof of her mouth. He screams, jerking back his hand. Serafine grabs her and drags her along, back toward the night and freedom.

He hurls himself furiously against the door behind them. They hear a crash as the wood starts to crack.

Sanne has no time to think before her hand reaches into her pocket and takes out the black container of pepper spray. The door gives, flies open, and smashes into the wall.

Her knees buckle. She wriggles free from Serafine's hold and turns.

He stands in the doorway then begins to stomp down the corridor toward them. Serafine stops behind her and again tries to make her follow, but Sanne shakes her off as she fumbles with the pepper spray. She manages to aim, but does not have time to press down before a powerful blow flings her against the wall.

He is standing over her when she finally comes around. The pain in her shoulder is indescribable. The flashlight lies on the floor some distance from her, the cone of light rolling back and forth, lighting up sections of the corridor that are covered in graffiti, feces, and empty bottles. She has dropped the pepper spray. She quickly rolls away from the boot that kicks out at her and gets to her feet.

Serafine is crouched down, back against the wall, and paralyzed. She is incapable of action. Now it is Sanne's turn to drag her along. She pushes Serafine past some boxes before turning around to see the knife in his hand. The long blade glistens in the beam of the flashlight, which continues to roll around the floor behind them. The knife's blood groove is thick and shiny.

For the first time, she realizes that they might die here tonight. And all she wants to do is say goodbye to Lars. Their pursuer lunges forward, brandishing the knife. She cries out, pushing the stack of cardboard boxes. He tries to ward them off, tripping over clothing, books, sewing machines, broken CD players, and blankets. The stack sways, before finally collapsing, forcing him to his knees and onto the floor.

"Quickly, Serafine," she shouts as she kicks broken electrical equipment, books, and saucepans aside, dragging Serafine with her. They run toward the end of the building, and get to the door that they first entered. She is sobbing with joy when her hands close around the handle — until she realizes that their escape route is blocked. He has wrapped a chain around the handle and attached it to a hook in the wall. They can hear the boxes crashing behind them as they are tossed aside. He is coming.

She pushes Serafine into the last room on the left, opposite the bathroom.

"Hide," she hisses. But where can she go? Sanne positions herself in the doorway, waiting for the knife.

Where can he be?

62

LARS TURNED THE corner, joined Luftmarinegade, pulled up next to Sanne's Fiat 500, and turned off the engine.

He had decided against going to *Ekstra Bladet*'s editorial office. Instead, he had met with Sandra Kørner in the 7-Eleven on the corner of Rådhuspladsen and Strøget, where he gave her a copy of the photograph of Mogens Winther-Sørensen with Serafine as a child, along with a brief outline of the story — including the most recent information from Søren Gjerding.

"This is a game changer, especially before the election." Sandra Kørner's eyes sparkled. "It makes me wonder if there's anything I can do for you in return."

"Just make sure it gets published. As long as you keep my name out of it, I'll be happy."

He got out of the car at Margretheholm and listened. It was so close to the city, and yet so very quiet. A black border hung in the night sky to the south, probably the cloudburst they had been predicting all day. He shuddered in the wind and pulled up his collar. Where were Sanne and Serafine? He scanned the area. It looked the part exactly—an abandoned ruin. Garbage and weeds fought for open space. High above and behind the old naval base, red lights flashed on the chimneys of Lynetten. He stepped over a partly burnt running shoe, then froze.

Sounds of quick footsteps and strangled shouting were coming from inside the building. Then he heard a crash and a howl of pain. Lars set off, running toward the door at the end of the building. He pulled at it, but it refused to open.

"Sanne!" he screamed, rattling the door. A faint whimper was coming from inside the building.

63

WHAT'S KEEPING HIM? The stocky figure blurs, disappearing into the darkness. Further away, her flashlight has started flickering irregularly in the corridor. Then she realizes why it's taking him so long to climb over the boxes: the pepper spray. She dropped it on the floor at the far end of the hallway.

"Who are you?" she whispers.

But there is no reply. Then the massive dark shape looms right in front of her, his knife pointing straight ahead. He is holding the shiny black cylinder with a firm grip in his other hand. Sanne lashes out at him, hitting something soft and squishy. He winces, aims at her face, and presses the button.

The muscles around her eyes go into spasms. She is blinded; her entire face burns. Now she knows how Lars must have felt when he and his punk friends were tear-gassed in the 1980s. *My eyes*, a voice screams inside her. *I'm blind.* She tries rubbing away the pepper spray, but it only exacerbates the pain. Then she is pushed aside. She falls into the corridor, rolling in the contents of the fallen cardboard boxes: glass, clothing, and plates are crushed underneath her. His heavy body smashes into the door frame, straightens up, and disappears inside the small room.

Run, Serafine, the voice inside her yells. But the satisfied grunt and the scream coming from the room indicate that Serafine has not escaped. And where would she go? They are trapped in here.

The scream rises and changes pitch. The vile, wet sound of a knife penetrating flesh. Serafine's death cries fly out into the hallway, mixing with her own. The door to freedom rattles in its frame, and a familiar voice calls out from another world:

"Sanne!"

But it is too late. It's all too late.

OCTOBER 1999

A **VEIL OF** fog engulfs the street lamps on Amicisvej. Mogens forces himself to walk up the four steps to the front door and rings the bell, shuddering. When Merethe calls, you obey.

It is cold, almost midnight. He is hungry. And yet, he has not been able to eat since this morning. Kirsten threw him out of her office; then she grabbed Sarah from preschool and drove to Hornbæk.

Despite the cold, he is sweating. He looks around, half-expecting to see TV cameras, microphones, and a furious mob.

He hears footsteps from inside. A silhouette appears behind the yellow glass in the heavy oak door.

Arne doesn't look at him when he opens the door, nor does he say anything. He just steps aside to let him pass.

"Hello Dad." There is no reply. The conversation they had at Margretheholm was less than three weeks ago, but Mogens doesn't bring it up. He just follows Arne into the drawing room.

"There you are, my boy." Merethe doesn't look at him either as she gets up from the sofa. Newspaper sections spill out of *Berlingske Tidende*, flopping onto the floor. A section ironically titled "Free" catches his eye. She air-kisses his cheek. Then she sits down again. It's not as obvious as with Arne, but it's there — the distance.

"I'm sorry." The words fly out of his mouth before he has time to think, but it's too late. They have already accepted Søren's version of events. They won't listen to him — not anymore.

"Now let's see how we can get you out of this mess you've got yourself into." Merethe brushes a crumb from the coffee table. "How is Kirsten dealing with it?"

Mogens sits down in the armchair opposite her.

"She's totally behind me, obviously — one hundred percent." It's not until now that he realizes: he is utterly alone.

"Of course, of course. I was just thinking...Never mind."

Arne has sat down behind them with his jigsaw puzzle.

"That kind of thing never used to interest him, but he has been busy with it all day, ever since..." Merethe raises her eyebrows. "Six thousand pieces."

The lid of the jigsaw puzzle is filled with an image of a benign God reaching out toward Adam, surrounded by a myriad of naked children. Arne turns and follows his gaze. Then he takes the lid and places it picture side down.

Mogens slumps, gripping the armrest.

"I don't know what you've heard, but—"

Merethe's gaze loses its focus and becomes steely. Her mouth is a line in her chiselled features.

"I'm not interested in your excuses."

"But I didn't do the things they say I did." Mogens wrings his hands. "You must—"

"I just told you I'm not interested. What you have done..."

Her eyebrows arch independently of each other. "There is no . . ." Her voice cools. "I want you to know that what I'm about to do is for the sake of the family."

A drunk staggers by on Amicisvej heading for Frederiksberg Allé, singing "Erase/Rewind" by The Cardigans at the top of his lungs. Merethe continues.

"I have spent all day in a meeting at the Town Hall with the Socialist People's Party and the Conservatives. Both parties are willing to break their coalition with the Social Democrats if you" — she points a finger at him — "return to local politics. Mogens, they'll make you mayor."

"Mother, we agreed—"

"Be quiet. You know perfectly well what this means for the party, both locally and nationally. You're a Winther-Sørensen, so help me God. And we respond when duty calls."

"But that would be the same as admitting the accusations are true." He rubs his temple. Everything is spinning; he feels nauseous and afraid. On the other side of the table his mother seems to expand and become two people.

The two Merethes get up.

"Let me make this quite clear: you will not get another chance. Either you leave here as mayor, or there's nothing more I can do for you."

They hear a crash from the other table. The jigsaw pieces rain down on the carpet.

Arne runs up the stairs, knocking over his chair on the way. Mogens half gets up, staring after him.

"Look at me. Look at me, I said." Merethe slaps him hard across the face. He blinks and touches his cheek. The skin burns under his hand. Just when he thought he was free and had finally escaped the suffocating embrace of his family.

"I . . ." He can't talk. He just shakes his head.

Merethe says nothing. She bends down over the sofa, picks up

349

the newspaper, and unfolds it. There is no picture, only a tabloid headline in a fat font that fills the whole front page.

100 YEARS OF SOCIAL DEMOCRATIC RULE OF COPENHAGEN HAS ENDED

MOGENS WINTHER-SØRENSEN IS THE NEW RADICAL MAYOR

Mogens has to read the words three times before the full impact dawns on him. Then he collapses on the sofa and buries his face in his hands.

64

"**S**O HE FLED when you arrived?" Allan was sitting on the other side of the table, reviewing his notes inside the well-lit mobile police unit.

Lars squashed his umpteenth cigarette in the ashtray, nodding. The area around the unit was teeming with police officers and curious onlookers from the terraced houses on Luftmarinegade. The first press photographers had already arrived.

Sanne and Serafine had been taken to Rigshospitalet—Sanne with a broken shoulder and temporary eye injuries. The attacker had used her own pepper spray against her. Serafine's condition was more serious: a deep stab wound to her left shoulder. She had lost a lot of blood. Bint believed the attacker had aimed for her heart, but she had managed to turn just in time. The act had saved her life.

Lars rubbed his face. He was tired. He hadn't slept properly since . . . well, since when, really?

"What are you doing here?" The voice rang out through the mobile unit. "I thought you had been suspended." Lisa was standing at the door, one foot placed inside.

Allan looked over his shoulder.

"Ulrik called. Staff shortage." He tried to placate her: "Have the dogs found anything?"

Lisa hesitated.

"They lost the scent somewhere along the embankment." She entered the mobile unit. "It looks like he ran through Christiania, and on through the community gardens. He's probably hiding in one of the sheds along Forlandet."

But Lars didn't think so. They were too late. He had gotten away.

"Allan leaked the pedophile story to *Ekstra Bladet*." Lisa folded her arms across her chest.

"All I did was confirm it. She already knew everything." Allan slammed his notebook shut. "But if that's how it's going to be . . ." He stormed out.

"Well, what did he expect?" Lisa sat down in the seat Allan had left. "Low-life snitch."

Lars held up his hand to stop her.

"Not now, please? It's for Ulrik to deal with."

"Sorry." Lisa sat down. "I'm guessing you want to go home now?"

Did he?

"Have the technicians finished inside?"

"Don't you think it's best that you let the rest of us handle it? You look exhausted."

"I'll just take a peek. Then I promise I'll go home."

"Okay. In the meantime I'll find someone who can drive you."

Lars walked across a small patch of grass and through the door at the end of the dilapidated building.

He had managed to remove the chain locking the door immediately after hearing the heartbreaking cry and the terrible moaning coming from inside. But the assailant had gotten away. Lars had found Sanne lying on a pile of crumpled cardboard boxes and old household items, screaming. Serafine was in a pool of blood on a bed. Her breathing was very faint, and blood was spurting from a stab wound to her shoulder, pouring along her arm and onto the floor. He had made a simple pressure bandage from his shirt before dialling 112. The dog handler had arrived a minute later, and helped him administer first aid.

Now the technicians were busy setting up generators and lamps. It was still fairly dark inside the building, but a single lamp shone just outside the room where he had found Serafine. It looked like something out of a war zone: upturned tables; a candle that had burned down to a black spot on the linoleum floor among all the red; blood spatters on the walls; books, papers, and clothing scattered all over. Serafine's blood had smeared when the paramedics took her away, and the red had turned into a viscous brown gloop.

Something was bothering him — something that didn't add up. He pressed the tips of his fingers against his closed eyelids and tried to work out what it was: the investigation, the murder of Mogens Winther-Sørensen, the initial, futile interview with Serafine in the victim's apartment.

"Lars?"

He turned around. Kim A was standing at the door.

"What happened?"

"Sanne and the witness to the murder of Mogens Winther-Sørensen were attacked. Fortunately, it looks like they'll both make it." Lars gave him a tired nod. "You're contaminating the crime scene. Go find the technicians and get yourself a face mask and some coveralls."

"What about you?" Kim A looked him up and down.

"I found them and scared off the attacker. My DNA is already all over the place."

Kim A dismissed his concerns. "Ah, well. They already have my profile. It's not the first time I've been at a crime scene, after all. It'll take less than five minutes to eliminate me."

Lars gave up. Kim A would have to take it up with Frelsén and Bint in due course.

"What are you doing here?"

Kim A stood next to him and studied the pool of blood. Then he walked across the room and stopped by the window, which was swinging open on its hinges: the attacker's escape route.

"The minister... you know." He flapped a hand over his shoulder. "I'm keeping her informed." Kim A let the sentence linger in the stagnant air. "He bled like a pig, the tranny, eh? What a mess."

Lars stared into space. It kept eluding him. He knew he almost had it. If only —

"What do think you're doing here?" Frelsén's fierce voice boomed from the door. "Get out of my crime scene."

They drove through the city from Margretheholm to Folmer Bendtsens Plads in total silence. Neither Lars nor the officer who drove him said one word. He was dropped off outside the Ring Café and was briefly tempted to pop inside the corner store to buy a bottle of what they claimed was red wine, but decided against it. He said goodbye, thanking the officer, picked up his bag, unlocked the front door, and entered the stairwell. He would have to go back for his own car tomorrow.

The apartment looked like it always did. Lars put his bag in the hallway, went into the living room, and opened the door to the balcony. The place needed to be aired out. He knew he should take the garbage down as well, but he was distracted by a crumpled packet of King's Blue on the shelf above the fridge. There were a few left. The pack he had opened only a couple of hours ago outside the SAS Hotel was already empty.

He flopped down on the sofa, swung his leg up over the arm-rest, and lit a cigarette while he looked around for an ashtray. An S-train approached on the overhead railway outside: they had been fitted with silencers and sounded like a whisper in the night, not like the noisy hell they used to be. The cigarette smoke wafted up to the nicotine-stained ceiling. He wondered how Sanne was doing.

He took out his phone and was connected to Rigshospitalet's switchboard.

"Lars Winkler, Copenhagen Police. One of my colleagues was admitted earlier tonight with a broken shoulder and eye injuries from pepper spray. Her name is Sanne Bissen. How is she doing? Is she still at the trauma centre?"

The duty receptionist at the other end mumbled something to herself.

"Sanne Bissen, did you say?" The sound of typing on the keyboard came through the phone. "I can't tell you where she is. I've just been rebuked for giving that information to one of your colleagues."

Lars sat upright.

"Someone else called to ask about her?"

"Her and the other one, the transvestite."

A tiny twitch began by his right eyelid. It continued, refusing to go away. Which one of his colleagues would have rung to ask after Sanne *and* Serafine?

"Did you get their name?" He got up and chucked the cigarette out onto the balcony.

"I'm sorry, I didn't. Listen. I'm afraid that—"

"She—they mustn't be left alone, do you hear? Neither of them."

Lars hung up. Then he called the duty office at police head-quarters while he stepped into his heavily worn Converse.

"Dispatch a car to the trauma centre at Rigshospitalet. Sanne Bissen and the witness from the Winther-Sørensen killing need protection immediately. And I need a second car to number two, Folmer Bendtsens Plads. Now!"

He ran to his bedroom, found the small steel-and-plastic suitcase, and fumbled with the key until he managed to insert it into the lock. The suitcase was intended for the storage of his service weapon, but it also contained extra ammunition. Lars found his Heckler & Koch in the case and removed the magazine. It was full. He slammed it back into the gun butt, took an extra magazine from the suitcase, and put it in his pocket. He tucked the gun into his belt at the back, put on his jacket, and ran down the stairs.

It started pouring the minute he spotted the patrol car coming up Lundtoftegade. He was soaked to the bone before it had driven the last twenty-five metres.

He tore open the door and flung himself onto the back seat.

"Rigshospitalet—the trauma centre. And we're blue-lighting it."

65

THE RADIO CRACKLED. Valmir swore, then wiped the sweat from his brow. Shqiptarë, the low basement that had been his home for the past seven years, was perpetually dark and narrow. It smelled of sweat, onion, and cigarettes. But that home-like sensation was gone now. It had been mayhem since Meriton and Ukë were shot. The Nigerians had moved in, taking over their territory and their girls. They had broken most of the bones in Goran's body the other day; it was a miracle he was still alive.

It was only a matter of time before they turned up here. This time it was serious.

He turned on the frequency selector. Radio interference and white noise filled the headset before a nasal voice suddenly came through.

"A police officer and a witness are on their way from Margretheholm to Rigshospitalet's trauma centre in an ambulance going down

Kløvermarksvej, heading toward Vermlandsgade. They need to be escorted by a patrol car. I repeat..."

Valmir closed his eyes and sniffed the air. Then he got up, downed a glass of raki, took off the headset, and tossed it on top of the radio. He opened a drawer and took out his Zastava EZ9. He removed the magazine from the gun with a click, checked it, and pushed it back in with the palm of his hand.

He nodded to Elvir.

"Turn off the lights when you leave." Then he crossed the floor in two long strides, ran up the stairs, and disappeared into the darkness.

66

THE WATER WAS already rising at the bottom of the concrete underpass that led to Rigshospitalet's trauma centre. The back of the patrol car skidded as the driver slammed on the brakes. A cascade of water sprayed out from the car. Lars pushed the door open and leapt out from the back, quickly followed by the driver. A group of porters were building an improvised dam of sandbags near the entrance to the trauma centre. Lars straddled the dam and showed his badge to the nurse in reception.

"A female police officer and a witness were admitted earlier."

The nurse was on the telephone, a panicked expression on her face.

"Hello..." Lars waved his badge in front of her. She blinked twice, then put the handset down on the counter.

"I'm sorry. Everything is in chaos, with the rain and all. We're busy moving patients higher up the building. Do you have their names?"

"Sanne Bissen. The witness is transgender. Her name is Arbën Bukoshi, but she calls herself Serafine."

The nurse scrolled through records on the computer. The ceiling lamps blinked.

She followed Lars's gaze. "Don't worry. We have emergency generators that will kick in. They're in a room right behind us." She gestured to a door on the left-hand side that opened onto another corridor.

"Have any other officers been asking after them?" Lars waved over the police officer who'd driven him.

She shook her head.

"Good. Is there anything we need to know before we move them?"

"I'd better come with you." The nurse showed them to Side Ward 2. Sanne was lying in the bed right inside the door, her arm in a sling and circular bandages covering both eyes.

"We've given her a sedative. She's asleep." The nurse removed the IV from Sanne's arm. "It's only fluid. You can ask the doctors upstairs to insert a new one. The other one is in a much worse state—did you say her name was Serafine?" She placed her hand on the other bed. Serafine looked deathly pale and her breathing was shallow. Her naked torso was covered with tiny white scars. The shadows between her ribs were eerily deep, the bones rising under her skin with each breath. Her left shoulder and chest were covered in a large bandage. She was conscious, and didn't take her eyes off the uniformed officer.

"We were discussing whether she was safe to move..." the nurse began.

"Her life is at risk if she stays here." Lars put his hand on Sanne's forehead. A faint tremor went through her.

The nurse hesitated for a second. Then she grabbed a

clipboard from a chair, turned over the pale green form attached to it, and wrote a lengthy message on the back.

"Give this to the doctors when you get upstairs. They'll know what to do." Lars thanked her and stuck the clipboard under the duvet at the foot of the bed. The nurse disconnected the electrocardiogram from Serafine. The police officer positioned himself behind Sanne's bed, unlocked the brakes, and started wheeling it toward the elevator.

"Where are we taking them?" he asked.

Lars followed with Serafine.

"Anywhere upstairs."

The elevator door opened and they pushed the two beds inside. Lars pressed the button, which closed the door, then picked a random floor and kept both buttons pressed. He didn't let go until the elevator was in motion. Now they would go straight up without stopping at floors where others might be waiting.

The fluorescent light in the elevator flickered.

"Are you sure he's coming for them?" The police officer was sweating.

Lars watched the floor counter above the door: second, third, fourth...

"He murdered Mogens Winther-Sørensen when the mayor tried to prevent him from killing Serafine. He's coming all right. Make sure you have your service weapon ready."

The officer gulped. His hand moved to the pistol holster at his side. He opened and closed the security flap.

"My name is Bent." He held out his hand. Lars stared at it without taking it.

"Lars. Winkler."

The elevator stopped and the door opened onto the twelfth floor, unit 2122: *Gastroenterology*. Lars quickly stuck out his head and looked both ways. The area was filled with patients in their beds. They were staring at him. There was no mysterious killer in sight.

"Calm down." Lars attempted to smile at them. "This is the police. We just need to..." He pulled out Serafine's bed, carefully moving a few of the others to make room. Bent followed with Sanne.

Lars looked around. He didn't like being out here; it was too exposed and close to the elevator. He forged a path through the patients, dragging Serafine's bed directly into the gastroenterology ward. People were lying in beds along the walls, as well as in the middle of the corridor. Two male doctors and a not very tall female doctor with a bob were walking from patient to patient, reassuring them. It took him a while to recognize the red glasses.

"Christine?"

Christine Fogh looked tired, but colour rose to her cheeks the moment she spotted him. Then she noticed the uniformed officer and the beds in front of them. Her professional attitude returned. "What are you doing here?"

He pointed to Serafine and Sanne.

"You know Sanne. Someone tried to kill her and Serafine tonight. We have reason to believe that the killer will try again, so we've brought them up from the trauma centre. Sanne just needs a new saline drip. Serafine, on the other hand..." He flung Serafine's sheets aside and handed Christine the clipboard. "The nurse from the trauma centre wrote a message."

Christine read it, her eyebrows buckling in concentration over her red glasses. She looked up after she finished.

"Your timing is perfect: we've just evacuated the top floors. The water was starting to leak in. Thankfully we have the emergency generators." She started walking. "Follow me."

They pushed the beds and followed her down the corridor.

The fluorescent lights flashed again and again, then went out for a few seconds before coming back on. They were wheeling the beds slowly, so that they didn't bump into the other patients.

"You can take them into the nurses' station—"

The lights went out again. And this time they didn't come back on. Lars registered the unease behind him: the sound of bodies stirring in their beds, groaning, and a voice calling his name . . .

"Lars?"

He turns around. His eyes scan the beds and the faces. Somehow Sanne has managed to remove the bandage covering one of her eyes and is staring at him. Her lips are moving. Is she trying to tell him something? He bends over her, turning his head so his ear is right above her lips. All she can muster is a faint lisp and croaky breathing. But somehow he senses what she is trying to give him: a name.

"Easy now. Don't exert yourself." He pats her hand. "I know. It's Kim A."

Outside, the sky is ripped asunder by a gigantic flash of lightning. The blue-white electrical discharge lights up everything and freezes all movement. Everything is double-exposed. The view of Copenhagen from the window is overlaid with a reflection of the hospital corridor on the twelfth floor. He sees himself bent over Sanne's face. Then the darkness returns.

"Lars," Bent says behind him. "Shouldn't we be . . ."

Lightning strikes again and tears the world apart. The thunder reverberates between the concrete buildings. Frozen movements; yet another double exposure. A door opens behind them. The black figure in the doorway is reflected in the window, a Heckler & Koch USP Compact in his hand. The balaclava conceals his face, except for the mouth and eyes.

And Lars recognizes those eyes; he was staring into them less than an hour ago.

67

SHE FLOATS ON her back across the grassy hills. The blades
tickle her back, thighs, and legs. Rays of sunlight caress her
body. She can't see anything, but everything is beautiful. The
pain in her right shoulder is a hollow thumping, far away.

The air around her is alive with singing voices. She is safe.
She hears a faint beep: a machine starting. She surges upward.
She is surrounded by music, a string section with long notes:
simple themes that merge imperceptibly.

She hears another beep and the grass blanket returns. But the
sun and the beautiful music have disappeared. She can't see. A
chorus of voices lash out at her. They are angry now and fright-
ened. Her shoulder starts to hurt. Where is she? Her left arm is
heavy, and twitches from her shoulder to the tips of her fingers.
She grits her teeth. One finger moves first, then her whole hand.
She raises her arm and fumbles for her face. Her fingers follow

the bandages over her eyes, picking at the surgical tape keeping them in place. Everything comes back in a flash: the abandoned naval base, the figure, the knife, and her pepper spray.

Serafine. Her fingers pick at the surgical tape. She has to see to get her bearings. The voice, it sounds close by. She recognizes it—recognizes him—it is . . .

"Lars?"

She manages to lift up the tape by her right eye and rip off the bandage. Her world is dark and chaotic. She can see only blurred figures. She blinks, trying to focus.

A searing white pain. Suddenly everything is lit up by a blinding light. Then the darkness returns and the world is shaken by a violent blast. She can see again. Lars is standing with his back to her, staring out of the window.

She tries again: "Lars." This time he hears her, bends down and puts his ear to her mouth. She tries to articulate the sentences clearly and logically: who, what, where. Another blast rocks the bed she's lying in. She looks at him, caught in the flash of lightning. Did he nod? Does he understand? His mouth is moving, but she can't hear what he is saying.

Then lightning strikes again. Her eyes have adjusted and she sees what Lars can see reflected in the window: the figure appearing in the doorway behind him.

She tries to scream, but she can't. Not a sound passes her lips.

68

"JUST PUT IT down. There'll be more officers here in a moment." Lars doesn't turn around; he tries to keep his voice under control. He may only get this one chance. Darkness has descended on the room once again. And yet he thinks he can still see the outline of Kim A's reflection in the window. Through the glass, the cascading water, Blegdamsvej, and the blurred contours of a high-rise construction across the road are visible.

"When you're gone, no one here will dare to contradict me."

Lars knows he's right; he can tell from the faces around him. Though it wouldn't surprise him if Christine told the truth.

Then he turns around.

"You stay just where you are." The order is barked immediately. Lars turns his back to him again and raises his hand. He slowly unbuttons the top button of his jacket.

"Put your hands on the bed where I can see them." The voice

slams against the wall. "I know you hate shoulder holsters."

What can he do? He is starting to panic. He can't reach his gun; there is no time to turn around before taking the shot. But what's the alternative?

Bent has moved a step away from Sanne's bed and is standing with his left side to the door. His right hand fumbles with the safety strap on his holster. Lars tries to catch his eye, shaking his head faintly. But Bent is sweating; his gaze is fixed on the figure in the doorway. The weapon leaves the holster. Bent's hand approaches the correct firing position. His left hand grips his right wrist and his elbow is slightly bent. His forefinger curls around the trigger, but he pulls too hard, yanking the pistol with him. The bullet hits the ceiling.

It takes only a fraction of a second, but to Lars it feels like hours.

There is a roar from the doorway followed by a second shot. Patients and doctors scream. Bent sighs, falls backward, and is thrown against the nearest bed before he crashes onto the floor. Bloody foam bubbles between his pale lips. Christine lunges, rolls him over, and puts him in the recovery position.

Lars tears open his jacket. He grabs his service weapon and spins around until he is face to face with his opponent. But he doesn't dare shoot — the risk of collateral damage is too great.

"Drop your weapon," he calls out instead, constantly moving to keep the firing line clear.

The figure is now in the hospital corridor next to Serafine's bed, the muzzle of his gun resting on her forehead.

"You don't have the balls. You never did."

Lars fires his gun. The other man wobbles and touches his head. Then he dives behind a bed before returning fire. The bullets ricochet. An old man next to him screams, but Lars can't decide whether he has been hit or is just petrified.

He sticks his head up. Kim A fires again. He has retreated

away from Sanne and Serafine, but Lars can't shoot for risk of hitting the screaming patients and doctors crouching on the floor. Lars sees the flame from the muzzle; the hair stands up on his head from the air pressure as the bullet whizzes straight across his scalp. Then his opponent gets up and staggers away, pushing the beds aside, before fleeing down the corridor.

Lars leaps up to give chase, and follows the trail of blood the other man is leaving behind. A doctor tries to stop the running man by blocking his path, but receives a blow to the head with the barrel of the gun and stumbles backward. There are ten metres between them, but Lars is closing the gap. Then Kim A disappears through a door and slams it shut. Lars is forced to waste costly seconds prising it open. The echo of the other man's clattering footsteps rises up through the stairwell.

69

THE STAIRS GO on forever; it is a long way down from the twelfth floor. He encounters a young couple around the fifth floor; their pale faces press against the wall as he passes them. The sound of the other man's footsteps rises up from the floors further below. His heart is pounding. He is gasping for air, but his legs move confidently underneath him, the muscles working.

They reach the ground floor. Lars pulls the door open. The reception area is filled with people and beds. Two paramedics are standing by the main entrance with a stretcher. Lars catches a glimpse of the balaclava further ahead, ploughing his way through it all. He is already past reception. Lars accelerates and starts to gain on him.

The fleeing man has already reached the exit at the opposite end of the hospital; he rips open the door and disappears out into the rain. Lars catches the door before it slams. He is soaked through the moment he steps outside.

The other man is about to cross the road. Lars chases him with his weapon raised, but trips over the curb. His arm and shoulder jolt as the shot goes off. Across the road, the big body twitches, and then stumbles onward on stiff legs before he is lost among the trees of Amor Park.

"Kim, stop! You can't get away." Lars runs across the road, past the parked cars. The rain is easing off and becomes a quiet drizzle. He follows Kim A into the park. The soil is soft and muddy. Water trickles everywhere, glistening on the leaves and in the grooves of the bark. He can hear twigs snapping over the sound of the rain. Someone groaning.

"You shot me in the ass, you dick." The voice is very close.

The other man is leaning against a tree with his head tilted back, sinking slowly down the trunk until he sits on the wet ground. He pulls off the balaclava. There is blood coming from his ear. The rain washes blood and soil from his throat and chin. Something red seeps out of his left buttock into the mud.

The pistol in his hand is resting calmly on his knee. It is pointing straight at Lars.

"Just drop it."

He has no choice. Lars is forced to let his weapon fall; it lands in the mud by his feet. He is wheezing, and his muscles are filled with lactic acid. Now that he's not running, it's starting to hurt. He rummages around in his pocket and finds his cigarette packet. It's wet and squashed. He tosses it aside with an irritated movement and watches as it lands next to his gun in a stream of rainwater, where it is whirled away. It's over.

He blinks in an attempt to clear the rain from his eyes. The traffic has started to return to Tagensvej. The car headlights and traffic lights colour the raindrops green and red. The sirens are coming closer. The figure opposite him sits hidden in the shadows. There is something about that voice, something that doesn't add up. A last flash of lightning strikes, bouncing between the tree trunks, and everything freezes in a white glare. And Lars finally sees, but can't believe his own eyes.

"You?" The horizon tilts. Lars reaches for a tree for support.

70

ALLAN RAISES HIS hand to his ear and rubs it. The movement makes his fleshy cheeks quiver.

"So you did have the balls after all." He wipes the blood on his pants and coughs. "Just out of curiosity, why did you think it was Kim A?"

Lars looks down and shakes his head. *Allan?* Finally all the pieces fall into place. Allan was the first officer to arrive at Margretheholm—because he was already there. Allan persuaded him to return Serafine to Sandholm for deportation back to Germany the day after the mayor's murder. He wanted her out of the way, far from the investigation. Allan leaked the information to *Ekstra Bladet*, not for money, but to misdirect them. Serafine was traumatized that first evening because she recognized him straightaway. She must have been convinced that police officers would cover for each other in this country as well. But, even so — *Allan?* Lars sweeps his hair away from his forehead. How long have the two of them worked together? Seven, eight years?

The gun in Allan's hand; Lars's own in the mud by his feet. Not the safest position in the world. He clears his throat.

"I learned that a fellow officer had called the hospital to ask where Sanne and Serafine had been admitted... And Kim A arrived at Margretheholm just after... And then he turned up at Mogens Winther-Sørensen's apartment, just after the murder. I thought it was so he could explain away DNA evidence once the technicians had processed the crime scene. But you were there too. Why?" Lars spits into the mud.

"Well, I guess you have a right to know — before we say goodbye." Allan's finger on the trigger is tense and white. He is shaking, blood mixing with the rain that washes over his face.

Neither of them says anything. The sirens are still too far away. Then Allan coughs and spits.

"One tiny mistake, one ridiculous mishap." His voice slips into a sob. "And I've been paying for it ever since. My girlfriend, the kids... Oh, you don't care." He breaks off. Lars can't work out whether they are tears or raindrops running down his cheeks. Allan sobs again before he continues. "Ukë and Meriton were busy pimping, even while they were still at Margretheholm. I found out by accident when I went there to follow up about some stolen bicycles. I let them carry on in return for me... well, I'm sure you can guess."

"But she was just a kid."

"She certainly didn't look like a kid. Anyway, one day it went wrong. A moment of madness — isn't that how all the perps explain themselves?" He laughs, wiping his mouth. "When I came to my senses, I had stabbed her with a pair of scissors. There was blood everywhere. And her brother was standing in the doorway."

Allan closes his eyes, then opens them immediately.

"Ukë and Meriton said they would help me fix it, and we buried her outside. But the next day they turned up at the police station." The hand with the pistol quivers and starts to fall. But he straightens up and continues.

"They had sent the boy out of the country and said there was no use trying to find him. They wanted information, or—"

"Or what?"

"Well, it's obvious, isn't it?"

"So you've been feeding Ukë and Meriton information about our work ever since?"

"They won't bother you again." The bitter expression turns into a small smile.

Lars wipes water from his forehead. That explains who killed the brothers.

"And the mayor?"

"I found Serafine in Hamburg through an Interpol contact and followed her back here. She was going to tell Mogens about her sister, about me. What else could I do?"

"I . . ." Lars leans against a tree. The sirens are closer now. Perhaps there is enough time after all? "I just don't understand why you leaked the pedophile story to Sandra Kørner. Surely you had no interest in that going public?"

"She already had the story from another source; she was just looking for confirmation. Seeing as Ukë and Meriton were dead and Serafine was the only witness, I thought—"

"You thought you could get rid of her too. But that wasn't how it worked out. It's over, Allan." Lars takes a deep breath and steps forward. *This is it.* "Give me your gun."

"Do you take me for an idiot? Goodbye, Lars." Allan raises the hand holding the weapon; his finger is on the trigger.

Lars stops two steps in front of him and flings out his arms.

"And then what? Where will you go? They'll never stop

374

looking for you if you kill a fellow officer; you know that just as well as I do."

"Lars." The gun is shaking. The back of Allan's head lolls back and forth against the tree trunk. The first patrol car pulls up by Tegner's sculpture on the corner of Tagensvej and Blegdamsvej.

"Over here," Lars calls out, waving.

"Screw you. Goodbye." Allan's finger curls around the trigger.

"Lars!" The cry cuts through the rain. It comes from behind him and to the right, not from the patrol car, which is behind him to the left.

"Here!" Lars holds his hands where Allan can see them.

Allan aims the gun at the sound, and peers into the darkness and the rain. A shadow passes on the left. Allan turns toward the movement, trying to follow it.

Then a shot is fired, and Allan's jaw explodes. Blood and teeth spill over his shirt. The hand holding the pistol drops into the mud. The ruined face gurgles, and his eyes roll into the back of his head.

"Lars." Kim A has reached him; he takes a look at Allan. The PET officer runs both hands across his wet scalp.

"You didn't have to shoot." Lars is kneeling beside Allan. "It was already over." He moves the pistol. Allan still has a pulse, but he is losing blood—fast.

"It wasn't me." Kim A peers in between the tree trunks, shaking his head. "It came from over there." He points in the direction of the Panum Institute.

"But then who...?" Lars looks up. The park is deserted and there is no one around, except two uniformed officers, who come running from the patrol car. Lars stands up. "Copenhagen Police. My colleague is a PET officer. And this guy here needs a doctor." He points to Allan. "And make sure he doesn't escape."

The police officers pick Allan up and carry him toward Rigshospitalet.

"If you didn't do it, then who shot him?"

Kim A looks around.

"Whoever it was is gone now. We'll get the dogs out here. Now let's take a look at you. I think you're in need of some dry clothes and a hot drink. You'll catch your death of cold."

It is only now that he realizes he is shivering. His jacket, jeans—everything is sticking to his body. Lars picks up his own gun as well as Allan's. Then he follows Kim A through Amor Park. The officers have already taken Allan inside the hospital. There is frantic activity behind the automatic glass doors.

"Have you seen *Ekstra Bladet*'s homepage?" Kim A lights a cigarette and passes it to Lars. "They've found a picture of Mogens Winther-Sørensen at a refugee centre, with Serafine as a child."

Lars says nothing and inhales.

Kim A looks up at the sky. Lars follows his gaze. The underside of the clouds is lilac, reflecting the neon advertisements, the traffic lights. The pulse of the city.

"I don't mind looking after the minister, keeping her name out of the press in the run-up to the election, if necessary; maybe even bending a rule or two as long as she assures me that no one gets hurts. But this . . . ?" He shakes his head and sticks his hand in his pocket. "By the way, I think this is yours."

Lars opens his hand to accept the object from Kim A. It is not until his fingers close around the knobbly, soft texture that he realizes what it is: the red, crocheted bookmark from *The Tempest*.

Kim A heads for the entrance to Rigshospitalet.

"If I were you, I'd quit that crap."

FRIDAY, OCTOBER 4– TUESDAY, OCTOBER 8

71

THE TIME AT the hospital passes in a slow haze. Nothing matters anymore. She has given up. Police officers have been to interview her, both the woman and the male officer she ran away from at Sandholm. She has told them everything she already told the female officer. What made him hunt her down. They assure her that he is gone and that he won't be coming after her ever again, but something inside her has broken.

"You must eat." The nurses are kind and helpful. No one looks down at her or calls her names. But the quiet flutter of butterfly wings has vanished. She can't hear them anymore.

She is lying in bed, staring out of the window at the faded colours and clouds, when the female doctor enters. It is not until they have spoken for some time that she remembers the red glasses.

The doctor has talked to her colleagues at the hospital and

the police. She is trying to help. They are looking into whether she might get the operation after all. And the flutter returns, only very faintly, but it is there.

It is the only reason she can summon the energy to get up when the nurse tells her she has a visitor. With a little help, she gets out of bed and puts on a bathrobe. The pain in her shoulder is manageable at last, but she doesn't know whether it is because of the morphine or whether the injury is healing.

A cooking show is playing on the TV out in the visitors' room. A small child plays with building blocks in a corner. The boy's mother sits beside him with a magazine. An old man sits at the table furthest away. His hair is white; his skin heavily lined. There is something familiar about his features. His whole face lights up when he sees her. He gets up, goes to meet her, and clasps both of her hands.

"Serafine."

The nurse helps her to the table and then leaves. Now she can see the family resemblance.

"You're Moo-genz's father. You took a picture of us."

He looks away. Something glints in the corner of his eye.

"You have a good memory. My name is Arne." He points to her shoulder. "Is it...?"

Serafine shrugs her healthy shoulder and scratches her forearm. Neither of them says anything. Arne looks down at his hands.

"For fourteen years I hated my son. I was convinced that I had created a monster." Then he doesn't say anything for a long time. Serafine waits. But when he doesn't continue, she has to ask:

"Why?"

"Because of what he did to you—or what I thought he had done to you." Arne turns to her. He has tears in his eyes.

"Moo-genz was my friend. He didn't do what I said back then. My uncles forced me to say it."

"I know that now," Arne whispers.

382

They sit together for a long time. They talk a little, until finally Arne gets up.

"I have to get back to work. But I'll visit you again."

Arne grabs her arm once they're out by the elevator.

"I can't tell my son..." He breaks off. "I know that Mogens wanted to help you. If there is anything I can do...If you need money...Promise that you'll come to me?"

What was keeping her? The press was waiting at Ny Hollænderskolen, keen to see the two of them arrive together to cast their vote. It was all arranged. Merethe Winther-Sørensen wiped her forehead and continued to channel hop. TV 2, DR, every broadcaster was covering the election—the feast day of democracy. Talking heads tried to predict the outcome. And even she had to admit that it didn't look good. The media was tearing down the edifice she had devoted a lifetime to building, aided only too willingly by her fellow party members.

They wanted to throw her out of the party. They seriously believed it would be enough to save the sinking ship. And that spineless nobody they wanted as their party leader? At the time when it was imperative they stand firm?

But a captain never abandons his ship. A Winther-Sørensen goes down with it. She intended to vote for the abolition of immunity for members of parliament herself, so the police could charge her with corruption, God help them all. What a farce. Her life's work in ruins—mocked, and reduced to entertainment for the rabble.

But youth was waiting in the wings. With Sarah the goal was still within reach. She was young and untainted; she would go on to achieve greatness. Merethe got up, poured herself a glass of Moët, and went out into the hallway. She raised her glass to the portraits of her father and grandfather.

And perhaps it would look more symmetrical with two of each sex?

The telephone rang in the drawing room. Merethe clattered through the hall and turned down the volume on the television.

"Merethe?" The voice on the other end was hard and shiny, an impenetrable glass barrier. You could see through it, but not reach the other side.

"Can I please talk to Arne?"

It was Kirsten calling. She could tell something was wrong from the sound of her voice. Was she drunk?

"Kirsten? What's keeping you?" Merethe put down her glass. "You were supposed to be here ages ago." She could hear a girl's silvery laughter in the background. Was that Sarah? "Where are you?"

"Don't bother waiting. Sarah isn't coming. But she would like to talk to Arne."

Something inside her tensed up, contracted, and threatened to explode. So they wanted to take this from her as well—her right. She tried to control herself and get the air into her lungs.

"Kirsten. I don't know what you think you're doing. Now just come over here, and we'll forget—"

"Don't you understand?" The voice was shrill. "We're not even in Europe anymore. You can't reach her here. You won't get her ever, don't you understand?" She was screaming now. Then she stopped and took a deep breath. Her voice was calm when she continued. "So could we please speak to Arne?"

Her throat burned. The room began to spin, and her pulse throbbed in her temples. Merethe heard herself snarl into the phone.

"Who do you think told the press about the pedophile charge? It was your *darling* Arne. I've thrown him out. He no longer lives here."

Merethe Winther-Sørensen hurled the phone against the wall, and lashed out at the fragments as they bounced back

384

without hitting them. Then she sat down on the sofa in front of the muted television and closed her eyes. The talking heads continued their pointless chatter on the screen.

"Allan followed Serafine all the way from Hamburg to Copenhagen on the train without getting a chance to kill her." Lars was sitting in Sanne's office. He had just reviewed the security footage Allan had gathered after the murder. He featured in it prominently, which explained why their former colleague had been so keen to examine the footage by himself. "He came running out from Burger King, just after Serafine and Mogens Winther-Sørensen had caught a taxi, and followed them in the next one."

Lars had spoken to the taxi driver, who confirmed that a passenger matching Allan's description had asked him to follow a taxi from Rådhuspladsen to Sankt Thomas Plads.

After examining Allan's computer, they discovered he had leaked information about the investigation to Sandra Kørner as early as the day after the murder. She hadn't exactly admitted as much, but nor had she denied it.

After Lars had been driven home from Margretheholm, the sniffer dog had reacted to something in the shrubs between the buildings and the road. Frelsén and Bint had found the skeletal remains of a young girl, whom they assessed to be around fourteen years old. A pair of rusty scissors was found between her neck vertebrae and collarbone.

The third set of fingerprints on the chef's knife, which had been used for the murder of Mogens Winther-Sørensen, belonged to Allan. And he had provided them with the motive himself—a motive he had confirmed during subsequent questioning. The injuries to his jaw and tongue were still too extensive for him to speak, so Allan had written down his replies to all of Lars's questions during the interview.

According to the doctors, he was facing several complicated and painful operations. But he would be able to chew again—which he would be able to cherish throughout his long prison sentence.

But the identity of the person who had shot Allan remained a mystery. Bint had recovered the bullet the following day in a mixture of mud, blood, and leaves near the tree, and had matched it to a bullet used in a killing that was traced back to Meriton and Ukë's gang. This was as close as they were likely to get. But they did know that Valmir had coincidentally vanished into thin air. There could be little doubt that he had likely avenged the killing of Ukë and Meriton.

It was Sanne's first day back at work. She yawned and doodled on a memo from Ulrik with her uninjured hand. Her other arm was strapped into a sling. The effect of the pepper spray had eased off after a few hours, but her broken shoulder would need more time to recover.

"Did you remember to vote today?" She stopped doodling, tossing the pen aside. "They're going to get wiped out, according to opinion polls."

"You know, me and politics..." Lars fiddled with a paper clip, straightening it out. "How about you?"

"I voted this morning...with Martin." She avoided looking at him. "So we'll just have to wait and see."

Silence.

Lars stuck his hand into his jacket and stroked the envelope in his pocket. Perhaps Christine was right? Maybe it really was time to let go? He got up, tossing the paper clip on the table.

"Fancy coming with me to visit Serafine?"

Sanne pushed back her chair, got up, and grabbed her jacket.

"By the way, this arrived for you earlier today." She took a brown envelope from a pile on the table. "I didn't know anyone still used the old police ranks..." She pointed to the yellow Post-it note stuck to the front of the envelope.

"*KA* stands for Kim A—not the old ranking system." Lars tore it open. It contained a batch of photocopied newspaper articles from the last quarter of 1999. He whistled. "So this was the information we absolutely could not see!"

There is a knock on the door to the side ward. The nurse is tall and blonde. She smiles and comes over to her bed.

"Serafine, how are you today?" The nurse takes her hand without waiting for a reply. "I have some good news that I've really been looking forward to telling you. We've had a reply from the GU clinic. They would like to offer you an initial appointment."

Serafine blinks, hardly daring to believe it.

"To begin with you'll attend a series of appointments with a psychiatrist, who will assess if you should be referred for hormone treatment with a gynecologist."

"And then?"

The nurse with flushed cheeks squeezes her hand.

"If the psychiatrist decides to refer you, you'll be treated over a longer period. You'll see a gynecologist and have regular blood tests. They'd like to see you about every four months, initially, and then once a year later in the process."

"But...several years?"

"Yes, of course. It's a major procedure, don't you agree?" The nurse pats her hand. "Once the hormone treatment is in place, you'll begin a trial period, where you'll live as a woman. If the assessment is positive, the GU clinic will recommend you for gender reassignment surgery."

The nurse is happy. But the colours vanish and time stands still. Everything inside her tightens. She can't breathe. What else does she have to prove? That she lives as a woman? She has done that for years. Nobody should have to wait that long. The nurse glances over her shoulder and smiles before leaving the side ward. The fluttering wings fall silent.

She would do anything to be able to hear them again.

Lars drove Sanne's Fiat 500 past Vesterport, down Farimagsgade, and along Ørsted Park. The cloudburst had resulted in massive flooding and traffic problems in the days that followed. But the city was returning to normal. It was warm for the time of year: the trees and ivy along the railway cutting and in the park glowed red and yellow in the autumn sun.

Life at Rigshospitalet was also slowly returning to normal. The patients who had been evacuated were taken back to their proper wards. The power supply had been re-established. Only the two top floors in the main building were still closed. Inspectors were assessing the damage.

A nurse came running toward them as they entered the ward. They could hear agitated voices from the corridor. Christine Fogh was standing opposite an older nurse behind the glass door. Lars had asked Christine to keep an eye on Serafine. It looked as if she had taken the responsibility to heart.

"What on earth were you thinking? If you had waited five more minutes—"

"We have our routines." The nurse's face hardened.

"Christine. What happened?" Lars looked from Christine to the nurse, while Christine stared at Sanne with an expressionless gaze.

"You had better ask the genius here."

The ward nurse took an indignant step back.

"This is a hospital, not a prison."

"What do you mean?" asked Sanne. "Can we please talk to Serafine?" The fluorescent tubes in the ceiling crackled.

"She—" The nurse tried to reply, but Christine interrupted her.

"I helped Serafine with her application for gender reassignment surgery. The reply came today. And you just couldn't wait until I had finished my rounds before you told her, could you?"

"And how did she react?" Lars was starting to lose his patience.

"It was positive, they said yes." The nurse defended herself. "How were we to know that—"

"Yes." Christine interrupted her again. "But first she'll have to go through years of hormone treatment and psychiatric assessment—again, information that could have been delivered with a tad more finesse and empathy, especially after everything she has been through." She turned to Lars. "She ran away."

"Ran away?"

"Well, we couldn't tie her to the bed, could we?" The ward nurse's face was red from suppressed rage. "Like I said, it's not a prison."

"But she . . ." Sanne took a deep breath. "Do you know where she went?"

"Sadly, no. She stole a purse with five hundred kroner from the woman she shared the side ward with."

"Do you see what I mean?" Christine's eyes were flashing. She squeezed Lars's arm and marched down the corridor.

The glue holding the coated paper on the jigsaw puzzle pieces bubbled in the heat; the coloured surface curled up and blackened in the flames. Merethe Winther-Sørensen threw the last handful into the fire. Michelangelo, a section of the Sistine Chapel—the image of God touching Adam's finger—flared up and disappeared. She rummaged around the embers with the poker until she was sure that the fire was raging. It was whooshing right up into the chimney pipe when she closed the grate and opened the damper.

A knot exploded inside a log. Merethe Winther-Sørensen turned toward the television. A young, female studio host with bouncing cleavage was laughing ingratiatingly at her male colleague's joke. Behind them, graphics showed the results of the latest exit poll. It really wasn't looking very promising.

The knot exploded again, or was someone at the door?

Merethe Winther-Sørensen hurried out into the hall. It could be the media seeking a comment—she checked her hair before she opened the door.

It took a moment before she recognized the emaciated, dark-skinned figure that half-fell inside, trying to avoid bumping her bandaged shoulder against the door. It was the little bitch who had gotten her son killed. What was she doing here? How had she gotten past the PET officer? Merethe was sorely tempted to slam the door in her face, but Serafine's hand was already on the door frame. Kim nodded to her from his position by the garden gate before turning his back on the house. So he was the one who had let her through.

"Ar-ne?" Serafine staggered inside, forcing Merethe Winther-Sørensen to step back. She shut the door behind her.

"Arne has moved out." Merethe's legs were shaking under her. She wanted to hit the girl, anything.

"He said he would help." The heavy eye makeup was smeared down her cheeks.

So that was where Arne had been on the days he had come home late—at the hospital. How very predictable. A pathetic bleeding heart like his son.

"Well, he's not here." Merethe Winther-Sørensen went to open the front door again.

"But...you don't understand. I need an operation...Arne... your son...They promised to help. They both did." The black eyes bored into hers, pleading and intense. A textbook photo opportunity. Merethe Winther-Sørensen put her hand on the door handle and paused. Perhaps this was a chance to showcase a different side of herself. She knew full well how people saw

her: cynical and hard. Every now and then it paid off to challenge that image a little bit. She obviously couldn't offer the girl
a sex change operation; after all, they were talking about an
asylum seeker and she was still a minister and member of parliament—for as long as that lasted. There were certain things
you just didn't do. But soon the press would be gathering outside
her house and perhaps...

She took the girl's forearm and helped her to her feet.

"Listen, I can't work miracles. But I promise to do what I can.
You can't stay here right now. I'll call for a taxi that will take you
to Sandholm. Then I'll see what I can do." She braced herself
and stroked Serafine's coarse hair.

The spark in the girl's eyes died and her shoulders slumped.
She'd gotten what she came for. There was no reason to pro-
long the performance. Merethe Winther-Sørensen had seen it
so many times before.

"Would you like a glass of water while I make the call?"

Serafine shook her head.

"Can I..." She leaned on Merethe's arm, then collapsed at
the bottom of the stairs leading to the first floor. "Can I use the
bathroom?"

For a moment, Merethe Winther-Sørensen thought that the
portraits of her father and grandfather were staring down at her
with disapproval. Then she shook off the sensation. What did
they know about handling the media?

The door to Amicisvej 17 was open. Merethe Winther-Sørensen
was sitting in the drawing room on the sofa with Ulrik opposite her.
Arne Winther-Sørensen was nowhere to be seen. The minister's
turquoise suit pulled crookedly across her back. The television
was on: exit polls looked grim for the Radical Party.

Ulrik looked up as they entered.

"That was quick."

"Why haven't you brought her in yet?" Sanne looked as if she wanted to spit at the minister.

"We... The prosecutor thought we had better wait until the voting finished. We wouldn't want to be accused of influencing... What's this?"

Lars tossed the envelope from Kim A on the table in front of Ulrik.

"The newspaper articles the minister didn't want us to see." Merethe Winther-Sørensen avoided Lars's gaze. Her eyes were fixed on the floral sofa cover. Ulrik picked up the photocopies and read through them. Then he looked up.

"So you awarded grants from integration funds to Ukë and Meriton, and to Shqiptarë, from the moment Mogens was sworn in as mayor—to the tune of several millions? To Shqiptarë!" He slammed the photocopies down on the coffee table. "So tell me: how does it feel to finance drug dealing and human trafficking using public funds?"

Merethe Winther-Sørensen flinched.

"That was the real reason Malene Rørdam was fired." Lars picked up the photocopies from the table and returned them to the envelope. "She thought it was because she had overheard something at the Christmas party—a fight, a revelation—but she was wrong. She was fired for doing her job, for trying to understand why the money had been allocated so she could explain it to the media. But she got too close, didn't she? She had to be stopped."

By the time Merethe Winther-Sørensen was able to speak, her voice had almost disappeared.

"You can't even begin to imagine how greedy they were. Mogens and I met with them here several times at night. Allan was the only one who could make them understand... that there were limits. Or we would be found out." Her shoulders were shaking. "It was hell."

"Politicians, gangsters, and a police officer feeding them information. Quite the party, I must say." Lars stuck his hand in his pocket, pulled out another envelope, and threw it on the table on top of the newspaper articles.

"What's this?" Ulrik picked up the plain white envelope and turned it over. Lars was about to reply, but Sanne couldn't wait.

"The duty officer said that Serafine was here?"

Ulrik nodded.

"She's in the bathroom. But Sanne—"

It was too late; she was already in the kitchen.

A brief scream pierced the drawing room. Lars followed the sound.

Sanne was standing in the doorway to a bathroom tiled in salmon-coloured marble. The taps, the frame around the mirror—even the lavatory brush—were all finished in gilded metal. Two identical deep red towels hung either side of the sink.

Serafine lay curled up on the floor; her empty eyes staring out from under her hair. She was clutching a jar of pills in her hand. The lid was off, and the remaining pills were scattered across the floor.

A butterfly had been drawn on the mirror and below it a single verse, both in pink lipstick.

Before I sink
Into the big sleep
I want to hear
The scream of the butterfly

"She arrived just under an hour ago." Merethe Winther-Sørensen had come up behind them, followed closely by Ulrik. "She claimed that my son had promised her that I would help. But...as a member of parliament—well, she's an illegal. I offered to pay for a taxi to take her to Sandholm." The minister leaned her head against the door frame. "She wanted to use the bathroom. When she didn't come out..."

Sanne knelt down next to Serafine and closed the girl's eyes. She didn't look at Merethe Winther-Sørensen when she got up, but dragged Lars with her.

"Let's get out of here."

Neither of them said anything on their way through the drawing room and the hall. Lars took a final glance at the three portraits of the minister and her father and grandfather.

Outside, it had started to drizzle.

"What did she write on the mirror?" Sanne stopped on the steps, and raised her gaze toward the grey sky.

"It's from a song by The Doors, 'When the Music's Over.'"

"But what does it mean?"

Sanne walked down the steps. Lars followed.

"To her? Who knows?"

They left through the garden gate. Lars pointed across the sidewalk to the other side of the street. The TV vans had arrived. Sandra Kørner's tall figure stood in the middle of a group of reporters behind the barricade.

"I have a hunch Ulrik tipped them off."

"It's a great PR opportunity." Sanne pulled a face. "I don't think he would want to miss out on it."

They turned right, to the white Fiat 500 that was parked outside number 23.

"What was in the other envelope you gave to Ulrik just now?" Sanne unlocked the car.

"A holiday cottage." Lars took out a King's and lit it. "I could use a cup of coffee right now. How about you?"

AUTHOR'S NOTE

This book is a work of fiction. The Copenhagen you have just been reading about has many features in common with the real Copenhagen, where I have lived most of my life. But the city and the universe depicted in this book do not reflect reality. So I offer you no guarantee that you can use this book as a guide or a key for anything other than a specific Copenhagen, the Copenhagen that exists in my mind and in my books.

ACKNOWLEDGEMENTS

The people below have in their various ways contributed to the realization of this book. I would like to take the opportunity to thank them here:

Camilla Schneekloth Melander · Julie Paludan-Müller · Cecilie Højmark · Find Sørensen · Stephanie Gaarde Caruana · Ulrich Sonnenberg · Sofie Voller · Jenny Thor · Lydia Constance Grønkvist Pedersen

JAKOB MELANDER is the author of the internationally acclaimed Lars Winkler crime series. Born in 1965, he entered the eighties punk scene as a bass player and guitar player in various bands. He lives in Copenhagen.

CHARLOTTE BARSLUND is a Scandinavian translator. She
has translated novels by Jonas T. Bengtsson, Peter Adolphsen,
Mikkel Birkegaard, Izzet Celasin, Thomas Enger, Karin Fossum,
Sissel-Jo Gazan, Steffen Jacobsen, Carsten Jensen, and Per
Petterson, as well as a wide range of classic and contemporary
plays. She lives in the U.K.